Candy and the
Broken Biscuits

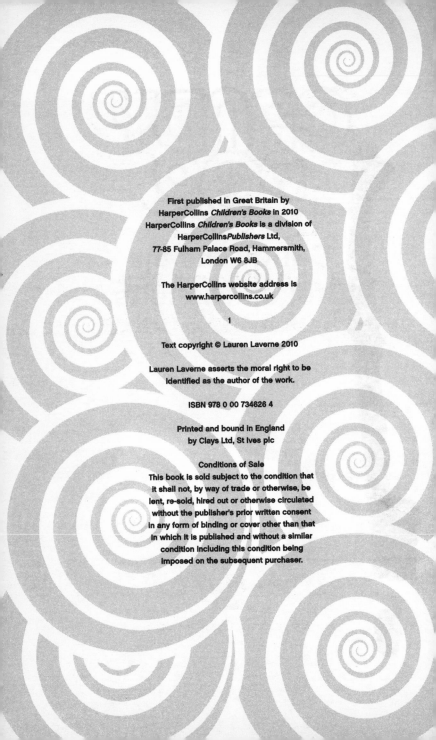

First published in Great Britain by
HarperCollins *Children's Books* in 2010
HarperCollins *Children's Books* is a division of
HarperCollins*Publishers* Ltd,
77-85 Fulham Palace Road, Hammersmith,
London W6 8JB

The HarperCollins website address is
www.harpercollins.co.uk

1

Text copyright © Lauren Laverne 2010

Lauren Laverne asserts the moral right to be
identified as the author of the work.

ISBN 978 0 00 734626 4

Printed and bound in England
by Clays Ltd, St Ives plc

Candy and the Broken Biscuits

Lauren Laverne

HarperCollins *Children's Books*

To Graeme, Fergus and Dot,
who put the song in my heart

I'm on the Pyramid Stage at the festival. In eight bars (thirteen and-a-bit seconds) my band is going to smash into our biggest, loudest, most stupidly catchy single yet. The crowd will jump so high, so fast, the field below us will shake. Lights will flash like the sky is on fire. People will spring out of the throng – sea spray crashing against rocks in a storm. I turn to Hol, she's on bass and coming in first. She starts playing… the wrong notes. DUN DUN DUN DUGGA DUN-DUN! What the hell *is that*?

ICE, ICE BABY…

Vanilla Ice. Mum singing along. The dribble-dribble of the shower. Experimentally, I raise one eyelid. Pale, cold sunshine pours in like vinegar eye drops. As I suspected: I'm alive. It's today. Unfortunately I'm still me.

1

Their Bloody Valentine
(the Morning After)

Hello. I'm Candy Caine (I know. I know. Didn't name myself, did I?) Bit of an odd moment to meet, but since my life isn't about to get any awesomer (and it isn't, It's *Monday*) I suppose it's as good as any.

Here I am in bed, seven-eighths obscured by my ancient *Forever Friends* duvet cover, hair exploding from the top of my head like a firework. A brown firework. My eyes are screwed up, as if I can somehow stop the day from starting by not being able to see it. The duvet cover of shame matches the too-short curtains on the window above my bed. One of Mum's exes put them up when I was seven. That's nearly half my life ago, people. Dave I think he was called. Or maybe Clive? There was a -VE somewhere in there. Anyway he's long gone, but his rubbish DIY is still here, in my bedroom, although his teddy-bear curtains are now framed by hundreds of pictures of my favourite bands. I also have a clear view through the gap, out of the window and up into the freezing blue sky. Gulls scream and circle overhead, delighted by the prospect of another day scavenging old chips and bits of kebab off the seafront.

I'm not slagging my home town off. Bishopspool is pretty much your average seaside settlement: small, cold and (I think) beautiful, tucked in beside the unfathomable depths of the sea. We only really ended up here because Mum "stuck a pin in a map" when she left London. So here we are. And it's... fine.

Reluctantly, I roll myself up to a sitting position before staggering over to the wardrobe, pins still wobbly and sleep-drunk. My extremely un-fetching maroon school uniform is hanging up, all scratchy and angry-looking. The thought of putting it on is about as inviting as swapping clothes with my maths teacher (and I'm including underwear in that).

It's not just the uniform, though. For me, school is like being forced to play a really complicated contact sport where nobody's told you the rules and everybody else is on the other team. So you'll excuse me if I don't get totally *jazzed* about it. All the same, I am basically a Good Girl (check my report, it says "bright, tends to daydream") so after drizzling myself clean under our no-power shower, I slip into my uniform's polyester embrace, ready for another six-point-five-hours of academic excellence and hearty banter with my classmates. Can't wait.

If it weren't for my best mate Holly (and Mum I suppose) I'd probably have stopped going to school by now. She's the only other sane person in Bishopspool. Holly, I mean, not Mum. Mum's as mad as a frog in a sock.

Speaking of which, I'm leaving my attic room at the top of our rickety seafront-house, the bottom floor of which is Mum's business – a beauty salon called *The Cutie Parlour* (you see what she's done there?) – when I hear her giggling and, is that... singing?

"Ice ice BABY! Ice ice BABY!!!" Insane laughter (told you). A man's voice joins in.

Oh no – Ray. That's put me off my cornflakes already. He must have stayed over last night (after their special Valentine's Day dinner. *Ick*).

Ray Hoppings is Mum's latest boyfriend. Ray is a life coach. What this involves, I couldn't tell you, although I have a mental image of him following people around the supermarket while they do their weekly shop yelling, "GO FOR IT! WAY TO SELECT CARROTS!" like a football coach at the side of the pitch.

I have actually heard him refer to himself as (DIRECT quote) "Bishopspool's answer to Paul McKenna". *Paul McKenna!* Ray can't even hypnotise people! I asked him about it once and he said, "I can hypnotise myself" like that was in any way remotely cool. Maybe he's hypnotised himself not to realise what a total dofus he is.

Opening the kitchen door, I am greeted – even by Our House standards – by an unusual scene. Mum, resplendent in her pink fifties-style salon coat-dress and heels (she's a dresser-up) is dancing around the kitchen with Ray. In her free hand she's holding a spatula, on the hob there's a frying pan, eggs and bacon sizzling away. They're both still singing *Ice Ice Baby*. Suddenly Mum shimmies back a few feet and then actually RUNS towards him. Ray holds his arms out. She leaps! And in one *Dirty Dancing* move, he hoists her into the air before spinning them both round, placing her gently down in front of the oven and kissing her on the cheek.

"Ahem." Seriously. I can't think of anything else to say.

"Candy! Morning darling!" says Mum, flustered. "We were just… celebrating! Sit down. I'm making us a proper breakfast."

Then I notice our big old kitchen table. The usual mess of glossy mags and science-lab salon stuff have been replaced by a smart checked tablecloth, a teapot, knives, forks and actual alive flowers in a vase. Something is clearly up.

"Celebrating what?" I ask, pulling out a chair and easing myself into it.

"It's a beautiful day!" Ray chirps, setting down a plate of toast. "On a day like this, anything could happen! Dreams could come true! Maybe they already have..." He looks over to Mum, who gazes back gooily. Ick.

"Celebrating what?"

Still humming that appalling Vanilla Ice song, Mum is dishing up slightly burned eggs and bacon with her back to me. She picks up two plates and plonks them down with a flourish on the table. As she lifts her hand away I notice a flash. There – gleaming and glistening on her fourth finger. Left hand. *Ice Ice Baby.* Oh no.

I feel the shock register on my face before it hits my chest. My eyes widen, my jaw drops open. Mum swoops down into the chair next to me and leans over to give me a huge squeeze of a hug. Beaming her beautiful, perfect-lipstick smile she clasps my hand in hers. Ray is saying something.

"...have decided to take our relationship to the next level..."

They're getting married.

"...truly make a lifetime commitment... be a family... create something non-traditional but special..."

Oh. My. God.

Ray is still talking but I'm not taking in the words. I pull my hand from Mum's grasp and drop it into my lap where it lies uselessly by the other one. For a moment I imagine them growing, superhero-style, to ten times their size, lifting Ray up and throwing him out of the kitchen window.

"Candy? Isn't it wonderful news?"

It's Mum.

"We're so excited, darling! I know this will be a big change for you, for all of us, but it's going to be wonderful! Like Ray says. We can be a family." She's holding my hand again, and Ray hers. For a second we look exactly as she wants us to.

"Mum, I'm fifteen! What's he going to do – adopt me? Walk me to school? Dress up as Santa at Christmas?"

Mum's smile falters. "I don't mean that, Candy." She looks at Ray. "Ray loves me. And you. He wants to be… part of your life. Maybe like a dad, maybe more like a friend. Is that so terrible?"

I can't believe this. There were always Rays. Rays, Daves, Larrys, Ians, Johns, Toms, Harrys and (total) Dicks. They might have stayed for a while but they were always THEM. We were US. And this is Our House. Suddenly I feel like a visitor.

Ray clears his throat.

"Candy, science has demonstrated that human beings only

use twenty per cent of their brains. Did you know that?"

I sulk harder, wishing he'd only use twenty per cent of his mouth.

"Before I met your mother, I was using only a fraction of my emotional capacity. But Maggie makes me the best *me* I can be. In terms of happiness, I am at saturation levels."

He pauses, allowing us to absorb the full impact of his wisdom. I look straight at my mum. She can't seriously want to marry this guy.

"I don't... I don't know what to say, Mum."

"Candy darling, Ray loves me and I love him! Don't you want me to be happy? Don't you think I deserve that?" She starts breathing a bit hard and I know she is trying to stop herself crying. I look at the clock – eight fifty. Clients in ten minutes. She doesn't have time to re-do her makeup, so we can't have an argument now.

"It's all right, Maggie." Ray puts his arm around her and leans in, touching his head to hers. Puke. "Candy's entitled to her feelings." He turns back to me, every inch the reasonable dad at the family meeting, dealing with the inexplicably moody child. I obviously must have missed the meeting where anybody asked whether I actually wanted to be *in* this family.

"Well we'd better get going. Start of a new day. Come on love."

He gestures to Mum, who is still too busy concentrating on not getting upset to actually say anything.

Mum has this thing called "poise". She developed it years ago, working as a model. It's the knack of walking into any room as if it's her surprise birthday party, no matter what kind of day she's having. Another gift of hers I have not inherited, along with unbreakable nails and consistently obedient hair.

Shaking her shoulders out slightly, Mum adopts her delighted-you-could-make-it expression. She doesn't even know she's doing it. She places her twinkling left hand on my shoulder and leans in close.

"Candy. Darling, I love you. Both. Please, please try to be happy for us. If you can't just yet then give it some time to sink in? It's a big change, I know." She stands up and they leave together. Be happy for us. The new us. One without me.

2
Gladly

I don't remember much about the next ten minutes. All I know is, by nine o'clock that morning I am sitting on the step of the East Bishopspool Pensioners' Day Centre under an empty blue sky. Believe it or not an OAP club down at the old docks is the only place I can think of going this morning. Yes, I'm *that* cool. There's nobody around but I turn the collars of my school blazer up anyway to make it look less like I'm wearing my uniform, in case anyone spots me. Do people still call the police about truanting? They might call the taste police, in which case I'm stuffed. Guilty of possession of aubergine polyester.

Hurry up, Glad.

I've never skived off school before. The world looks weird, like it's the wrong colour or something. I'm freezing and starving. Why couldn't we have had all this upset after breakfast?

Where is Glad, anyway? She's always here first. You know what old people are like for timekeeping – fifteen minutes early for everything. Sometimes, when I can't sleep I look out of my bedroom window at the seafront about 6am and there are old guys out there. Why are they up so early? It's not like they've got work or a train to catch.

The sudden crunch of enormous wheels approaching accompanied by a rapid crescendo of ear-bleedingly loud hip hop pulls me back into the present. Hurtling down the deserted road towards me is a tank-sized 4X4. Its windows are completely blacked out, indistinguishable from its gleaming inky frame. The music inside pulses louder, the throbbing track turned up just loud enough to make it indecipherable.

It's pulling up. Someone inside kills the music. The black door zzziipps open with that exhalation sound spaceships make in films. I scramble upright. Have I stumbled into the middle of the weirdest drug deal ever? *(I'll meet you at the OAP club at 9.)* Somebody is getting out of the car.

The tinted windows and glossy black door make it impossible to see anything apart from their feet.

Plop!

A little sausagey leg with a white plimsoll squashed on to the end lands on the ground, quickly joined by another one –

apparently their owner is short enough to have to actually jump out of the car.

Scccrrriick! A familiar walking stick joins the sausage-legs. Little metal coats of arms are screwed into its length, indicating that whoever it is might need a bit of help, but still gets out and about on her travels, thanks very much.

Glad.

"Thanks for the lift, Calum!" she trills, sounding (as always) like a little Scottish cockatiel. The door swings open and a large square white plastic handbag appears, attached to an elderly lady of similar dimensions. "Candy! What on earth are you doing here, lassie? In the name o' God! You're freezing! Aren't you supposed to be at school? Something's happened – what is it now? An argument with your mother again? You're as bad as each other, that's the trouble. That's it, Calum, just down there, I'll get the door open…"

Without pausing for or expecting any kind of response, Glad reaches into the cavernous depths of her white bag and produces a huge prison-warden-style bunch of keys. As she immediately selects the right one from the bunch I recognise the driver of the car for the first time. Calum Stainforth. I sort of remember him from school. We all do. I mean, he was one of the wildest pupils in his year. Legend has it that he was eventually expelled for releasing not one but *two* dogs slap bang into the middle of his English Lit GCSE exam. Nobody knows how he got them in there, but the resultant chaos was so intense that Miss Aitken who was invigilating, had to have a fortnight off and some tablets from the doctor for her nerves. Since then Calum has been trying to make a name for himself as the baddest bad boy MC in Bishopspool. It is somewhat at odds with this precise moment. Calum has removed a fully-stocked tea trolley replete with cups, saucers, teaspoons and two urns from the back of the 4X4. He pushes it along in as manly a fashion as possible, towards the Day Centre. Two saucery-eyes peer out from deep within his hoodie. They meet mine and he stops dead.

"Hey," I say.

"All right?" he mumbles, not waiting long enough for an answer, then presses on towards the door, with his head bowed even lower than it already was.

"Descaling," Glad tells me, as if this explains everything, then she turns back to Calum. "Good boy, Calum. I'll tell your granda what a help you are, he's so proud of you!" She gives his arm a small pat of approval. Somewhere deep inside his fluorescent hoodie, Calum smiles wonkily at her and nods at me, before hopping into the car, reigniting the music and screaming off into the distance.

"Do you remember Calum from school?" Glad asks.

I squint and nod in a non-committal kind of way that tries to avoid saying, "Yeah, I heard he was a headcase!"

Glad smiles, apparently oblivious. "He used to be a bit of a wildcat but he's a good boy these days."

Glad fixes me with a beady glare, which makes her look not unlike Yoda from *Star Wars*. She taps one of the urns with the top of her walking stick. "Right you. Let's fire this lot up and you can tell me all about it."

So this is Glad. We go inside and she settles into her favourite chair in the corner of the optimistically named 'Sun Room' in East Bishopspool Pensioners' Day Centre, clutching a proper cup of tea with saucer (very important).

"Well?" She Yoda-glares at me again over the faint steam and hiss of her cup.

"Mum's marrying Ray."

A pause. "I see."

"What do you mean, you see? It's a disaster! I feel like I'm in a badly updated fairytale. It's *Cinderella*, but instead of a wicked stepmother I get David Brent as a stepdad. And she barely knows the guy! It'll never work Glad, you know what Mum's like as well as I do! She's not... She's never going to... to *settle down.* She's not that kind of person!"

"Well, I would have thought not. But... people change. Maybe she knows herself better than we do, lassie."

"She's doesn't! That's just it. She's not herself at all! She's gone temporarily insane, or he's hypnotised her, or... or... I can't do it, Glad. I can't! It's only ever been the two of us. I don't want her bringing a stranger in. A nuclear family! With a dad who pronounces nuclear 'nuc-u-lur' and thinks he understands me because he likes Coldplay!"

Glad sips her tea, does a whisky-grimace and chews over my news. She's fond of a mull, is Glad. So while she's thinking, let me fill you in on how a Little Old Lady ended up being the only person in the world (apart from Hol) who actually understands me.

You might not have noticed this about my mum, so let me spell it out. She is unusual. By which I mean NOT NORMAL. I mean, I love her and everything, but she's unreliable. Take my name. Depending on what mood she's in when you ask her, Mum either claims I'm named after Candy Darling from the Velvet Underground song *Walk on the Wild Side* or the Jesus and Mary Chain's *Some Candy Talking.* Which means I'm either named after a vulnerable transvestite or a song that everybody thinks is about drugs. Brilliant. She forgets things (I don't think I have ever got a permission slip to school on time). She doesn't really know how to work our oven, even though we've had it since I was two. She makes bad choices (from shoes to boyfriends – neither ever fits – she walks home barefoot a lot to cry about being single). If the job of Me had been left entirely to Mum I would be a mess. OK, more of a mess.

Luckily, for the last thirteen years we have lived next door to Glad, the closest thing I've ever had to a nan. (The real Granny Caine lives on the Costa Brava. All we get from her is a card at Christmas with a new photo of her and my grandad and their shiny mahogany tans).

Glad is the opposite to Mum in every way. A piano teacher by trade, she has been as steady as the metronome on her upright ever since I can remember. Always next door. Most days after school she would pick me up and, back at hers, I'd plonk-plink-plonk my way through *Twinkle Twinkle Little Star* before being rewarded with a strawberry milkshake. That was how I first found music.

Playing gave me a sort of filled-up feeling, heavy and satisfied. And no matter how all-over-the-place things were at home, Glad was there in her front room, sheet music open at something I could dive into. Over the years my fingers got quicker and lighter until I felt they could almost play anything and then, eventually, I could just sort of think the music out of my head and into the keys and it wasn't anything to do with my body at all.

So I live in the world, but I also live somewhere Glad calls Candyland – a place I slip in and out of all the time. I'm very susceptible to the power of a tune. A song floats by out of a car window and suddenly I'm lost in my imaginings. And my biggest imaginings of all are that I will one day make music of my own. The songs in my head will be out in the world.

How could Glad not be my mate, when she introduced me to all that? Anyway she's finished thinking and is about to deliver her verdict. "Sabotage is out I suppose?"

"I'm sorry?"

"You heard me, lassie. If you're THAT unhappy maybe you could sabotage the wedding?"

"What, in the 'if any persons here present can think of any lawful impediment blah blah speak now or forever hold your peace' bit I get up and say something? Like what? 'He's an idiot, Your Holiness! He calls having a chat *dialoguing*! His favourite film is *Ghost*.' Glad. Seriously, what do you mean by these dark mutterings? I know you're part-witch but can you let a mere mortal in on the secret?"

She cracks a smile – I can always get one out of her, even when she's trying to be a grown-up. "I'm saying, Candy, I think your mother deserves some happiness. If it's with Ray then so be it. He's not of her usual stamp, I'll grant you, but do what you've always done... And?"

"...and you'll get what you've always got. I know." Glad has been drumming this particular pearl of wisdom into me since I was as tall as her piano stool.

"I don't believe you when you say Ray is wrong for your mum, Candy. He's been a good influence on her, admit it." She sips her tea, observing me over the top of the cup.

I try to think about the last time Mum did anything preposterous. "She made me miss our school trip, to go on the road with a Kiss tribute band!" I huff, remembering the mortifying week I spent touring the seaside resorts of Britain with Smooch.

Glad makes a face. "That was down to that awful Brian laddie."

Oh yeah. Brian. Mum's boyfriend before Ray. He was Smooch's drummer. Mum was desperate for me to sample "the magic of life on the road". The reality of watching her boyfriend dress up as a cat and play metal every night almost put me off music for life. Almost. "What about the Guinea Pig thing?" I ask, in the style of a lawyer making a spirited case for the prosecution.

A few weeks ago Mum bought twenty-five of the things from a pet-shop because "they looked sad".

Glad smiles, casting a glance at the cage in the corner where her own two dozy furballs (Winston and Adolf) are snoozing contentedly. "He was away that weekend – remember?"

She's right, dammit! He was on a course called *Becoming Your Own Biggest Fan.*

Glad smiles kindly. "I think what you're finding hardest about all this is what it means about who *you* are. You're just starting to work out who you want to be and now you're going to belong to somebody you never asked for. It's tough, but can I let you in on a secret?"

Like I have a choice. I do an if-you-must eyebrow at her.

"None of us get to pick. That's how family works. And there are much, much worse fathers to have than Ray."

"He's not my *father!*"

"He's the closest thing you've got. And he wants the job. He's not what you'd call 'cool' but so what? Dads aren't cool. If he's not so terrible a choice that you'd sabotage the wedding maybe you just need to accept him."

A silence descends as Glad allows this newsflash time to percolate. I hover glumly over my tea. She's right – this is my life. A man so uncool he makes my geography teacher look like Jay-Z has been cast in the role of The Dad. I'm skiving off school for the first time ever and I'm in the East Bishopspool Pensioners' Day Centre. I look round and my eyes come to rest on a poster on the noticeboard.

RESTRICTED MOVEMENT? CHAIR-OBICS COULD BE FOR YOU! TUESDAY 3PM.

Oh God. This cannot be it. I love Glad. I love my mum. But this cannot be my life...

Can it?

3
Operation Awesome

Instead of going to school, I head home. Not ideal as Mum's salon is a mere creaky floorboard below but that's where I go. Partly because I'm not sure what else to do and partly because I've got to get out of this uniform before I can think straight. I feel anchorless and a bit floaty. It's beginning to sink in that Mum is going to go through with this. Her life is separate from mine. I suppose that looks obvious written down, but I've never really thought about it before. It's a horrible thought but the other side of it is... a bizarre kind of freedom. Why should I go to school anyway? I can make my own decisions too.

I walk home via the quiet streets, so that I'm not spotted. The floatiness turns to giddiness and then something approaching hysteria. The world is spinning out of control and nothing is the way I thought it was when I first opened my eyes today. I'm out of school on a Monday morning! I feel, in a surreal way, daring. Spy-like.

I flip my MP3 player to a David Holmes' film soundtrack. As it thrums into action, pacy and tap-tap-tappity everything suddenly looks monochrome. I cling to the sides of cars Jason Bourne-style as I pass, subtly checking over my shoulder for double agents and imagining myself seen through the sights of a weapon. When I place my hand on an imaginary gun, I have a word with myself. Luckily I'm back. I pop out my headphones and, quiet as a mouse, sneak into our yard, through the back door and up to my room.

My bedroom is as much like the inside of my head as anywhere could be. Pictures line the walls. Mainly they're of musicians but there are some of places, too. Each one takes me somewhere or pushes my thoughts further out. Towards? Just away, I suppose. I have a bit of a thing for stars and my collection decorates the ceiling. Every time I find a picture of one I have to cut it out, otherwise it's unlucky. Cartoons, scientific diagrams, wierdy mathematical line-drawings of ones by an old Dutch dude called MC Escher (not *actually* a rapper as it turns out!) and a 3D model I stole from the school science block that I still feel bad about.

My bed is tucked under the window, with its sea view and embarrassing curtains. Mum is obsessed with old stuff. Clothes, records, furniture: anything, really. So obviously our house is full of it. She calls it "vintage" but we sensible people know it as second-hand junk that's often broken. Like the people in it, our house's furniture is charming but doesn't really do what it's supposed to. I have an old 1950s bedroom set, made of white melamine with a sort of grey tiger-stripe pattern going on. There are a couple of handles missing and one of the dressing table drawers won't open (Holly, has speculated that it may contain the ashes of a murder victim). At first I thought it looked uber lame but I must admit, now that it's got all my stuff on it, it's pretty cool. A rainbow selection of clothes peek out of the wardrobe, lounge on the bed and curl up on my dressing-table like old friends.

My phone beeps. Text: PIRATE. It's Holly. Her surname is Rodgers. Holly Rodgers. Jolly Roger? Pirate. Don't blame me. I didn't invent the rules about nicknames. Why do they always have to be something insulting? When people try to start their own nickname it's always so obvious. They give it away every time by trying to make it sound cool like 'Laser' or 'Hawkeye'. It never sticks. Fart in PE once, though, and you're 'Napalm' for the next hundred years.

Anyway Holly has decided to "own" Pirate. It actually really suits her. She's the most genuinely rebellious, take-no-prisoners, close-to-the-wind-sailing girl I know. Definitely the funniest. She got detention for titling her homework 'A pain in the Pythagoras' last week. Which shows you how much she hates authority. And maths, which is where she is now.

"Whr ru? M in hell pls snd hlp. X"

I picture her texting from her pocket without looking at the screen.

I message back. "@ home but going 2 the blue. Can u get out? X"

I know, I know, inciting her to truant. Well trust me – today may be a first for me, but for Holly it definitely isn't. How Mr and Mrs Rodgers produced her I'll never know. She's from a family of nine and they're very religious – they go to one of those churches with singing, clapping and lots and LOTS of smiling but NO ACTUAL SENSE OF HUMOUR. Our pirate friend is very much the cuckoo in the crow's nest. She actually keeps a change of clothes at school for sneaking out.

"Cu in 20. X"

I'd better get changed myself. It's funny – the things I wear make me even more of a freak to people round here but dressing up makes me feel better about it. I've tried toning it down but it's like holding your breath. You can only last so long.

Ten minutes later, I am wearing a tea dress that in my head belonged to Drew Barrymore in around 1993, long woollen socks that come up past my knees, battered Nike hi-tops and a 1980s knitted hat made of sparkly lurex wool. Like all the best outfits it's wrong on paper and right on the person.

By the time I get there, Hol is already standing outside The Bluebird Café dressed head to toe in black except for an enormous fuschia scarf which, being wrapped around her neck numerous times, makes her look like a gothic cupcake. She is jiggling up and down against the cold and... is she playing *a kazoo*?

"What the flip is that, you loon?"

"I believe the standard greeting is HELLO. Nicotine inhaler."

"Hello. Why have you got a nicotine inhaler? You don't smoke."

"No smell. Mum and Dad." She grimaces. "And I don't *smoke*" but I was feeling so *stressed out* I started to, like, feel addicted to the *idea* of smoking? Except I don't want to end up with a raisin face. So I half-inched this."

She flicks imaginary ash from the end of the slim, white tube before going in for another drag, the cold air puppeting her blonde bob around her pixie-face. There's a flash of blue as she looks up at me through her fringe. Blowing out non-existent smoke, nature plays along and freezes her breath which floats away in little clouds. She is an angel in eyeliner. Not that you can say stuff like that to her. She's enough of a handful as it is.

"You look like you're smoking a tampon. Get a hold of yourself, woman."

I lead the way inside and pretend not to notice as she mimes putting out the ridiculous prop before tucking it behind her ear. The glass door slips shut behind us and we are suddenly in 1982 which is approximately when 'The Blue' was last redecorated.

Brown and red plastic predominates – booths, laminated menus, those tomatoes with ketchup inside and then the brown ones with brown sauce, their non-tomato status serving only to highlight the mysterious nature of their contents. At the back of the café is the reason we (and everybody else in town with a clue) come here. Racks of records and CDs frame a large hole in the wall behind which, illuminated by strings of fairy lights and an angle-poise lamp, is a small room stuffed from floor to ceiling with singles, albums, CDs and merchandise from bands-gone-by. MGMT are playing on crackly vinyl on the stereo. The Blue Room, at the back of The Bluebird Café, is the only non-chain record shop in town and apparently evolved from the days when The Blue was a 1950s ice-cream parlour with a jukebox at the back. But that's not the reason we come here. The reason is perched on a high stool behind a book. *The Dice Man*.

"That Dan Ashton. *So* unbelievably hot. Hot!" Hol stage whispers behind her menu.

The book is readjusted momentarily revealing a black eyebrow, a mop of hair to match and one chocolate-brown eye.

She doesn't notice. "So what gives? I take it you're not ill. Ill people never wear hats." I give her a quizzical look. "They haven't got the energy to accessorise." Hol tips a dose of sugar out of the dispenser on to the table and starts drawing in it with her fingers.

"Mum and Ray are getting married."

"Shut up!"

"They are."

"SHUT UP!" This time she reaches across the booth and punches me in the shoulder, sprinkling grains of *Tate and Lyle* down my chest in the process. I brush them away.

"No. Seriously. A wedding – cake, singing, a really embarrassing horse and cart. Me probably being forced to wear a lilac dress. Them *dancing* together." I shudder, recollecting the scene I walked in on earlier. "It's a nightmare."

Holly pouts her bottom lip. "Oh, Can. That's terrible. That's... Ooh! I forgot! I brought THESE for us!" She reaches into her enormous yellow pleather bag and produces two pairs of sunglasses. Hers are electric blue with glittery frames in the shape of two butterflies, mine are white with red stripes like a candy cane. The frame contorts into a letter L on one side of the lenses and K on the other.

"And these are?"

She throws her hands up, universal sign language for "Duh!"

"They're a *disguise*? So that we can, like, *do stuff* today without attracting too much attention? I got them from the arcade on the way over." She slips hers on and turns butterfly-eyed to the surly waitress who has just appeared beside our booth. "A pair of cokes and one chips, please, *garçon*."

The waitress, who is about nineteen but looks way older, purses her lips, shakes her head and stalks off in disapproving silence.

To be honest I didn't expect much sympathy from Pirate. Holly is not great at bad news, operating a blanket policy of "tuning out negativity". I think of it as just ignoring stuff. She must read my thoughts because she reaches across the booth, gives my forearm a rub, then a pat before finishing off with a few more firm slaps on my shoulder. I feel like a sofa having its cushions plumped.

"Chin up, soldier. It sucks, you know? But parents... they're nuts. Well, ours are. Come and live at my house! I'm sure Mum and Dad wouldn't notice one more!" I smile in spite of myself. "Why don't you, like *channel your feelings into our art*?" Hol waves her arms around in what she obviously imagines is an arty fashion.

Hol is one half of said art project – our (as yet unnamed) band. She doesn't write songs. She claims her role is "more of an actualisation deal. Like, you provide the raw materials – I bring the magic." What this actually means is that I spend every night wigging out on my own in my room like a loser (singing along to my knackered old keyboard in apparent silence via my gigantic orange headphones) writing songs for which Hol then has to create a four-note bass part. Like she says – magic.

"What was that one you wrote last week?" she asks, sucking a few grains of sugar off her index finger.

I cast my mind back to last Wednesday, when I stayed up late writing about this really annoying girl in our class who has a secret tattoo. The chorus was particularly satisfying ("You've got your boyfriend's name in ink on your bum/ And if you don't shut up/ I'm telling your mum").

"Er... *Inkspots*?"

"No! The one about Ray!"

"Oh! *Chairman of the Bored*."

"Yeah – you could adapt that and make it about this. You know what John Lydon says, 'Anger is an energy'. Use it to your advantage, Caine. Now put on your regulation issue disguise and let's discuss Operation Awesome."

She may not do sympathy very well, but if you want cheering up, Pirate is the girl for you. "Sir, yes sir!" I slip on my extremely 70s Elton John eyewear, my head now inviting the empty café to LOOK.

Operation Awesome is our plan for world domination by our band, using the weapon of amazingly brilliant music. Holly and I spend most of our time together discussing logistics, tactics, album titles, who we'll tour with, which cities we'll play in and what we'll wear onstage. The fact that we are the only members, own one battered old Casio and a borrowed bass does not figure in any of this. We have a Facebook page called Operation Awesome inviting the public to help us on our road to superstardom. So far we have three friends, two of whom are us. The other one is Glad.

Removing a tattered notebook and pen from her skip of a handbag, Holly flicks through the pages until she reaches the list of potential names we were working on yesterday lunchtime.

"So… where did we get to? The Neon Girls, Play, The Twister Sisters…"

"I hate that one. And there's already a metal band called Twisted Sister."

"…Daydreamer, Ice Scream…"

"And that one. Cross it out – people will think we're a screamo band. Totally wrong."

"Totally!" agrees Holly, who refuses to acknowledge her enormous emo phase which finished three months ago (her wardrobe has yet to catch up with her music taste). She puts a decisive strike through the offending moniker. "But we do need something. It needs to say who we are and what we're about – it needs to show that we mean *business* and – CHIPS! WOO HOO!"

Surly Girl plonks the plate down between us. Hol turns beaming towards her. Surly Girl is wearing a badge that says, 'My name is Nicola. Ask me about our FREE REFILLS!'

"*Danke, Camarero!* Could we possibly have another fork, *sil vous plait*? And what's the deal with these *free refills* I've been hearing about?"

Surly leans in close enough for us to catch the surprisingly pleasant scent of perfume and cigarettes.

"One fork per order only and the free refills is only for a family party who get the lunchtime special. Not timewasters and *broken biscuits* who haven't got nothing better to do with themselves than hang around here making one order last all day."

A crescent-moon smile spreads across Holly's impish face.

"Ooh, you're good! Nicola, is it? You're GOOD!" She starts scribbling in the book.

Taken aback by Holly's apparent delight, Surly straightens up, gives a derisory snort and stalks off.

"Thank you!" Holly calls after her with a wave. She turns to me, still beaming, before doing her best Professor Higgins, "By George, I think she's got it!" She turns the notebook round. The entire list of band names has been scratched out and underneath in letters as big as her grin she has written THE BROKEN BISCUITS.

Before long we're laughing and the world almost feels the right way round again. Pirate can do that to a person.

We stumble out of the café and take the bus up the coast. As we bump along, Hol gives a particularly animated account of her escape from double maths and a life in which she might have grown up understanding long division.

We end up in a little village a couple of miles out of town. Its selection of shops is pretty odd – a tearoom, a fancy dress shop and a newsagent that also sells reproduction antiques. Somehow Holly convinces the owner of the fancy dress place that we are fashion students looking for kitsch accessories for our end of term show. We spend an hour trying things on. Wigs, feather boas, clown noses, witches' hats... In the end we buy a pair of cat ears (me) and rabbit ones (her). We add them to our disguises, Holly promising to return to buy more "when we're closer to curtain up." There's nowhere else to go and no more money. So we walk down to find a bench on the freezing beach and split a packet of bubblegum.

Glad once told me there is actually no definitive line where the sea ends and the sky begins. They are made of the same thing. I didn't understand at the time but today I know just what she means. I can *feel* the sea in the air, like silk. We watch the waves throw themselves one by one on to the sand, each trying to escape the sea. Failing. That's how the tide comes in, I suppose.

Still in our comedy ears and sunnies, we sit huddled together blowing orange bubbles that look like plastic Halloween pumpkins. We hunch together in the cold for a long time, looking out to sea as if we're waiting for a ship of loons to come and rescue us, to take us to a place where people wear rabbit ears and sunglasses every day and love music as much as we do. I think about Operation Awesome – Pirate's the kind of person who's just about mad enough to manage to make that happen. I need her help with something else. I take a deep breath, the damp February air is cold enough to sting my teeth.

"I think I need to find my dad."

Hol's bubble freezes mid blow, then she sucks it back in

thoughtfully, bursting it with a smacking sound.

"Is this cos of the wedding?"

"Yeah, kind of. I mean, I've always wanted to know who he is. But in a way, not knowing was cool before. Like, he could be anyone. He could be Johnny Depp or Brad Pitt or something. Stupid."

She smiles and resumes chewing. "It's not stupid. I used to wish I was adopted for the same reason. Then I realised that it was unlikely my mam would have wanted to adopt, like, her *fifth* baby when the others were still little. Unless my dad actually *had* been Brad Pitt. He loves that kind of thing."

I roll my eyes at her. "Ha ha. The thing is, now that Ray's going to be my stepdad, I care. He's taking my dad's place. Whoever he is. But I can't do this on my own. I'm going to need help. From you."

"Of course! *Mi casa su casa!*"

"Thanks, Hol. I don't think '*mi casa su casa*' actually means—"

She cuts me off, pointedly blowing a bubble in my direction. "Does when I say it. What about your mum?"

"Useless. Everything she says about when she was young contradicts everything else. All I know is, she lived in London, she was going to be the next Kate Moss and then..."

POP.

"Have you ever just, like *asked*? WHO IS MY FATHER?"

"I can't."

"*Pourquoi pas?*"

"I just kind of... *can't*. She doesn't want me to."

"How do you know?"

"Just do."

"OK, dude. I'm on board. We now have *two* projects. *Operation Awesome* and *Operation Who's-the-Daddy?*" She grins. I frown at her.

"Do we have to call it that?"

"Yes," she says finally, before unfurling a bubble the size of a space-hopper between us. We get my MP3 player out of my bag and take a headphone each. I scroll through to a really old album I just discovered. *Marquee Moon* by Television. Apparently they are the band who invented punk, which is funny because they totally look like teachers. My favourite track comes on, *Friction*. Tom Verlaine starts screaming, "I don't wanna grow up/There's too much contradiction!" and looking up at the sky I feel like gravity could just switch off and I could step out into it. In my other ear the sea keeps breathing. Wave. Wave. Wave. Keep trying.

On the bus back, I think about Mum crying sometimes when I was little. Wet eyes and a big smile on my birthday. Hiding it but not very well. I heard her at night sometimes, through the bedroom wall. The day after something bad had happened, when she wouldn't get up. She always said it was a headache but I stopped believing that ages ago. The answer I need is underneath those tears. I have always known not to ask. About any of it. Suddenly it strikes me that I haven't heard her cry for a while. Definitely not since… I push the thought back down. He's an idiot. And he's not my dad.

The bus drops us back at the stop outside The Blue. It's quarter past three and already it's beginning to get dark. Navy spreads through the empty sky like ink in water. Hol fluffs her hair with the back of her hand and stares into the dimly lit café window, half at her own reflection, half through it trying to catch a glimpse of Dan Ashton. "Want to come to mine?"

"Nah. I'd better go home."

My stomach gives a little lurch at the thought. Holly notices and gives me another conciliatory pat.

"OK soldier. Listen, tomorrow we begin a new phase. We have a name. We are the Broken Biscuits. I think it's time Operation Awesome went overground."

"Meaning?"

"We start recruiting. This isn't a two-woman operation. We need band members. At least two more."

I salute. "Yes sir."

I hug Hol and watch her stride away purposefully. I suppose I'd better get home before anyone notices I'm gone.

I arrive back to an empty house. Mum is still down in the salon and Ray... he's probably teaching some business-dude to pretend he's a tiger so he can go in and 'kill it' at his presentation tomorrow. Lame-a-rama. I try to imagine him actually *living* here, bursting through the door with a "Honey, I'm home!" every evening, like a character from a bad sitcom. It's the end. No more TV nights, lounging around in our pyjamas watching films. No more Pizza Wednesdays. No more Mum practising salon treatments on the pair of us, candles and wine glass balanced on the side of the bath; The Pixies on the stereo. The bathroom will probably stink now. Man-stink. In fact that's the best way to describe Ray's arrival – a bad smell emanating through the house. Everything *looks* the same, but the whole place reeks. The flowers sit on the table from breakfast, smiling out at the kitchen with the stupid optimism of things that don't even know they've been hacked down and will soon be dead. Stupid flowers. Stupid tablecloth.

I stagger up into my room, overcome by a weary mix of misery and powerlessness. I kick off my trainers and flop down on to the bed. The clock-radio blinks 15:55. I blink back. Once, twice and then fall headfirst into a black-hole sleep, the deepest I have ever known.

When I wake again it is almost midnight and the house is enveloped in velvety darkness. A glass of juice and a sandwich sit outside my bedroom door. I pick them up and tiptoe down from my little attic room to the floor below. The door is ajar. I call Mum's room 'The Museum' because everything in it is about a hundred years old. It being hers, none of it in any way goes together. Ancient floral quilts clash with old leopard-print lampshades. Twinkling Indian saris frame the window and a costume shop array of frocks are slung willy-nilly over a battered Chinese screen. In the middle of it all is Mum asleep on her bed in a pool of lamplight. Dark hair framing her beautiful face, long eyelashes flickering mid-dream, the gentle rise and fall of *Brides* magazine on her chest. If she hadn't been snoring it would have been just like an advert.

I sit on the third stair and eat my sandwich, drink my OJ and watch her sleeping. I can feel the fact of her *engagement* (sounds so weird – she's thirty-five!) sitting in my chest like a stone, heavy and cold – a boulder thrown into a lake, the surface of which has now become calm. I think about her almost-crying this morning "Don't I deserve some happiness?" Like she'd never had any until now. Was life really so unbearable when all we had was each other?

After eating, I walk into the room to turn off her light. She doesn't look too much like me. Her eyes are brown and mine are green. I suppose our cheekbones are the same. Sticky-outy – but hers make her look like a film star, whereas mine make me look like an alien. Her hair is smooth and unfurls itself like a shampoo ad when she takes it down. Mine seems to defy gravity and if it has been in a ponytail it stays there when you take the elastic out. Wondering if anything about me will ever make sense, I flick off the bedside lamp and sneak out, leaving Mum snuffling away contentedly in the darkness.

4
The Beast and the Godbrother

A feeling of numb calm stays with me for the next few days, punctuated by sickening moments when I remember that the world as I know it is about to end. In science I draw Ray's face on the textbook illustration of the meteor that caused the Big Bang hurtling towards earth. The dinosaurs were lucky – they didn't know what was coming to take them out. Then I start daydreaming about my *real* father (who Hol and I have christened BioDad). Maybe he's a film star! Mum's always telling stories about the flash company she was in down in London. "He could be Johnny Depp or Clive Owen," I suggest to Hol at lunchtime, "maybe even Daniel Craig! James Bond could be my dad!"

"Dude, BioDad is *so* not James Bond. Judging by the way you're turning out, he's more likely to be some freaky brainiac who's in the jungle looking for a cure for cancer or locked in a laboratory building robots that can, like, think for themselves and do wees and stuff."

"Why would anybody invent a robot that can do wees?" I ask incredulously.

"I'm just saying... who knows why these scientists do what they do. Anyway, don't blame me. He's *your dad*," she huffs, taking a cross bite of her chicken wrap. We settle into a glum silence but I can't stop thinking about it. Maybe he won't be amazing, maybe he'll be even more of a loser than Ray. *Impossible,* I tell myself. Then I think maybe he'll think I'm a loser! That thought's much harder to shake.

Bizarrely, the very moment I am paralysed by misery, Holly has been gripped by a renewed sense of purpose, like an anti-authority Girl Guide. Within an hour of stealing Sarah Andrews' librarian's pass, she has photocopied a hundred of our flier advertising for band members proclaiming **"WANTED FOR GLOBAL TAKEOVER BY THE AMAZING BROKEN BISCUITS: WORLD'S ACEST DRUMMER/BEATBOXER. ALSO, ANY GUITAURIST WITH OWN INSTRIMENT. WORLD DOMINASION GARUNTEED. CALL OR TEXT NOW 07977..."**

She proudly unfurls a copy on top of my uneaten lunch in the canteen, seasoning my inedible curry, rice and chips with her atrocious spelling. Holly's convinced advertising like this will find us some bandmates but I'm too miserable to work out whether I agree.

"Dude, chillax," Hol says, placing a conciliatory arm around my shoulders, "*Operation Awesome* is totally the key to *Operation Who's-the-Daddy!* Think about it – we get rich, famous and wildly successful, then we get the press to do the hard work for us! Put out an appeal? Or hire a private investigator or something..." she tails off and I rub my eyes, managing a weak smile.

"Sure Hol. Whatever you say." Even though I'm shattered, I haven't slept in days. It's like I've exchanged the traditional states of awake and asleep for one, long stretch somewhere in between. At home I say as little as possible while Mum fizzes away like an asprin, chattering about her wedding plans. At night I lie awake, staring at the fake stars on my ceiling.

Mum and Ray have decided on a June wedding. Three days into their engagement, the whole house is already overrun with catalogues, magazines and books called things like *Wedding Planning for Dummies*. Still in my pyjamas and barely awake, I sit at the kitchen table and plonk my cereal down on the top magazine in the stack before me. Milk sloshes on to the satsuma-tanned face on *Celebrity Brides Revealed!* I'm not sure I'd be as chuffed if I looked that much like an Oompa-Loompa on The Happiest Day of My Life™. Mum breezes into the room with all the upbeat industriousness of Snow White mid *Whistle While You Work.*

"Morning, Can!" she trills, unloading the dishwasher with the clatter of a one-man-band. "There's so much to *do*! Nineteen weeks is such a short lead-time these days. I've got some fabric swatches coming over today and I was thinking maybe I could make the favours? Something crafty and cool?"

What is she on about? This has been Mum's tactic the whole week. Keep asking questions, don't wait for any answers and pretend everything is hunky-dory. I stop listening to the actual words and get lost in the music of her voice until I realise she is saying my name repeatedly. "Is it, Can? Candy? Candy! You haven't forgotten. Have you?"

"Hmm?"

"It's Glad's birthday! The party? This afternoon at the Day Centre. You're playing something?"

"Mmm hmm." I had totally forgotten but am too tired to even feel bad.

"So you've got it sorted, yes? What are you going to play?"

"Debussy." I think I say it because I'm halfway through a yawn that already sounds like his name.

"Right, then. Have a lovely day. I'll see you at Glad's. And so will Ray."

I smile weakly. "Bye, Mum.". She pulls on her old fur coat and click-clacks out the door into the weekend. Four inch heels and snow outside. If she's not careful she'll be going up the aisle on crutches.

I look at the clock: it's almost nine. Hol is out of the picture today – her parents make her play in the church band on Saturday *and* Sunday mornings, so she'll probably be mid-*Kumbaya*. I flip through my mental address book of social engagements, fabulous friends and must-dos. Blank. Blank. Blank. Debussy it is. I pad through to the front room and go to the shelf with my sheet music on it, although I could play Glad's favourite piece in my sleep. It's an easy choice, *Clair de Lune*.

I trudge upstairs, back to my room. It's dark: the curtains are still half-drawn but the pale winter sun can barely make it through the clouds this morning anyway. Thick flurries of snow billow pointlessly towards the ground. It never lies round here – there's far too much salt in the air. I switch on the lamp on my dressing-table and that's when I see it. Lying on the bed is a large black oblong decorated by an enormous shining scarlet ribbon. A guitar case. A guitar. Like an idiot I look around, as if somebody is going to leap out of the corner shouting "SURPRISE!" while Party Poppers explode all over the room. I catch Iggy Pop's eye in a poster and feel sheepish. Cautiously, I step forwards like I'm creeping up on a sleeping bear. There's a small black envelope tucked neatly under the bow. I tear it open already knowing who it's from.

Darling Girl,

Here is something from us to help make your dreams come true like ours have, M and R xxx

The heavy bow slides apart smoothly. I spread my fingers out and brush my hand across the word indented into the pitted plastic of the pristine case. *Gibson.* Reaching down I find four cool metal clasps. They flip up one by one like locks on an enchanted treasure chest. I notice that I seem to have stopped breathing. The lid weighs a ton. I lift it up a fraction, slowly pulling apart the weighty body of the case, forcing myself to breathe in, out, in, out... silently praying, *Please let it be beautiful. Please let it be beautiful.*

My first glimpse is of the retina-scorching electric-blue fur lining, which is – pretty unnecessarily – also leopard print. It's so bright it's practically neon. The room fills with a heady scent – musty wet-dog with an undertone of stale tobacco. I cough. Nestling in the bed of blue fuzz is the shabbiest, oldest, most scraped, scratched and beaten up, *ugliest* guitar you have ever seen.

Oh crap.

The guitar, or what's left of it, is an old Gibson SG. Three strings stretch up its warped neck (there should be six) and the figure-of-eight body appears to have been in a war. Most of the glossy cherry-red paint that once covered it long ago has gone. Patches of bare wood stare up at me, bone through wounds. A series of deep gouges run diagonally below the bridge and indecipherable marker-pen scrawl, stickers and peeling glitter glue are everywhere, giving the overall impression of a psychotic five-year-old's art project. Its elegant curves have been chipped and dented beyond recognition and two of the four volume and tone knobs have been replaced. One with a huge leather-covered button and the other with a badge that may long ago have borne a witty slogan but is now so utterly ruined that only three letters are visible. "G US". As in "disGUSting".

Ick.

Gingerly, I reach down and pick it up as you might a run-over cat at the roadside. I've been desperate for a guitar forever and now I've got one. Only it's *this* one. Typical. I place the beast of a thing on my lap and – awkwardly – curl my fingers into one of the chord positions I managed to learn one afternoon on Hol's dad's church group guitar. Being very religious, Alan would only teach me hymns. I decide to start with *Victory in Jesus*. I hit the first chord, an atonal G that sounds like the wail of a depressed cat. Sticking my tongue out in childish concentration, I make a

B chord with my left hand and strum with my right.

KAKAKAKAKBBBLLLOOOOWWWBBBAAAABBBOOOOOMMM
MMM!!!!

There is a huge explosion – a deafening blast, accompanied by a blinding flash of light that throws me back against the wall. Everything is plunged into bright white silence. I start to hear ringing in my ears. And then… a voice. So high I think it's a noise at first – the kind of noise the neck of a balloon makes when you stretch it and let the air escape. But it's somebody shouting – shrieking in fact. With delight.

"WOOOOAHHH! FREEEDOMMM! HALLELUJAH! I'M OUT AND PROUD, MOTHER! WINGS DON'T FAIL ME NOW!!!"

As my eyes recover from the blast of light or… whatever it was that just happened, they start to make out a figure. Zipping through the air at speed, bouncing off the walls like a rubber ball and emitting a light so brilliant it doesn't so much shine as *sing*. He is a small (sort of handspan-sized), apparently *flying… man*. And he's *shouting at me*.

"I'm out! You let me out! At last! Candy Caine! Let me have a look at you… Do you know how to take your time or… WOW. Nice outfit. You are obviously in the middle of an, um, emotional *situation*? Never fear, I am here now. Speaking of which, where am I?" Four tracing-paper wings crinkle and buzz as the shining creature flies over to the window. "Urgh! Snow! The worst weather for dressing well. Perhaps I shouldn't be too hard on you, then."

I try to speak but nothing comes out. Shakily, I push myself up to stand. I'm trying to work out whether anything hurts but if it does I'm too shocked to feel it yet. I'm in the middle of the room, goldfish-mouthed and speechless in my pyjamas, my beaten up old beast of a guitar hanging limply around my neck. The creature hovers in the window, snow swirling behind him.

"I... I..." I manage to lift my finger and point. Quite what I am hoping to indicate I don't know.

"Don't point, Candy Caine. Terribly rude. I can see my entrance has caused quite a stir. Can't say I'm surprised. But can still say more than you, it appears. In which case allow me to do the introductions. Before you and about you and in fact especially for you, I am Clarence B Major at your SERVICE!"

He throws both arms open in a highly dramatic fashion. Apparently his name should be enough to elicit a reaction.

I manage a weak nod. Personally, I'm still caught up on the fact that he's a... is he a...?

Clarence B Major flies down to the windowsill and paces up and down as if onstage. His wings bristle and hiss behind him like an old record. Although his entire person is a shimmering mass of glistening almost light, I can now see that he is in fact, wearing clothes. An elaborate outfit consisting of a tattered skin-tight jumpsuit, a headband, wrist cuffs, three belts and pixie boots. Each item is as luminous as the moon. His shining hair is immaculately tousled beneath his headband and although he's definitely a *he*, he has a face that could only ever be described accurately as beautiful. He also appears to be wearing makeup in the shape of a lightning strike over one eye.

"Naturally, my dear girl, your little head will be stuffed full of questions. STUFFED! Time aplenty for each and every one of them. For now I will give you the bare bones. The facts as they are on a need-to-know basis."

I feel as if my entire head has been dipped in glue. I shake it, trying in vain to get the cogs in my brain going again. I'm still pointing, mainly because I'm so shocked I've forgotten to stop. With a great effort I manage to slur, "You're a... You're a f... You're a f... f... fai—"

"Hush, hush my dear. I'll do the talking for now. And in future do try to avoid speaking with your mouth open. Most unattractive on you. As you may have noticed, I am a creature imbued with both human and superhuman traits—"

My brain and mouth simultaneously come unstuck. "A fairy! You're a fairy!"

In a bristling flash, Clarence B Major zooms from his place

on the windowsill and delivers a sharp kick to the end of my nose, then hovers at eye-level to shout. "I am not and never have been a *fairy*. How DARE you!"

"OW! Sorry." I squeak through my hand. Clarence B Major looks at me as if *he's* the wounded one.

"So..." I ask, checking for blood. "What are you then?"

Clarence taps his finger on his chin, thoughtfully and says, more to himself than me, "Ah. A poser. How to explain my nuanced state to one so febrile as you. Let me see..." He clears his throat and addresses me once more, "In terms you might be able to grasp, Candy Caine, I was once alive, but now I am not. I am caught between two worlds, the visible and the invisible—"

"So you're a... ghost?"

Clarence makes a face. "Oh my dear, no! The stuff of Victorian melodrama and nothing more. And they can't do half of what I can. Look!" There's a little flash of light and for a moment he is a dragonfly, then a further flash and he is himself again. Clarence B Major smiles a twinkling smile. "Magic, you see! I had a lot of it when I was alive and now that I am dead it has made me into something else. Let's just say that I am an echo of a person who once was, without really *being* that person. I am now partly Clarence and partly... magic. But most importantly of all, I am totally and entirely here for *you*."

I try and fail to think of something to say to this. Luckily, it seems that Clarence B Major is on a roll and requires no further prompting. He places his hands on his hips.

"I have been assigned and apportioned the role of your mentor, protector and guide. You have summoned me by playing the chord named in my honour." I look at him blankly, he rolls his eyes. "*B Major*? It is my duty to help you fulfil your destiny. Do you wish me to provide this service?"

Clearly the sane answer is no.

"Er... *yes*?"

Mollified as quickly as he became enraged, Clarence taps my tender snout with his finger. It goes *ting!* like a bell. I cringe but the pain instantly disappears. Clarence flutters back to the windowsill, resuming his position centre-stage, hands clasped behind his back, chest puffed out like a small army general. With wings.

"But what are you doing here? What *destiny*?"

"As I was saying, you and I are bound together, Candy Caine. I have been charged with the task of getting you out of this..."

He looks about him, clutching for a word that will accurately encapsulate the hopeless grimitude of my freezing box room on a friendless Saturday morning.

"...this poky little life of yours and getting you one that fits."

"A life that *fits*?" I ask, sarcastically. *Who does this... person think he is?*

Clarence B Major meets my glare, returning a look as cool and clear as iced water.

"Well? Haven't you ever felt that your life was too small?"

"I..." I leap into speech, ready to tell him how wrong he is. Only he's not. Every single day I have dreamed of something bigger, more, brighter, louder, faster. My life is a sleeping machine plugged in and waiting to go, switch firmly flicked to OFF. Clarence flutters closer, his light warming my face like a spotlight. It feels wonderful.

"This is not your destiny, Candy Caine. There is too much music in you."

"Music?"

"Yes, music." Clarence flies over to the guitar around my neck. It shimmers under the light he casts – the remaining paint on its body coming alive: an intense scarlet glow. In a weird way it sort of *feels* alive too, but not quite. Asleep maybe. He indicates that I should play something. This time, my hands find their place instinctively, my right across the bridge, my left lightly holding the neck. There's a *rightness* to the feeling, like putting your arm around someone you love.

"My dear girl. If I told you I was the possessor of an invisible power which could change your day, your mind, your life, the world—"

"I'd believe you. You're a flipping f— You're... made of magic, apparently."

"Not just I. Music, Candy. Music is magic. It is in me as it is in you. You possess this power. You have summoned me with it. The chord of B Major to be precise. And your music, your magic, is going to get us out of here and into your wildest dreams. You do have dreams you wish to come true, don't you?"

An image leaps into my head, a scene from the dream I always have: me and Hol up onstage in front of a crowd we can't even see the end of.

"Yes," I say. "My band. I want to make music." Then I think of Mum and Ray and the missing puzzle-piece that is BioDad. "And there's... there's someone I want to find."

Clarence B Major leans in close, smiling. "Your father."

I actually gasp. Then nod. Although why the fact that the magical fairy made of moonbeams that is flying round my bedroom knows I haven't got a dad is such a shocker, I'm not sure.

"Don't look so surprised, Candypop! I've never really been one for homework but I did do *some* research before I got here... I sense that he is intrinsic to your destiny. Whoever he is, he gave you your music. This guitar will help you find him and it will help you fulfil your wildest imaginings."

I look down at the car-crash of metal and wood in my lap. Accidentally, a little snort of derision jumps from between my lips. Clarence is not amused. His expression clouds with anger. He brings his shining hands together and starts to rub his palms.

A luminous not-quite-liquid begins to bubble between them. A shimmering mess of every-colour light, it's accompanied by the gelatinous hum a fat drunk bee might make. Clarence opens his palms into a circle and blows. The goop separates into six bubbles, which hover in the air for a split second before shooting towards me.

POP OP POP OP POPPOPPOPPOP!

Smashing into the guitar the bubbles explode, releasing a crackling cloud of sparks, smoking colour and noise against the bridge. It's somewhere between a mini fireworks display and an electrical storm in a snowglobe. The instrument seems to respond, shuddering in my grasp.

Alive with the cloud's strange energy, the guitar's three old strings start to glow, pulling tighter and tighter against the neck which pushes out in the opposite direction until...

DONK! DAANG! DUNNNN!

The old strings snap tunelessly and flashing out of the cloud like lightening six perfectly luminous threads appear across the length of the neck. With a triumphant flourish, Clarence strums his little hand across them. They resonate with the most beautiful ear-trembling sound I have ever heard.

"This guitar is your Excalibur, Candypop. It will lead you to your destiny."

"You wouldn't think that noise could have come out of such a... beast of a thing," I say, somewhat in awe.

"Not *a* beast," Clarence corrects, "*The* Beast. Now – get those pyjamas off and let's get started."

5
Squashed Bananas and Stew

It transpires that Clarence B Major is a rock star. Or was.
Or should have been, if he wasn't dead. Which he is. Sort of.

"Very cross-making, you know, dying. Especially if you're in the middle of something. Now this finger pulls back a fret and there you are... a C chord."

Four hours after our initial meeting, I'm sitting on the bed, dressed in an outfit he handpicked (I look like Amy Winehouse in her darkest hours) being taught the guitar. Clarence is flitting back and forth checking the position of my hands as we work through chords, all the while filling me in on what it's like to die and transmogrify into a fairy. Actually, it seems that Clarence can transmogrify into anything he likes – he gives me a demo which involves him turning himself into a kettle, a frog, a ridiculous hat and finally a tiny planet with rings that looks like Saturn. Each change is accompanied by a blinding flash of light which leaves me feeling like a welder who's forgotten to put his goggles on. I search through the whiteout in front of me and can more or less make out Clarence, who has gone back to his original fairy-shape. "My favourite form," he says, "is a scaled-down version of the one I inhabited on earth. With a couple of useful additions!" He buzzes his wings, momentarily lifting himself a foot or two into the air.

So my flying friend has thrown himself into the role of mentor and I have found my tongue and then some. I'm still sort of trying to figure out (a) whether this is actually happening and (b) if it is – what the heck is going on. So far, via the medium of relentless badgering, here's what I've figured out:

According to Clarence, since he met his untimely end twenty-three years ago, he has been in a kind of limbo, not-quite-on, not-quite-off earth, waiting for the person to come along whose 'music' chimed with his. This person would become his charge and anchor him back to the land of the living. A twin soul who he could watch over, guide and protect. Someone whose successful union with all that is meant for them will override Clarence's unfinished business and allow him to move on. "But to move on where?" I ask. "To, like, heaven?"

"My dear girl, there is no such place. Or if there is, it is strictly metaphorical. There are only two states. The visible and the invisible. I have, by dint of misfortune and truncation of life, one foot in each realm. When my work here is done I may graduate *to the invisible*. I spend some of my time there, but you can call me back here by playing my chord – B Major – on this fine instrument." He pats the guitar on my lap fondly.

What's weird is how un-weird all this feels. Maybe it's his natural skills as a conversationalist, but it feels a bit like I'm chatting to my hairdresser. I'm also amazed by how quickly my fingers fall into place against the sparkling strings Clarence created. I barely have to think about it and they find chord after chord as Clarence shouts them out. It's as if a bigger force than me is in control. I've been building up to my next question for a good half an hour. I wince in anticipation but ask it anyway.

"How did you die, Clarence?"

He sighs, but whether from real emotion or to create a bit of dramatic tension, I can't tell. "There I was, amid the razzle-dazzle and stardust of London (well, my bedsit in Barnet to be precise) about to hit the big-time. It was Sunday night and I was all set to sign my record deal the next morning. I saw it, you know, on the way *up*."

He gives me a meaningful look.

"The contract, I mean. Sitting on my A&R man's desk, open at the page I was due to go in and make my mark on. I was due to start a new life, I just didn't know it would be *this* one." He flexes some mysterious muscle, spreading his wings even wider so that he can examine them which he does, glumly.

"Gentle pressure on the strings, my dear. Don't grip the neck. You're playing the guitar, not strangling it. Where was I? Oh yes, dying. So anyway that night I was, quite naturally, celebrating. 150 or so of my closest friends and I were having a costume party in the heart of Soho. Things were about to change so the theme was REVOLUTION! Naturally I had decided to go as Marie Antoinette."

Now it's my turn to give *him* a meaningful look. He ignores me.

"So there I was, face full of makeup, pearls, enormous gown fashioned from an old peach satin bedspread." He giggles at the memory. "Anyway, I was perfecting my *coiffure* (that's French for hairdo) when I fell foul of an appliance. My accommodation in those days being somewhat insalubrious, my measures for bathing were somewhat... primitive."

He falters. I catch his eye and he looks away shyly. I stop playing for a moment. "What do you mean, primitive? Don't be embarrassed, Clarence. In case you hadn't noticed, I hardly live in Buckingham Palace myself."

"I most certainly am not embarrassed, Candypop, I wouldn't know the meaning of the word! F minor! Move those ape-like digits of yours down a string. There... Anyway Marie Antionette's hair was terribly *high* and I was crafting a spectacular bouffant with the use of my hairdryer. As I mentioned, my conveniences were most *in*convenient at the time. Unfortunately, I had to bathe in an... um... well..." A look of disgust clouds his pristine features, "A *bucket*. In any case my bucket was still sitting there and I had quite forgotten about it. I was doing the tricky part at the crown when I lost my grip and the hairdryer tumbled out of my grasp. I instinctively went to catch it. I succeeded. The very moment it hit the water, that was it," he sighs, adding in a whisper, "*Poof!*"

I stop playing. Clarence is sitting on the windowsill now, hugging his knees, wings tucked in behind him, looking defeated like crumpled sellotape.

"I'm sorry."

He's quiet for a moment, then shivers throwing off his gloom like a cloak. "Thank you, my dear. In any event it led me here, to this..." he looks about him, aiming for a smile that lands more in the region of grimace, "...*delightful* seaside hamlet. And to you."

"So we're destined to be together, and you were sent here to look after me from a magical invisible world. Does that mean you're my..." I leave a pause where the word *fairy* should go "...Godfather?"

"God*father*? I should say not, darling. I was a mere handful of birthdays above you when I met my end. But God*brother*? Perhaps. Now. From a party that never got started to one that is about to begin; I believe you have a soirée to attend?"

"Glad's birthday! I completely forgot!"

"Luckily, I did not." He raises an eyebrow and flutters over to my dressing-table, where he extracts from the bric-a-brac a toy tiara Holly bought for me last Christmas and plonks it on top of the already-enormous hairstyle he has created. "The finishing touch to your outfit and, if I do say so myself... *fabulous*."

It's not until our front door bangs shut behind me and the freezing air hits me in the face like a bucket of cold water that I realise Clarence is actually, like, *coming with me*. He swoops into the air in a reverse swan dive with a "WHO—HOO-HOOO!" shooting so high into the snowy sky he could almost be mistaken for a particularly shiny flake.

I do an immediate 180, simultaneously hissing over my shoulder in a shouty whisper, "*Clarence! What do you think you're — Get back here NOW!*"

My Fairy Godbrother, meanwhile, is soaring high above like a demented shooting star. "Clarence! Come down here NOW!"

Nothing.

"CLARENCE!"

A faint giggle.

"CLAREENCE!!"

With a whoosh, he drops like a stone from the sky, a streak of light in his wake. I brace myself for a crash-landing on the roof of next-door's car but somehow he brakes, stopping a fraction above it, then lowering himself delicately on to the frosty bonnet. He spreads his arms as wide as his Cheshire-cat smile. "Sweet freedom, Candypop! Has there ever been a better day to be practically alive?"

I sigh. "Look, Clarence, I know you're happy to be out, I mean, back in the world and everything but..."

His grin shrinks a little.

"...but you can't come to Glad's party! You can't just go flying about everywhere! People will *see you*! This is Bishopspool – there are no fa... I mean... we don't do *magic* around here!"

Clarence smiles mischievously. "If we are going to agree on anything, my little Candypop, let us begin with this: we are not 'around here', here is 'around us' and we do precisely as we please!" And with that he zips off down the street, leaving me to run to catch up.

I wince as we enter the Day Centre. Clarence flits through the door ahead of me and off into the bowels of the building which is pulsating to the sounds of cheesy 70s disco and friendly chatter. I brace myself for a scream but none comes. Unsure of what else to do, I take my coat off and hang it up, then place Glad's gift atop the growing present pyramid on a nearby table.

Clarence zips out of view momentarily, then returns asking loudly, "What kind of soirée *is* this exactly? Where are the *cocktails?*" before settling on my shoulder. I hear a gasp, then turn to come face to face with the gaspee – Calum Stainforth, who dropped Glad off the other day. He is staring at me with his mouth hanging open. *Oh God! He can see Clarence!*

"Candy!" Calum breathes, "Is that...? Is that a..." it seems like a phenomenal effort for him to get the words out. There's a second's silence that feels like an eternity. Clarence's wings bristle beside my ear. Calum swallows hard. Just then, Glad appears by his side looking similarly shocked.

"Is that a new dress?" Calum manages to ask before Glad bursts into a peal of laughter and I remember that I have accidentally turned up dressed as a Guns 'n' Roses groupie from 1987.

"By God, lassie!" she chuckles. "It's not *that* kind of party! You look like you're dressed up for a night out there on the docks! Come inside and defrost!" She leads the way and I'm left with Calum who smiles awkwardly.

"Just trying a new look!" I laugh nervously, tugging down my mini-dress.

"I like it," he says, almost in a whisper.

At this point, Clarence takes off and performs an elaborate loop-de-loop around Calum's baseball-capped head, shouting (somewhat unnecessarily, because I'm already starting to figure this out), "Don't worry about him *seeing me*, Candypop! In my present state I am quite invisible to anybody other than you. It is only when I make myself into a physical object – a *thing* – that lumps like this one can spot me. Or hear me." He zooms round and round Calum's head, who obviously senses something as he shivers. Clarence laughs wildly. "I am incognito! Imperceptible! Undetectable!"

So, happily, Clarence goes unnoticed. Unhappily this makes me look as nuts as my outfit – try as I might, I just can't keep my eyes off him. He whizzes around like a gust of wind through the busy Day Centre, delighted to be at an actual live party with real human people (even if the birthday girl is eighty-four). Clarence might be out of sight but he isn't out of trouble. My gaze flits around the room in search of him. People can't see him but they flinch as he whooshes by, wondering what just happened (especially Glad's friend Alf, whose toupee is left spinning round like a record after one of Clarence's fly-pasts).

I'm keeping one eye out for Clarence among the dancing crowd (who are getting stuck into *YMCA*) when Mum and Ray arrive.

"Superb event!" Ray says to Glad, shaking her hand.

A dose of dullness is exactly what this party needs. So – strangely – as he and Mum cross the room, I find I'm almost glad to see him. "Where have you two been?"

"Hello darling!" trills Mum a little bit more loudly than necessary. Is she a little bit tipsy? "We've been celebrating!" She's tipsy. "You'll never guess. Ray has bought me an engagement present. A holiday in the Lake District! Very romantic."

"Skiddaw," says Ray, evidently very pleased with himself.

"Come again?"

"Skiddaw, Candy!" choruses Mum. "It's the fourth highest mountain in England and our hotel is just below it. Did you know some of the greatest literature our country ever produced was inspired by those views?"

Ray nods, "And the bass player from Jethro Tull."

"Anyway, darling," Mum continues, breezily, "I told Ray that I couldn't possibly consider leaving you on your own for seven whole days."

As she's already quite clearly had a celebratory glass of something-or-other and has therefore decided she *is* going, I leave a pause for her to fill.

"Unless…"

Bingo. "Unless what, Mum?"

"I mean I couldn't. Unless you were happy on your own? I mean, Glad's right next door and your little friend can come over and keep you company. What's her name again?"

"Holly, Mum."

"That's it! Holly. Such a sweet girl."

And my only friend in the world for, like, four whole years. Would it kill you to remember her name? I think to myself.

"So it's decided then? We're going?" Mum squeaks in excitement, putting her arms round Ray and giving him a squeeze.

"Apparently so," I shrug. "Have a great time. When are you going?"

"T minus fourteen days!" beams Ray. "We'd better get our crampons ready!"

"Excuse me?"

"I said we'd better get our crampons ready. And other climbing equipment. Your mother and I are going to scale Skiddaw."

"You. And Mum. You mean *my* mum? You're going to climb..." I turn to Mum confused. This is a woman who last wore flat shoes to her first Holy Communion. The most practical item in her wardrobe is made of PVC. I try to picture Mum dressed for a freezing March hike up one of England's tallest peaks. Can't. I take a swig of punch (which Glad *claims* is non-alcoholic, although on a day as mad as this, frankly, how would you know?) Mum's eyes begin to mist.

"We're going up the mountain, Candy! So romantic, don't you think? A metaphor for our new life together! I've always loved the great outdoors as you know..."

"HA!" It's a goose-like honk of a laugh, and it escapes before I can stop it. She looks hurt. "Sorry, Mum." I put my hand on her arm, fighting to submerge a particularly buoyant smile and not quite managing. "I'm sorry, but *when* have you always loved the great outdoors?"

"I've always loved getting out and about, up and down the coast, breathing the fresh sea air..."

"Yeah. Through the window of a car!"

"That's as may be. But now I'm ready to get out among it all, and Ray is quite the rambler."

"He does go on a bit, I'd noticed," I mutter under my breath. Ray doesn't hear but she does. There's a pause, during which Hot Chocolate's *You Sexy Thing* starts up. Ray slinks off to dance. I make a conscious effort not to look.

"That's *not* what I meant, young lady. You're impossible! Can't you just be happy for me about this one thing?"

"I am happy, Mum. You and Scott of the Antarctic go off and

enjoy yourselves. Just make sure you take the number of the local Mountain Rescue with you when you go."

A few hours, eighty-four candles, lots more cups of punch, a very loud chorus of *Happy Birthday* and one tearful (on the part of Glad) rendition of *Clair de Lune* later, it's time to leave. Ray escorted Mum home a while ago. "She's a bit tired and emotional," he explained, pulling her arm over his shoulders in a bid to keep her vertical. "It's been quite a week for both of us. Do you want me to come back for you with the car?"

Awkward – him doing Dad-stuff. I suppose he thinks that's his job now. For a second I imagined BioDad coming to pick me up and take me home instead. I pictured him driving a monster truck with massive wheels that rolled straight over Ray's Mondeo until it looked like a tea tray. I twisted my mouth to one side and shrugged. "Nah, I'm walking home with... um, with a friend." I extricate Clarence from the mobile DJ's CD collection which he is flipping through making comments of the "Ugh!", "Pah!" and "Bo-*ring*!" variety. I wish Glad one last 'Happy Birthday' and head out into the night.

6

The Magic Bus (Stop)

A few moments later we're outside in the darkness, wending our way up from the old docks to the coast road. The snow has stopped, but there's a thick, white blanket over everything but the sand. The place is soundless except for my footsteps and the slurp-slurp of the sucking black waves. I pull my collar up and (for the millionth time) regret that I am wearing so few clothes underneath my coat. Whatever Clarence turns out to be, I think we can rule out personal stylist. He's hovering ahead looking out to sea, outshining the pale winter moon above him.

"Quite surprising. And quite, quite beautiful."

I look around, picking up my pace to keep warm. "I s'pose you're right. The snow and stuff. It's pretty."

"Not this! Ha! Beautiful. Well, I suppose you've never really been anywhere, so how could you know? No, I mean *life*, Candy.

Your life. Too small. But it has… the makings of something."

We've reached a deserted bus shelter – my stop to get home, across the road from The Blue (currently slumbering like the rest of the street: lights off, shutters down). I check the bench for grossness – negative – and perch on the edge, joined by Clarence. We're both staring out to sea. That is, I presume we are. The view is so dark we could be looking over the edge of the world.

"So you're really real, then? And you're staying? I won't wake up tomorrow and this will have all been a dream?"

Clarence stretches a small sparkling hand forward and places it on top of mine. "Quite the reverse, my dear. You will wake up tomorrow and *that* will *become* your dreams. Your music is going to cure your ills and answer your questions. And best of all, it's going to make you a star."

"Clarence, you might be, like, magical, but I hope you realise what a big job this is. I've got no idea who or where BioDad is. My band have got one messed-up guitar, there are only two members and all our songs are about school. *Glad's* more likely to become an internet sensation than us."

Clarence contemplates this. He makes a circle with his thumb and forefinger and through it, blows three hovering bubbles into the air in front of us. There's a swirl of sparkling colour inside each: one blue, one red, one yellow; and each emits a harmonic little hum that together makes a chord.

The glittering colours whirl and eddy inside, like marbles come to life. Clarence pushes a gentle breath through pursed lips. The bubbles react like pool balls breaking – ricocheting off each other they burst as they hit, releasing what's inside – colour, light and sound. Alive and delighted to be free, the music mixes and mingles, eventually coming to rest in the most incredible cloud. A glowing rainbow of every note and shade you could ever imagine (and a hundred more) is suspended in front of us, shimmering and swirling in the streetlight. I look over at him and he smiles. "My magic is made of music, Candy. It has the same possibilities and restrictions as a song. Entirely subjective, it can change the world for one person but it might leave another cold. That's why I've waited such a long time to meet you." He raises his hand, palm up. International sign language for, "Have a go, then."

I take a breath, close my eyes and push my head inside the cloud. Instantly, it fills with music – major and minor all at once, happy, heartbreaking, quiet and ear-splittingly loud. Suddenly I'm not at the bus stop: I'm in the middle of every moment that ever meant anything to me. I'm out in space as big as a planet. And tiny: lost deep inside my own imagination. I hear Clarence speaking in the distance. "Think of it this way – you have the numbers, I know the combination. Together, we'll make your life a work of art!"

As I take in Clarence's words, the cloud around me starts to move. Little smoky plumes of colour pull themselves into shapes, scenes, faces. The people I love, the things I want. I see a door and know BioDad is on the other side of it, waiting for me. Then suddenly I'm back on the Pyramid Stage at Glastonbury, like in the dream I always have. Only this time it feels less like a dream and more like…

"Ahem!" A loud cough behind me. A very un-Clarencelike cough. The cloud evaporates along with my Fairy Godbrother. I plonk back down on to the bench and spin round.

"Evening… Didn't mean to interrupt you. I thought you were on your phone there but, um…"

Oh. My. Freaking. GOD! Dan Ashton. Dan Ashton scratching his head.

"Who were you talking to?"

My heart is beating like a kick drum but he can't hear that. Can he? Scratching the nape of his neck, brows knitted in confusion, Dan steps into the shelter and sits down next to me, placing a battered leather bag between us. I'm too nervous to look directly at him so I look at it instead. It isn't properly closed; I see the spine of a book, the title begins *Psychotic Reactions and Car…* white headphone wires and a plastic bag.

"Hey – I know you! You come into the café sometimes. With that emo girl!"

Emo? Sometimes? I practically LIVE THERE!

"Uh huh. Holly you mean. She's not an emo. Not now anyway." With the concerted effort of ripping off a plaster, I flick my eyes up for a second, taking a snapshot of his face I will always remember. Brown eyes made as deep and black as the sea by the streetlights; that dark mess of hair falling into them; an expression something like a question mark; half-a-smile and frozen breath. A shadow under his cheekbone so perfect it looks drawn on. I get a sudden urge to reach out and touch it. I sit on my hands. The half-smile gains a quarter.

"And you?"

Oh God, questions. I'm so nervous. Note to self: BE COOL. DO NOT TALK TOO MUCH. I REPEAT, BE COOL.

"Emo? No way! I mean I like all kinds of stuff. Some of it's all right, I suppose. Apparently it all started with The Smiths and I like them. My mum used to play *Girlfriend in a Coma* a lot, which I always thought was really freaky, though…"

What are you going on about? Stop talking now.

"…She had a boyfriend once who used to sing it to her, which was just *wrong*. He had a quiff. Before, like, before it was OK again…"

STOPTALKINGSTOPTALKINGSTOPTALKING!

"No, I meant your name. What's your name?"

Oh. God.

"Oh God. I mean... Oh no. No... it's Candy. Candy Caine."

"Candy Caine." My name on his lips: half as good as a kiss.

"I'm Dan. Ashton. Pleased to meet you." He extends a hand towards me, I pull mine out from under my leg as gracefully as possible (which is not very, it squeaks on the plastic bench) and slip it into his. We shake, palm against palm and it feels like we really are on the edge of the world and have just jumped off. "Been somewhere cool?"

"A party. Birthday party."

"Where are you heading now?"

"Home."

"Yeah? I thought a girl like you would have more options than that on a Saturday night."

What does that mean? I give a non-committal laugh and hope it's something good. We sit in silence for three seconds. My chest feels like an overstuffed birdcage. If this goes on much longer I might cough up a feather. I'm trying to think of something to say next when Dan speaks.

"Ah... bus!"

It is indeed a bus. With impeccable timing, the 160 thunders towards us and into our stop. A hen party are piled into the back few rows, big girls in small clothes and pink cowboy hats giggling over half-hidden bottles. Dan stands, shoulders his bag and gestures for me to go ahead.

"After you."

I'm one step on to the bus home with the boy of my dreams when I remember: Clarence. I can't leave without Clarence. I turn around just as Dan starts to step up and smack straight into him. His nose whacks into my cheek and even through my coat I feel the mortifying squish of his hand against my boob. The contents of his bag go flying and he follows them down, attempting to retrieve them from the snow. I crouch beside him but I'm not sure whether he'd mind me touching his stuff so I just make 'helpy' arm movements without actually doing anything useful.

"Oh God! Oh no! Sorry! I'm sorry. Is anything broken? Listen, I can't... I mean I just remembered. I've got to..."

"You've got to what?" Dan brushes snow off his iPhone then presses the button to check it still works. It lights up.

Thank God.

"I've got to... to get the next bus!"

"What?"

"Yep. The one after this. I'm going with a friend. He doesn't really know his way around here so I've got to meet him and..."

I look out at the empty seafront, snow and blackness and nothing else. I sound completely mental.

The bus driver, who looks like a potato and is evidently just as romantic cuts in. "Are you two getting on or getting off?"

We straighten up. "Getting off," I say. Just as Dan says, "Getting on... Shame. Hope you and your 'friend' have a great night, Candy. It was nice meeting you."

Oh no! 'FRIEND'? He's annoyed. His eyes wander to the back of the bus. One of the younger prettier hens notices and starts to giggle in his direction, chugging on a bottle of something fluorescent.

"No! No, he's not that kind of... he's a friend. You know, like, *just friends.* I don't have a – I mean, I'm... single." His eyes find me again and there's a flutter in my chest. I try to sound casual. "Single at the moment."

By which I mean FOREVER.

"Oh, right. Well... I guess maybe I'll see you in The Blue sometime?"

"Sure, yeah. Definitely. See you there. You will see me too! Unless there's a freak accident and you go blind. Or I go invisible. Or both. Hopefully not, obviously. Do we have a nuclear power plant around here I don't know about? Ha..."

Stop. Talking. Now.

I bite my lip. As the bus doors swing closed, Dan says, "Great dress, by the way."

"What?"

What?

The doors hiss closed and I look down to discover that in the commotion my coat has come undone, revealing... well, revealing pretty much everything. As the bus pulls away I fingers-and-thumbs my coat up, frantically scanning the moonlit street for Clarence at the same time. Suddenly he appears, hanging upside down from the top of the bus stop.

"Clarence! It's a miracle! I spoke to Dan Ashton!"

He smoothes his right eyebrow with his finger. "And what's more unlikely it appears you can *almost* flirt!"

"*Flirt?*" I attempt a casual dismissal of the accusation with an accompanying hand gesture; but I'm so flustered it comes out as a fit of spluttering, choking and arm-flapping. Like an angry ostrich trying to start a really old car.

"Well," says Clarence, when I have eventually come to an embarrassed stop, "I don't know if I'd really call it *flirting*, either, that being a delicate and balletic art. Whatever it was, that young man was lapping it up. He likes you!"

The words light a little candle somewhere inside my chest. The sensation is so strange – a quiet ache as sweet as it is strong – that I hardly hear Clarence say, "And that is going to be very useful indeed..."

7

Bravery, Cunning and Feats of Daring Do

"What is going on with you today, Can?"

Monday. I'm at Holly's, in her room. We're supposedly doing homework but actually listening to last.fm and laughing so hard we almost wet ourselves. Still in our school uniforms, Holly has fashioned a 'Ramboesque' headband from her tie and I am wearing my jumper as a turban. And people say kids have nothing to do these days. We lie side by side on the bed. Pirate being somewhat funsize and me lanky, her feet just about reach my knees.

"Nothing! What? I'm fine! Finer than swine drinking wine!" I dissolve into another fit of hysterics.

"That's just it, though. You had the biggest mope *ever* on all last week and now you're..."

"I'm ridiculous!" I squeak, before being swept away in a tide of convulsive giggles. Holly is absolutely right, of course. Since actually *speaking*, and I mean *actual words* to D. Ashton, the world has been made of marshmallows and someone appears to have switched off gravity. But as is so often with Holly, it is unwise, nay, impossible to give her the full facts. If I told Pirate that Dan and I had spoken and specifically mentioned seeing each other at The Blue, she would march me down there instantly and force me to talk to him, probably insisting I start with a ridiculously implausible lie.

"Hello Daniel Ashton! Our car has broken down – is it all right if we shelter here in your special music-shop, cubby-hole thing until the AA arrive to tow us to safety? What's that you say? Aren't we fifteen and unable either to drive or indeed buy a car?"

No. No. Nonononono.

Previously, I would have caved and told her everything, but having Clarence to talk to has got enough Dan out of my system to stop that happening. Clarence has a fantastic ear for music as well as listening and put both to full use yesterday. I am now able to play pretty much any chord on guitar (although getting from one to the next sometimes takes a while). Late last night, I wrote a song. This time I actually think it might be a quite good song. Later last night Clarence also extracted and digested the entire story of my Dan obsession, chewing over each titbit of information like an olive from the bottom of a cocktail. I don't know how, but Clarence B Major knows exactly how it feels to be a teenage girl. He has also managed to bring together my improved musical and romantic talents to hatch a genius plan – a plan that will light a fire under Operation Awesome and take the whole deal stratospheric.

This is where Pirate comes in. I am marginally terrified about almost all of it but I'm 100 per cent convinced that it will work. Since Clarence put my head in that cloud on Saturday, anything seems possible. I feel like I've been given a preview of my future and I'm giddy at the thought.

Stomping over to the computer, Hol turns up *Battle Royale* by Does It Offend You, Yeah? Her bedroom is bigger than mine, but mostly pink and covered in pictures of princesses and ballerinas as she shares it with her two little sisters. On her way back to the bed she steps on a pointy, plastic doll.

"Bloody Norah!" she screams, face gripped by cartoon agony. I start laughing again, only just ducking out of Barbie's way as Hol flings her at my head. I retrieve the doll and putting on my best Miss World voice.

"Pirate, don't be mean to your friend Candy. She has news happier than dancing kittens and smiling unicorns!"

Hol ignores Barbie and levels her question at me. "What news is this, then?"

I jettison the thing into the toy landfill on the floor and scootch down to Hol's end of the bed, removing my jumper-turban so as not to compromise either the gravity or brilliance of Clarence's idea. Sensing something significant is about to happen, Hol removes her Rambo band.

"News of an unbelievably excellent plan. For The Biscuits. We need other members, right?"

Holly pushes her tongue under her bottom lip, crosses her eyes and screws her face up into a village-idiot expression, "NNnnuuh!!"

"A simple 'yes' will suffice, Rodgers. We need members, yes?"

"*Yes.*"

"And our efforts to get Operation Awesome off the ground have so far proved... well, useless really."

She scowls.

"Although the OA concept has been fantastically executed and possessed of huge artistic charm."

Placated, Holly gives a queenly nod. "Proceed."

"Anyway I was thinking – you've got the right idea but maybe the wrong medium!"

"Medium?"

"Yeah – we need to reach out to people but in a way they're going to, like, get excited by?" I take a little breath and feel a pang of guilt for passing off the ideas Clarence and I had talked about yesterday – Clarence's ideas – as my own. "Hol, listen. What are the biggest music shows on TV?"

She gives me her trademark bored stare, one that you and I might throw at a wall of drying paint but that Hol reserves for teachers, siblings and other inferior life-forms. "There are no music shows on TV."

I clear my throat. "Talent contests. *Britain's Got Talent. X Factor...*"

"Are we counting those noises as music now?"

"OK the music's terrible, but people love it. Millions of people! And the bit they love best is...?"

The Stare again.

"It's the auditions, Holly. People love an audition – the chance to show off, the chance of success, the risk of rejection. Something about it captures their imagination. And even more than auditioning, people love to *watch auditions.*"

Half The Stare, half a frown of genuine confusion.

"Look. In two weeks, Mum and Ray are going away, right? On holiday to some mountain or other."

Hol's expression shifts to one of slyly amused intrigue, like a detective finding the scent of guilt on a suspect. Pirate smells fun.

"We'll have the house to ourselves for seven whole days. We could hold auditions. Well... a party. An auditions party."

Hol raises an eyebrow. "Aren't the people who volunteer for that sort of thing *not* what we're looking for, though? They're '*ow you say, un peu fou*? Loons? Oddballs? Fruitcakes?"

I see her eyebrow and raise her my other. "You could call them Broken Biscuits?"

"Touché." She mulls, then laughs. She's almost in. "I'm not in yet, Can. I mean it – we need proper cool people in our band. Me and you are the misunderstood eccentric geniuses who will come to be appreciated in our later years. But you can't have more than two of those in any one musical ensemble."

She's right. As I understand it, those *are* the rules.

"Hol, that's where the party bit comes in. Maybe a few freaks will turn up, but loads of other people are going to want to come and watch. Some of them are bound to be secretly curious, they get into the party mood, step up themselves and I think we might just manage to get a band together!"

Holly runs both hands through her blonde mop. "Our watchwords, Candy, are *enigmatic* and *talented*. Now where do you suggest we find *that* in Bishopspool?"

This is the bit where I think I might be sick. As I say it, I remember the words coming out of Clarence's mouth yesterday afternoon.

"Daniel Ashton."

I'd laughed at first. Then I realised he was serious. "That young man is the Pied Piper of this particular Hamelin, my dear. To get the right following, you have to play the right tune. Besides, you have to speak to him sooner or later. And I told you – *he likes you.* For my part, of course, I will aid and abet you in every way."

I'm not sure whether it was the undeniable truth of Clarence's statement (Dan *is* the coolest person in town. He just is) or his promise to help when I next speak to Dan or breathing in fumes from that cloud at the weekend, but I found myself agreeing. I had left for school this morning with a strange mixture of fear and excitement – that my life was up and running at last. Even if he is a stress-related hallucination (which I still haven't ruled out entirely) Clarence has switched the power supply to ON. If I'm brave enough to effectively *ask Dan Ashton out,* my band taking over the world should be easy.

I clear my throat. "I'm going to get Dan Ashton to come. We get him, we've got everyone we need."

Hol nods thoughtfully before reaching down to her ankle, extracting her nicotine inhaler from inside her sock and placing it to her lips. "Yep. I can see that. But how will you get him? I mean, I know you like him but you'll never... do you want me to, like *have a word*?" She takes a meaningful drag and gives me a saucy look from beneath her eyeliner.

What I lack in confidence with boys, Hol more than makes up for. Her current flame, Bruno, is a DJ from Buenos Aires who she met through his music blog. Not that she has actually, like, *met* him. That's what the piggy bank under the bed is being fattened up for.

"I'm going to ask him," I say quietly.

There's a pause as we digest the audacity of the proposal.

"You mentalist," Holly pronounces authoritatively. "Operation Awesome has been appropriately named. This party. Is going to go. Down. In. History."

And we both start laughing again, first at all of this, then at each other, harder and harder until we can't stop even when we try.

8

Operation Who's the Daddy?

"It's a gold-to-bronze tonic sateen with chantilly-insert here. Classical style but with a little bit of a *funky twist*! Hee hee! All your ruffles, bit of fullness where nature has yet to provide! Tee hee! Hnnn hnnn..."

"You're sure it isn't a bit... orange?" Mum asks, squinting uncertainly at me.

"Goodness NO dearie! Trust me – I've been doing this for twenty-seven years and I've never sent a Bride to the altar unhappy! Think of it in that June light... and it's on special offer."

Mum softens (presumably in the head). "Oh well, if you say so... What do you think, Can?"

Why are we here again?

I'm standing on a box, glaring at myself in three giant mirrors angled in to one another to give an almost 360-degree view of how hideous I look, wrapped in a suffocating cocoon of orange fabric so manmade that I started sweating as soon as I looked at it. In the left-hand mirror I can see Glad, settled into a white wicker chair, feet not quite touching the floor, sipping a cup of complimentary tea and smiling. Mum is following the lady circling my feet. Round and round, pin, pin, tug, tuck.

"Why are we here again, Mum? It's not for ages yet!" I finally say.

Mum and the lady look at each other and exchange knowing simpers. The lady speaks through a mouthful of pins, plucking them out sporadically and piercing them deep into the ever-tightening dress. Death by taffeta, boa-constrictor style.

"Luvvie, you're lucky you've come now. We usually pop in an appointment with our Brides-to-Be six months before their Big Day. Luckily your mam here is sample size." She shoots Mum an even more simpering look of approval, "so we can more-or-less go off peg. But eighteen weeks is very tight for providing the standard what we do."

I glance out of the window of TOP CLASS BRIDES to the retail park outside. A lorry reverses into the loading bay of the twenty-four-hour supermarket next door. The driver swears loudly as a stray dog runs out behind him.

I turn back to my reflection. I look like a person-sized Quality Street. All afternoon the three of us have been referred to in a capitalised fashion – Bridesmaid, Bride to Be, Mother of the Bride (Mum and me didn't correct the lady on this one and neither did Glad. We all know she's as good as). We have been poked, prodded and stuffed into a variety of dresses, heels, hats, tiaras, boleros, cinchers, winchers. Every one of them hideous. Or at least they are to me. Mum normally looks quite cool but as soon as we started shopping for the wedding it's like she's had a taste bypass. It's like modelling at the fashion show from hell. In fact, if I wasn't so comprehensively pinned into this frock horror right now, I'd be tempted to turn it round and have a look at the label. *Maison de Satan*, I bet you.

Inexplicably, the more horrendous the dresses, the more Mum seems to be enjoying herself. She's so filled up with happiness it seems to be spilling back out – a sort of glow. I sneak a glance at the ornate clock on the back wall. It's almost five – I've got stuff to get on with today. Important stuff. Plus, if we don't get this over with sharpish, Clarence is going to suffocate in his current hiding place (can you die twice?) At any rate there is a distinct possibility I am going to die of boredom. "I... er... I think she's right, Mum. This one's OK," I say, trying not to look down in case I actually throw up.

"Really, Can? You really like it? I'm just not sure about the colour..."

"I love it!" I lie. "It's so... um... zesty!" I throw a quick smile and a few nods at Mum, then the lady, who smiles back carefully around the tacks in her mouth. I catch Glad's eye in the mirror. Rumbled. She knows I'm lying but doesn't say anything, just places her teacup back in the saucer and steadily returns my gaze.

I deposit Mum and an unreadable Glad into a taxi. I can feel Glad wanting to talk to me as I help her into the car. Escape is imperative. Mum winds the window down and pops her head out, "Aren't you coming with us, darling? I've got a bottle of Cava in the fridge so we can celebrate!"

"Mum, I'm fifteen! You're not supposed to encourage me to drink."

She pouts, crestfallen. "It hardly counts if it's fizzy, darling."

"*Special Brew* is fizzy, Mum. Anyway I've got to meet Holly. See you!"

Waving, I watch the taxi go before turning on my heel and running round the back of the supermarket to the bus stop.

It's almost March and while it's still too cold to say spring is in the air, it's definitely round the corner: almost five o'clock and still light. I catch the bus along the seafront and stare out into the watercolour sky. The world is stirring, growing, changing. Seven days ago, Clarence exploded into my life. In seven more Holly and I are throwing a party like Bishopspool has never seen. Seven after that... who knows? I take a deep breath – it feels cold, fresh and full of possibility.

This week I've played guitar until my fingers bled. At night in my room, Clarence has taught me some of 'the greats' ("the primary colours of pop music, Candy Caine.") The Who, The Kinks, The Clash, The Fall, Bowie, Blur. He has stories about them all too. I haven't slept much but I feel fantastic. Music is feeding me and I don't need anything else. At lunchtimes and after school, Pirate and me have planned and schemed and imagined and dreamed. I've written six songs; taught Holly three; stolen a whole extra life out of the one I already had. Hol can't believe how fast I'm learning – she thinks it's to impress Dan at the party and maybe there's some truth in that – but I'm looking for something else too. Someone, to be precise. It's time to take the next step.

I get off a stop early and take a detour into the back alley behind The Blue. The delivery van from the florist's pootles past, then I am alone. Opening up my overstuffed handbag as if I'm looking for my keys, I whisper.

"It's OK. You can come out now."

In a flash, Clarence shoots out of the open zip leaving a trail of old bits of paper, pencil shavings and elastic bands as he goes. He dusts himself off, an expression of disgust on his face.

"Quite how you expect me to be imprisoned in that foul maw for hours on end I have no idea! When did you last clean it out anyway? A *handbag*? It's more like a scrapyard..."

I roll my eyes. I knew he was going to be difficult about this. "Clarence I told you! It's too distracting to have you flying about all over the place! People are going to think I'm even weirder than they do already. So you can either stay invisible or be something everyone can see, at least in public." He pouts but I persist. "Those are the rules. Do you want to come or not?"

Clarence shakes out his hair. "My dear, as we both very well know, I am indispensible! Are you ready?"

I exhale. Time to exchange one set of possibilities for certainty. We're about to find my dad. Despite searching the house from top to bottom, we can't unearth my birth certificate and according to Clarence, BioDad is "of pivotal importance" to everything so we're going to look for one online. Our computer at home (by which I mean the one in the salon) is off-limits for work this sensitive, especially during the day, so we're off to The Blue. As a keen observer of action here on earth for the last couple of decades, Clarence knows what the web is but he doesn't really actually get it. Talking to him about this stuff is like one of those conversations when somebody's telling you – in extremely boring detail – the route they drove to get to wherever you are. He feigns polite interest but I suspect he's thinking about something else. I'm not entirely sure how helpful he's actually going to be but I appreciate his company.

"You going back in the bag?" I ask.

"Thank you, Candypop, but I would rather eat glass," he replies lightly. Clarence's face creases up in concentration. From somewhere he emits a crystalline hum. He reaches his arms up above his head and then, before my very eyes, rolls up into a shining white cylinder which then reveals itself to be a long slim glowing fountain pen, lying in the palm of my hand. I lift it closer to my face and notice that there is a tiny head on top of the lid – Clarence's. He is smiling in a self-satisfied fashion.

"Well I think that went well!" he says, smugly. "Now how can you possibly say I'm distracting?"

"Clarence you're a *talking pen*!"

"Would that such a useful invention were available to the masses!"

"So, will people be able to see you?" I ask.

"They will now that I am an *object* rather than myself. But why should they notice? I am practically incognito – I mean, what could be more workaday than a pen? The accoutrement of any conscientious pupil? And at least I won't have to go back into that appalling attaché of yours. Now hurry up and get in there!"

Hesitantly, in case I either hurt him or touch anything gross, I clip Clarence to the strap of my bag and make my way into the café. It's Saturday, so The Blue is pretty packed. Dog walkers, families and metal detectives all chat and bustle over fish and chips, old ladies in clothes older than my mum sip milky tea and watch the world go by outside. I make my way to the back and the Blue Room, where Dan is behind the counter, hunched over a magazine. The stereo behind him pumps out the cheerful *Best of The Byrds* into the café. They always make him play old stuff on Saturdays. I take a deep breath and do one of those unnecessary throat-clearing coughs to announce my presence.

He looks up and, seeing me, smiles. I can't help thinking it's more to himself than at me.

"Bus girl! I was wondering when I'd see you again."

"Hey." I smile, holding his gaze as long as I dare.

It must be a bit too long because he says. "So... what can I do you for, exactly?"

And for a moment I have no idea.

"Oh! Oh yes. Um... I need to use the computer." I scrabble around in my purse for change. "How long for three pounds?"

Dan slips out of a side door in his little record booth and re-emerges next to me a moment later. "It's supposed to be an hour but I'll do you two. Mates rates." He winks. I try not to faint.

Clarence and I settle into a little brown cubicle in the corner of The Blue and start searching for a copy of my birth certificate. Before long it is completely obvious that I am not going to be able to find it, at least not for free (which is the amount I have to spend). I suppose it makes sense. If any old Tom, Dick and Candy could view birth certificates online, identity theft would be pretty easy. I feel even stupider than usual. Clarence, who is beside the keyboard watching me tap away, sighs. "The leisure age is really terribly *dull*, isn't it?"

"*Clarence!* Sssh!"

"In my day we were promised a thrill-ride powered by the white heat of technology!" He glances around himself, which – in pen form – is not easy. "What a joke!"

I'm trying to work out what to do. But Clarence is on a roll. His whisper rises to a crescendo. "A simulacrum of a life is not a life, Candy Caine! That much I know from bitter experience. One must get out there and *taste the world* in the flesh!"

"Clarence!" I hiss. "Will you *shut up*!? I'm trying to concentrate! I've got two pounds seventy-five left to go on here and for two pounds seventy-four of it I want *complete silence*! OK?"

Clarence huffily rearranges his features to look pen-like. I get back to Google and go through more searches. Missing birth certificate? Replacement Birth Certificate? Where can I view my birth certificate? Bishopspool birth certificates?

Another twenty minutes and nothing. At least nothing I can afford. And judging by the forms I've got to fill in to get a new one, I'm short on information as well as money. I don't know the address Mum was living at when I was born (at least not the house number), her occupation (would she still have put down 'model'?) and – obviously – the *father's* name is a bit of a mystery. I shove the keyboard away crossly and sink my head into my hands. "This is useless! I don't even know any of the stuff it's asking! I mean, if you're trying to find out who your dad is, you're hardly going to be able to type in his flipping name, are you?"

Clarence maintains the silent demeanour of a writing implement.

"I said *are you*, Clarence? I know you can hear me! I know you're dying to speak! I said what am I supposed to do? I don't know the answers to any of these questions!"

Opening his eyes, he wrinkles up his nose and in a voice heavy with scorn, whispers, "Had I not taken a *vow of silence* – which I have – I may have been able to make a suggestion. As it is, I couldn't possibly comment."

"Clarence! *Clarence*! Come on... I need your help! Aren't you supposed to be my mentor here?"

But it's no good. Clarence in a mood is deaf to reason.

OK. So, the only people I know anything about are me and Mum (and with her there are definitely patchy bits). I'll start with her. I type in *Margaret Claire Caine*. A Canadian actress, a company CEO in Houston, Texas... Seven pages in and someone from Dumfries is searching for Margaret Caine, their long-lost scout mistress back in the 1960s. Mum is mysterious but she's not *that* mysterious. I decide to see if any of her old modelling shots are online. She did a couple of biggish ad campaigns and shoots before I popped up to spoil the party. What was that conditioner one again? Oh yes – *Nature's Lustre*! Mum has, on occasion, been known to refer to herself sarcastically as 'the Nature's Lustre Girl'. Image search. *Nature's Lustre girl Maggie*. Nothing. (By which I mean a hundred thousand photos of people who aren't Mum). That's weird. Idly, I skip through about fifteen pages of stranger-faces. The names below the images start to reshuffle themselves slightly as the results become less relevant. I look at the clock. Only the inbuilt thriftiness I learned from Glad is keeping me going. Must... use up... full... three pounds...

"BLOODY HELL!"

The words pop out of my mouth at top volume before I even have a chance to think them, causing a bit of a stir among the patrons around me which takes a moment to abate. Cutlery is rearranged, bums shift in seats. I bow my head slightly lower.

Clarence – who has evidently decided to break his vow of silence – strains to get a look at the monitor.

"What is it? What? CANDY? SHOW ME! SHOW ME!"

I lift him up to the screen. "Oh! Oh my! Valentine? That's your Mother all right. But that can't be… That can't be who I think it is with her? Is it?"

In front of us is a photograph. Underneath it says:

…happened to **Maggie Valentine**??? Our **Nature's Lustre girl**! Xmas 94! Good times!!!

Slightly bleached out by the camera flash, Mum looks impossibly beautiful if sort of frail (even thinner than she is now). She is looking just off camera, laughing – a laugh so huge it breaks her face in two. Her long loose shiny hair is the opposite to the way she wears it now, her neat vintage 'do'. Here it almost reaches her waist. Further than her black crop-top anyway. Is that a pierced belly button? I didn't know about that. So 90s. She's even wearing a choker. There is tinsel and streamers all over the place. It looks like someone is firing Party Poppers into the picture – yes, that's what she's looking towards. What she's laughing at. Her arms are wrapped around a man. Well, he's a man now. Everybody knows that. At the time he was sort of a boy. His eyes have found the camera, of course. Green and piercing, straight down the lens. Something people like him have an inbuilt talent for.

He's hugging Mum back but there's something territorial in it. He's smirking, not laughing. A cigarette trapped tightly in the corner of his mouth. Casually dangling his bottle of beer by its neck. Clarence – now completely forgetting himself – takes three good hops so that he is nose-to-nose with the screen. Even he is awestruck. "*Is* that who I think it is?"

I nod. "Nathan Oxblood."

I knew that Mum knew a few movers and shakers but *Nathaniel Oxblood*? As in Nathan Oxblood from *The Rain*? As in *only the biggest bloody band in the world ever since this picture was bloody well taken*?

Not wanting to lose the photo, I open up a new window. Image search. Breathe in. Out. I type each letter slowly… M-a-g-g-i-e- V-a-l-e-n-t-i-n-e. The name has changed but not as much as she has. I click search.

This time there are lots more photos. Of course there are still some stranger-faces in there but most of them are Mum. Or whoever she was then. And almost all of them have something to do with The Rain. After a while I start doing searches on The Rain 1994 or Nathan Oxblood 94. Sure enough, Mum is in the background of lots of those pictures, too. Beautiful and silent. Smiling in sunglasses. I suppose anyone else wouldn't even notice her. You kind of expect it in that type of photo. Band? *Check*! Grumpy-looking lead singer? *Check*! Anonymous pretty girl? *Check*! She's just a prop denoting *this dude's job is being a rock star*. Like a guitar or a bottle of whisky. And there are others. Lots! They all sort of look alike and – to be honest – sometimes even I can't quite work out who is Mum and who isn't.

The one thing I know for sure is that the first photo I found is the last one of them together. It's from a blog by some lady called Christie who works in London at a place called Awesome! PR Apparently, she was at Reckless Records (The Rain's original label before they moved over to EMI and went stratospheric). The picture is one of her old photos, taken at the Reckless Records Christmas party in 1994. Most of the blog is total gibberish. This is what it says about my mum.

Whatever happened to Maggie Valentine??? Our Nature's Lustre girl! Xmas 94! Good times!!! Mags and Nate were soooo cute!!!!! She really was mad for it though!! Does anyone else remember the time she broke into EMF's dressing room at the Camden Palace and nicked all their beers??? Naughty naughty girl!!!

That's it. Evidently Christie loves exciting punctuation marks as much as Mum loves a drink. So not everything has changed. An image pops into my head of Mum back then trying to placate EMF (whoever they are) about their stolen beers.

"It hardly counts if it's fizzy, darling..."

The sky outside is darkening now. I look up and notice that everybody else around me has gone and Surly Girl is making moves to close up the café. I've scribbled down a few URLs so I can find some of the pictures again but I don't have any more money to print anything off.

What does all this mean? For one thing it looks like Mum's life back then was much more exciting than I ever imagined. She was at the epicentre of a musical earthquake! I close down all the other windows, leaving only the original picture onscreen. Mum, limbs pretzelled around the biggest rock star on the planet. Him happily claiming ownership in return with a look to camera that says *Hands off! She's mine.* "Vulpine", Clarence calls it, "Like a fox who's just broken in to a henhouse." This is the last photograph of my mum before she disappeared from The Rain's entourage. December 1994. Eight or so months before I was born. Technically, I am *in* that picture. Someone appears at my side lugging a leather bag.

"I've got to close up now, Bus Girl. Would you like to print a copy of that off?"

It's Dan.

"I don't have any money."

"No biggie." He smiles. "My brother owns this place. He's just out the back on *Second Life*. I'll get him to come and sort you out." He crosses to the food counter, ducks underneath it past Surly Girl and shouts upstairs through a beaded curtain at the back.

"Jay! JAY! JASON! Come and give us a hand down here so we can close up, mate? Got a printing job." Then to me he says," Just so you know – he's a weirdo."

Seconds later a small slight pot-bellied bloke in his mid-twenties flounces through the beads. Over his T-shirt and tracksuit bottoms he's wearing a long black cape accessorised by something resembling a Viking warrior's helmet. Only it's made of plastic and with what looks like a headset microphone on the front. In his hand is a toy sword with a USB wire coming out. He speaks without pausing for breath, like this:

"WhatareyoudisturbingmeforDan?I'minthemiddleofaBATTLE!"

"Mate, we all want to get home and the printer's bust. Candy there needs to print something off but the thing... er... ate her money," Dan lies.

Without saying another word, Jason stalks over to my computer and presses a couple of keys without looking. Apparently, Dan's brother is entirely unembarrassed by his outfit. I can't decide whether to find this sad or impressive. He stomps over to the printer and removes the photograph. It isn't until he's about to hand it over that he says, "Hey! That'sthatguy! NateOxblood! ThispictureisWAYold! Beforehe grewthatLUDICROUSbeard!"

I give it a moment just in case Jason realises he has made this comment while essentially dressed as a baby Darth Vader.

He doesn't, continuing, "Where'dyoufindthis? Doyouknowhim? Doyouknowher?"

I look down at the photograph. Unsure what to say, I opt for the truth. "I don't know either of them." Suddenly I think I might cry. Grabbing my stuff, I jump up and manage to squeak, "I've got to go. Thanks. Thanks Dan."

Looking a little nonplussed, Dan waves at me as I run out of the door and into the darkness.

The cool air is like a bucket of water over my foggy head. What am I supposed to make of this? The top deck of our bus home is entirely empty, every window completely misted up. We take a seat right back and Clarence resumes his usual form, although he is unusually silent.

"He's got green eyes," I say eventually. More out loud than to him.

He smiles, sort of happy-sad.

"I know. Like you."

9

Bus Girl, the Dream Boat and Pants Stain

That night I dream about the party. There is a queue of awesomely-dressed kids all the way down the street, waiting to get in. I'm dressed up too, looking through the window of our darkened front room where the auditions are going to be held. I should be excited – only I'm not. I'm scared. Every aspect of the dream is permeated by this acute sense of fear. Something terrible is going to happen. One by one the kids outside start making their way into the house. It's at this point that I realise I can't see anybody's face. They're all hidden – muffled up in hats, scarves and hoods (one of them is even wearing a plastic Viking helmet and cape). A sickly dread slips its fingers around my throat and squeezes. My stomach drops to my shoes. Run. I need to run. But my feet won't move. Mum appears beside me. "Don't go!" she laughs, grabbing my wrist and throwing me down on to the sofa. "This is what you've been waiting for!"

"Music!"

It's Clarence. He claps, throws his arms wide and is suddenly wearing a guitar. My guitar – only pristine and scratchless. The room starts to spin. Clarence starts to play a drunken merry-go-round version of *She's Only the Only One* by The Rain – it sends firecracker sparks out into the room which is quickly filling with people. One by one at first then in twos and threes and more: silent, faceless, looming. Clarence flutters above them noodling on his guitar. Then, like an overexcited sports reporter, he shouts: "Aaaannnd if you don't want to know the results... LOOK AWAY NOW!!!"

With one enormous flourish the crowd unmasks itself. Hats fly across the room, scarves whip and whirl into the air. A hundred faces all belonging to one man. Every photograph and TV image I've ever seen of Nathan Oxblood, grafted in 3D on to the teenage bodies of the crowd.

A skater boy wears the head of the hungry-eyed poet from the picture with Mum, smirking and smoking. Next to him is a fake-tanned skinny girl in a gold prom dress. Her head is Nathan Oxblood in black and white. The famous, heartthrob-in-waiting picture from the cover of The Rain's debut album *Yes I Do*. She keeps shouting "COME ON YOU LOT! HAVE IT!!"

A nerdy kid in his school uniform is swearing at the top of his lungs. His face is from a grainy newspaper pap-shot, twisted with rage. Nathan falling out of a nightclub and into a fight. All the Nathans have the same eyes – green, piercing and laser-bright.

The noise is cacophonous. Rock Beast Nathan is belting out *Saviour* in wraparound shades. Off-to-rehab Nathan is babbling, bloated and grey. Haunted and hunted, the head from a long-lens shot of his escape to L. A. five years ago keeps shouting "*Leave me ALONE!*" Then there's Nathan now – the yoga-loving recluse, tanned by the L. A. sunshine and sporting a mid-life crisis haircut, chanting "Ommmm…"

I cover my ears but there's no escape. The noise is inside my head. I'm uselessly trying to block it out as the Nathans start to advance in my direction. Pair upon pair of burning green eyes turn on me, red-hot needles pricking my skin.

"NO! NO! NOOOO!"

I come to, flailing like a confused ghost, standing up underneath the teddy-bear-duvet-of-shame. After a few seconds wrestling, I manage to find daylight. The soft spring sun is up and about, small sounds of a day in progress outside leak in through the window. I have slept late.

After failing to wash any of my confusion away in the shower (but at least making myself look a bit less like a Furby) I go downstairs to look for Mum. I find her in the back yard doing yoga. Quite how much Mum's version of yoga resembles the ancient Indian discipline I'm not sure. She has done it daily for a while now and definitely looks the part – layered vests, wraparound top, leggings, headband. She is, however, also smoking a fag and drying a pedicure. I try to imagine Ghandi doing his asanas while puffing away with wads of cotton wool between crimson-tipped toes. Mum pauses for a swig of her gigantic black coffee and a long drag on her cigarette. Then she spots me and hastily throws it into a nearby plant pot. Officially, Mum is a non-smoker. The truth is no news to me, of course. She often goes outside after dinner "for some fresh air" and re-emerges smelling of fags (and mints and Chanel No. 5). But now I'm starting to see how much there is about Mum that I really *don't* know. She's like an iceberg. 'Mum' is only a fraction. What was it we learned in biology? The top ten per cent is visible. The real iceberg – Maggie *Valentine* – is lurking underneath, frozen and cold. Hiding beneath deep black water.

"Morning, darling!" Mum says, trying not to sound startled. "I didn't see you there! How's my favourite girl? Hungry?"

If this was a film, I'd probably be too emotionally overwrought and confused to eat. What with me and my Fairy Godbrother uncovering my mother's secret life and the news that I am possibly the long-lost daughter of one of earth's biggest rock stars. But it's the actual world, almost 11am and I'm fifteen. I'm starving.

In the kitchen, Mum makes me peanut butter and banana on toast with honey, and tea. Like every other Sunday she has the radio on that love songs show. She *looks* the same. And sounds it – chatting away about my bridesmaid's dress. She's being *nice* as usual. I don't want her to be nice. I'm angry. As she speaks I keep thinking *Iceberg. Iceberg. Iceberg. Iceberg...* Like sharpening a pencil to a point. Twist, push, twist. I need to stay cross with her otherwise I'll never ask.

Mum is emptying the dishwasher and telling me a story about her work. Andy Williams' *Can't Take My Eyes Off You* is on the radio. "...and her son is in your class! James, I think he's called. Her first facial. Such a lovely lady..."

I swallow the last of my toast and just say it. "I want to know who my dad is, Mum."

She freezes. I look up. Mum is holding a sieve in one hand, her mouth open mid-sentence. She gives a little winded pant and grabs the kitchen worktop with her free hand, steadying herself like she's on the deck of a ship. We stay this way for what feels like a long time. The radio, oblivious, pumps out the high-kicking Las Vegas chorus of the song. It's so ridiculous I almost want to laugh. I say, "I want to know, Mum."

"Candy, it's complicated." Her voice is cracking. I think of icebergs again, great chunks of them breaking off and falling into the sea.

"How complicated can it actually *be*, Mum? You do know who he is? My dad? You do remember him?"

"Of course! Of course I do!" Her eyes fill up with tears. She turns them on me, to show me she is melting. I don't care. There's still ninety per cent of her left to go.

"Well then? Who is he? I want to know! You think you can just decide how my life is going to be! You think you can just marry Ray, make him my dad? Well you *can't*. Somewhere out there I already *have* one. Who is he, Mum?"

She's really crying now. Big quiet drops rolling down her cheeks. Unsteadily, she lowers herself into a chair. She wipes her face with her hands, hard. Breathes in, swallows, tries to regain control. "Candy. I know you think you're grown up. One day I will tell you. I promise. But your... your father and me. It was complicated."

I huff in disgust at the word.

Mum reaches out pleadingly. "Candy! It really was! I wouldn't know how to explain to you at the moment. When you're older you'll understand!"

"I already understand. I understand that you don't want to tell

114

me because it doesn't suit YOU. You're so selfish! You only want to acknowledge the things YOU care about! Like your stupid boyfriend and your stupid wedding and stupid... stupid YOU!"

And then I'm crying. Hot loud angry tears, the opposite to hers. I grab my bag and coat off the sideboard and run out of the back door, slamming it behind me. I can see her silhouette through the frosted glass, shaking shoulders and unsteady hand reaching for the concealed packet of cigarettes in the cutlery drawer. She thinks she's so good at hiding things but she isn't. I don't need her to tell me who he is. I'm going to find out for myself.

I run as fast as my legs will carry me without really knowing where I'm headed until I get there, clattering through the door of The Blue and into a booth inside. Gulping down air, I sit staring hard at the ketchup dispensers. Somebody slides into the seat opposite.

"Hello, Bus Girl."

It isn't the nickname I would have chosen. I mean, it's hardly attractive. But like I said before, with real nicknames you don't get to pick. I look up at Dan. He's smiling. My face must look like a boxing glove. Screwed up with anger and cold, red and puffy from the wind outside and crying. He is as cool and unruffled as a marble statue.

"I was wondering when I was going to see you again after

you disappeared last night. You look like you need a drink."

Daniel H Ashton has had a very bad week. He knows what it's like to have family strife, knows how I feel. He's been slaving away nonstop for his brother (you may remember him as Baby Vader) with no thanks at all and he seriously needs to let his hair down. He tells me this as we sit on the floor behind the counter in The Blue Room, his little, record-selling cubby-hole in the back of the café. He won't tell me what the 'H' stands for, though. We're leaning against approximately a million CDs under the counter – our spines on theirs. I think of all the music behind us, what Clarence has taught me about its power. I can almost feel that energy send a pulse down every nerve in my back. But maybe that's something else.

We are drinking coffee from his flask. It's disgusting but I'm pretending I love it. After talking nonstop for a while, the conversation has hit a momentary lull. Maybe I was staring at his eyebrows too much, instead of thinking of stuff to say. He has really perfect eyebrows. I mean eyebrows are eyebrows usually. But his are just so…

"This coffee's amazing, isn't it?" Dan asks.

"Amazing!" I smile.

"Better than the crap they serve here, anyway. Jason says I'm stupid, bringing my own in when I could have it on tap for free…

but I'd rather have the good stuff, you know? My brother has really bad taste, though, so what would he know? He thinks Muse are cool."

Suppressing a grimace, I swallow another mouthful of black tar and make a mental note to take down the Muse poster in the top-left corner of my room. I never really liked them. I just liked the picture. And it's from ages ago anyway.

Dan tells me Jason is in his final year of business studies at Leeds Uni and (believe it or not) their Dad actually *bought* this place for him as a kind of practical project. I knew Dan was from a rich family but not *that* rich. I ask how come Dan ended up behind the counter. His face creases in thought (thereby elevating his eyebrow-perfection to new heights) and he says, "Well, Jason's at uni in the week so I help look after the place for him. I'm on a gap year."

"A gap year? Isn't that, like, between college and uni? You only left school last summer."

"Did I now?" he smirks, flashing a smile that is equal parts sarcasm and amusement. "Don't you know a lot about me!"

My face prickles in embarrassment – I turn away quickly, huffing back over my shoulder, "Hardly! And anyway, like... way to not answer my question."

I hear the smile get bigger, "You'll have to go on *Mastermind*.

'Specialist subject?' 'Dan Ashton from Bishopspool!' You can do a PHDan when *you* go to uni."

Now I really *am* going red. I turn back to face him and hope I can pass it off as anger. "We live in a small town, Dan. It's hardly amazing that I happen to remember how many years you were above me in school!"

"Then how come I don't remember you?"

I aim for a penetrating glare of crossness but can't manage it. *Bloody hell* I think *I'm on the floor with Dan Ashton. Actually talking to him. And Clarence hasn't even helped!* Not that I know of anyway. Dan moves his face a fraction closer, pulling my gaze deeper into his, warm breath reaching my lips as he speaks. "Then again, maybe you just looked different. Maybe you didn't look as good as you do now."

If Dan's nose was any less bumpless and generally perfect it would be touching mine. Our faces are magnets, pulling together harder the closer we get. From the outside it probably looks kind of cool, but I can't make my brain shut up. It's going *Oh God, he's going to kiss me! Is he? He is! Isn't he? It better not taste of that stuff we were drinking. Blah! What if I taste of it and he doesn't? I had mints in my bag. Where is my bag anyway?*

Suddenly there's thunderous explosion of noise directly above our heads. As if in an earthquake we fall away from one another, covering our heads with our hands. Actually only I do that. Dan just sort of rolls himself away from me looking slightly cross and stands up, leaving me cowering on the floor. Someone is banging on the counter yelling, "YOYOYOYOYO! D-MONEY! Where are you, man?"

It sounds even less convincing in his accent than it looks written down. Dan straightens up, his crossness vanishing and face returning to its resting state of quizzical amusement. "All right Cal, what can I do for you?"

"Stain! Call me Stain, man! Have you got that bootleg I was after?"

Curiosity gets the better of me and I stand up too. On the other side of the counter is Calum Stainforth. He is evidently shocked to see me. So shocked that for a moment he seems unable to speak.

"Candy Caine! Is that you? What are you doing down there?" He flushes pink with embarrassment. "I mean here?"

"Don't be a *sack*, Calum," Dan admonishes. "This is Candy." I do an awkward wave as if he was all the way across the room and not, like, actually standing directly in front of me. Calum doesn't notice, though. He's too busy being exasperated with Dan.

"Dude! For the last time! Call me *STAIN*?"

"Why do you want him to call you 'Stain'?" I can't stop myself asking. He's about to answer when Dan cuts in, sarcastically. "It's his *M.C. alias.*"

Everything between Stain's expertly angled baseball cap and the headphones around his neck flushes red. "Shut up, Dan," he mumbles.

"What? Mate, I'm just telling her. She asked! He's a pretty good MC, actually."

Stain is somewhat placated by this. Seeing my chance, I take a deep breath and decide to bring it up. "An MC? You should come and try out for my band," I say to Stain. "I'm having an auditions-party-thing next weekend." I grab a pen and scribble down the details for Stain.

"Sounds badass," he says softly. "Thanks." The bootleg exchange between Dan and him goes down as planned ending in an extremely complicated handshake and mini-bodyslam. Stain bids us goodbye with an unconvincing "Peace!" We watch him exit, his gangly frame fighting the bracing wind as it puffs up his XXXL hoodie like a parachute, almost lifting him off his feet.

Dan nods in his direction and gives a little snort of laughter. "One all."

"Sorry?"

"That's one mate each who's ruined things just when we

were in the middle of..." He takes a moment to decide how to phrase it, "...an interesting conversation. Pants Stain there and your mysterious friend last weekend." He moves over to the knackered-looking stereo which is so camouflaged by promo stickers that it almost disappears into the flier-covered wall behind it and changes Bon Iver for a bloopy electro tune I don't know.

I shoulder my bag. Back to surreality – Pirate will be making her way to my house by now, we're due to rehearse. "So what about the party? It's an auditions party for my band. I was going to ask you yesterday but... but I had to go. Do you want to come?"

He turns to face me wearing his usual mask of wry amusement. That face! How am I supposed to tell what he's thinking? It's as if the entire cosmiverse is one gigantic pun brought into being so that Dan Ashton can find it *slightly* funny. He moves in close; we are eye-to-chin (he's a bit taller than me). "You want me to audition for your band?"

"No! Nonononono! I didn't mean you should audition. You can just come for the party bit! We can hang out. You know... talk?"

"Talk?" He considers this for a moment. I fiddle with the strap of my bag and make myself not look at him. "OK, Bus Girl. I'll come to your party."

"Great!" I say aiming for a nonchalant tone that lands closer to hysterical gratitude. For some reason I add, "Be there or be square!" God I hate me sometimes.

"Cool," says Dan.

"Cool!" I echo. Although I think we can all agree, cool is something I will never be. I fish my sparkly woollen hat out of the bottom of my bag along with a pen and scribble down my number and email. "Bye, then," I say.

He takes the hat out of my hands and puts it on my head, pulling it so far down it almost covers my eyes. "That is a good look!" he teases. "Saturday then, yeah?"

Deciding to quit while I'm ahead, I more or less run away as I am. My hat pulled down to dork-degree, my heart as giddy as a funfair.

⚬

I spend the afternoon telling Holly my news and teaching her my new songs. She has come straight from a morning spent in the Rodgers family church band. The rainbow guitar strap of her bass is adorned with badges that say things like "CH CH – WHAT'S MISSING? UR!!" and "GLORY GLORY GLORY!" She normally turns it the other way round when she's finished there but today she's forgotten. On the flipside there are badges too, but different. Bands (including a few of her former emo favourites she's forgotten to take off), retro numbers picked up doing our charity-shop rounds, even one from a Teletubbies birthday card from when she was little. I think about Mum. I have glimpsed the other side of her. If she doesn't want to tell me about my dad, so be it. She can't make me un-know things. And I know what I'm going to do next. It's obvious. Simple even! Find Nathan Oxblood.

I hand Holly the folded-up picture of Mum and Nathan. She unfolds it carefully and looks at it for a long time.

"*Sacrebleu*! Move over Brad Pitt, eh? Wow, so, I guess that means you have brothers and sisters and stuff?" she asks. The idea hits me like a wet fish round the chops. Having spent last night in shock, this morning arguing with Mum and falling in Like with Dan Ashton I haven't had the chance to find out anything more about Nathan. But Hol's right. Nathan has kids – two at least. One's almost my age. That girl who's always in the newspapers wearing clothes that probably cost more than my house. She's a spokesmodel for Original Girl, the "makeup and lifestyle brand". I try to answer Hol but nothing comes out. I have brothers and sisters. And a *stepmother*. We drift back into silence, both staring at the picture as if one of the people will tell us what to do.

Eventually Hol speaks. "Question is – how on earth are we going to find him?"

I shake my head. No idea either. Hey, said it would be simple. That's a different thing to easy.

Six days and a lot of covert internet research later, I'm on the hunt for one of the biggest and most reclusive and elusive music legends on the planet. It might not look like it to the untrained eye but that's exactly what I'm doing.

We're planting pansies in the garden out the back of the East Bishopspool Pensioners' Day Centre. 'We' is me, Glad and Ernie, propped up in a wheelchair nearby. Ernie is so wrinkled I suspect he may have no actual bones left and just be skin. He knows everything there is to know about plants and is here to supervise. I am here to do what I'm told, which at the moment is pansy-planting. I extract the budding blooms from their miniscule garden centre pots – sad roots dangling – and transfer them to Glad's best terracotta where there's plenty of room to stretch and grow. A life that fits. The cool, damp soil soothes my burning fingertips, tender from another week of constant guitar practice. They sting less than they did, though. Hard little pads are starting to develop on my left-hand digits like mini animal paws.

I run my finger along them, thinking *concentrate*. The important thing right now is to get the information I've come here for without arousing suspicion. This is difficult because Glad is a naturally suspicious person. She considers the question I've just asked, secateurs momentarily idle in her crêpe-paper hand.

"Why? Where do *you* think she got the money, Candy?"

I swallow nervously but keep planting. "Dunno! No idea, I mean... It's just, if I'm going to do a school project about an inspiring businesswoman and that's going to be Mum then it makes me wonder, you know? She was only twenty when she had me."

Glad nods, gravely "Three days after her birthday, aye."

"Yes, I know, and when I first came out you all thought I might be a monkey..."

"You were so hairy!" Glad chuckles, chiming in to finish the well-worn tale. Mum and her monkey-baby. I've heard it a thousand times. It's the bit before that I'm interested in now.

"So I mean, how did she afford to buy a whole salon?" I try to sound casual. "Unless she had a secret multimillionaire backer stumping up the cash! Ha ha!"

Glad trains a glare so beady upon me, I could make a necklace out of it. Gulp. "Why are you asking me this and not your mum?"

"It's... I'm asking you and not her because... because it's a secret! I want the project to be a surprise for her." This, at least, is true. It is a secret. And it will be a surprise. It's just not a school project. I must speak with enough conviction because Glad seems satisfied by my answer.

So I'm not just here for the pansies. Not just here to see my tiny yet terrifying pal. I'm trying to find more links between Nathan and Mum and honestly – where *did* a single mother only just out of her teens get the money to buy a whole salon with our house on top? As rickety as the place is, it's all Mum's. She'd been living in London, a wannabe model. She was making a name for herself but she certainly wasn't making big money. Not big enough to disappear off the face of the earth and then suddenly buy a salon. My guess is Nathan bought Mum the business to keep me alive and keep her quiet. Maybe part of the deal was that I would never find out who he was.

"You're right." Glad interrupts my thoughts. Weighing each word carefully she explains, "There was someone. Someone who loved your mother and wanted to see her right. They put up the money."

My heart gives a trill of excitement like a bicycle bell. Don't blow it. Stay calm. Poker face. Breathe. "Who, Glad? Who was it?"

Glad looks at me. She knows. And she knows I know. In her silence I notice the sound of birds busy in the sky above us, feel the sun's warmth making it through the wind, just a little bit. It's spring and everything is changing. Suddenly Glad says, "Ah – speak of the devil!"

"Hellooo! Candy darling! Morning Glad!" I spin round to see Mum, trotting across the substantial lawn towards us. A truce has been called the last few days. I'm letting her think that a combination of hormones (mine) and wedding (hers) led to a one-off explosion of BioDad-related curiosity. Mum promised to tell me everything "when you're older." For my part, I am allowing her to think that I accept this as a reasonable and mature offer, not the total lame-o cop-out it so clearly is. *In case you hadn't noticed, Mum,* I think, *I am older.*

As Mum approaches I try to work out what she is wearing. She and Ray are off on their holiday this morning. I couldn't picture her in full-on hiking gear and I was right. She's wearing a red wraparound dress and matching hat. Closer up, though, I realise she's also wearing thermal trousers and a warm top underneath and – shock horror! – properly proper walking boots. I picture her little tiptoe Barbie-hooves inside, squashed flat as pancakes.

"Bye then, my darlings!" she chirps. "We're off into the great unknown!"

"At least it looks like I don't have to worry about you freezing to death," I say, giving her a hug.

"You don't have to worry about me at all!" Mum smiles. "I'm going to be with Ray!" I feel a pang somewhere beneath my ribs.

Looking after Mum used to be my job.

"Watch out for the Mountain Fairies!" Glad jokingly intones, giving Mum a peck and a pat. Her voice quakes with mock gravity. "The appear out o' the mist intent on nothing but mischief! Don't let them lead you astray!" *She doesn't know how right she is.*

Ray strides up and bids us goodbye, dressed in what appears to be the entire contents of a camping shop. There's so much mysterious equipment clipped and strapped to and strung around him that he is actually jangling. I catch Ernie (who during the war camped for eight months in the North African Desert with a rucksack smaller than my schoolbag) shooting him a look of disgust.

"Hi-de-Hi Campers!" He waves, dislodging a Swiss Army knife so small a mouse could probably use it. Glad smiles warmly, giving Ray a hug and a pat like she did Mum. "Ho-de-Ho!" she laughs. What is this – old person code?

I pick up his toy knife and hand it back. "You're not going *camping*, Ray, you're staying in a B&B." I mean it to sound bored but it comes out angry. Ray just smiles. "Quite right, Candy. Now, are you sure you'll be all right 'til we get back?"

I shoot him a look that can only mean Duh? As in, *of course* and also *like you care*?

"She'll be all right!" Glad answers breezily on my behalf. "She's doing the overnights in my guest room anyway!"

That's true. I am. I think about Glad's guest room – also known (in my head at least) as the Doily Graveyard. After a last-minute panic on Mum's part about leaving me alone overnight, I am supposed to be popping next door to sleep, which won't be a problem any other night. Not tonight, though. Tonight is the night. And I mean The Night. Luckily, Clarence has a plan to sort that out. No Doily Graveyard for me this evening. At 8pm our party is open for business. By tomorrow, if all goes according to plan I might have a band. I might even have a boyfriend. I think of Dan and there's a flutter in my chest. Tonight is what matters, not scoring points over Ray. I adopt my most even grown-up tone. "Don't you worry about me, Ray. Go off and enjoy yourselves I promise you, I'll be having the time of my life…"

10
5-4-3-2-1... Blast Off!

4pm

Pirate arrives with the drinks: five massive bottles of something called BLAST OFF! I examine it suspiciously. "Where did you get this stuff?"

Holly is midway through the third stage of her highly complex eye makeup process. It involves pulling her lower eyelids down and colouring bits I can't help thinking should only ever be blood-coloured. She stops for a moment, peepers watering. When the lining portion of her task is over, Pirate will be blind for 3–5 minutes until they adjust. "Spar. It was on offer. Pound each. Apparently it's got guava in it. For energy."

I gaze through the brown plastic at the fizzy contents within. "Looks more like it's got gravy in it from here."

5pm

In my room, I pick up my guitar and summon Clarence (by playing a B Major, naturally). He appears with a little POP. He seems annoyed. "Oh for the love of...! Really! Really? It can't be time yet! I was in the middle of a conversation with someone!"

"It's five o'clock, Clarence! People are going to start arriving soon! Glad will see them going past her window if we don't do something about it!"

"Yes, yes, very well. Let's put Miss Marple to bed," Clarence says irritably, flapping away the remainder of the smoke with a flick of his shimmering wings. "It's just that my dear friend Jimi was in the middle of a *hilarious* anecdote about something *unspeakable* Ginger Baker got up to in the back room at the Bag O'Nails. If I can't find him again to get the rest of it, I'm blaming you."

I'm nervous. We're about to make sure Glad doesn't interrupt the party. I already feel bad about it but what choice have I got? To be honest, I'm more worried about her busting us than Mum. At least she was a wayward teenager! Glad was a teenager before they were invented. She was only a couple of years older than I am now when she married Billy (I can just about remember him – he died when I was little). She won't understand. "Clarence, promise me this won't hurt her."

He shoots me a look.

"Clarence! Promise!"

"Hurt? *Hurt?* My dear child you really are quite the most featherbrained deliriant I have ever come across. Of course it won't hurt! If anything it will be a pleasant and peachy holiday from beastly, boring old reality. Lord knows you could do with one yourself!"

He's right. I need to get in touch with my inner delinquent. If anything this kind of crazy activity is my *job*! I tell myself to go with it and stop being a loser.

"Back in five minutes!" I call to Pirate over the noise of the hairdryer as we pass the bathroom. She is still beautifying herself. You would have thought that the less of you there was to apply products to, the quicker the getting-ready process would be. Apparently not. She pokes her head round the door. Every one of her blonde hairs is standing completely on its end. The sight stops me in my tracks. "Whoa! That's a good look! Is it by any chance troll-inspired? Should I stroke it for luck? Are you, like, also a keyring?"

"Ha ha Candy*tard*! I'm not finished yet. You going to the shop? Will you get us some matches? I can't find any anywhere."

"Matches?" I'm confused. "You do know you don't *actually* smoke, Hol? I mean, you light the end of that inhale-y thing and it will just melt." Her plasma-ball head vanishes behind the door momentarily, reappearing along with her hand and a large plastic bag which she thrusts in my direction.

"Matches for the mood lighting, dafty! I brought these!" I look inside. It is stuffed with candles, some of which are adorned with religious symbols. They look suspiciously like they might have come from a church.

"Holly, do you really think combining a house rammed to the gills with teenage hedonists and a bunch of naked flames is a good idea? It sounds like the setup to an episode of *Casualty*."

Pirate rolls her eyes. "Don't you *want* this party to have ambience?"

"I do." I say. "Honest. I just don't want it to have an ambulance. Now do you promise not to do anything with these until I get back?"

"I've just told you! I haven't got any matches! God! You're such an old lady!" Flipping her head upside down, Holly resumes blow-drying with a new viciousness.

She's right, I think. *So is Clarence. I am a fifteen-year-old old lady*. The sensible voice in my head has always been in charge. But it's Glad's voice not mine. I feel a penny drop. Am I going to let it tell me what to do forever? Is this the way for a potential heir of one of rock's all-time bad boys to act? This is my life we're talking about! I should be in the driving seat! And if not tonight, *when*?

I bound over to Mum's bedroom and extract the ornate silver lighter from her bedside-table drawer. Stomping back over to Hol with renewed purpose, I thrust it before her upside-down face. "Here you are," I boom decisively. "Get on with it. I'll be back shortly." I can almost hear *Independent Woman* by Destiny's Child strike up in my head as I skip down the stairs and out of our front door into the embers of Saturday afternoon.

⬤

I slip into Glad's house as quietly as possible. It feels strange. Wrong being here secretly, in the only house I know as well as my own. But today I am a typical carefree teenager. Impulsive! Wild! Intent on having a good time! I'm not having a particularly good time as I sneak towards the lounge door to be honest with you. But I've only just started. *Yes*, I remind myself, *I need to stick at it. If I practise being rebellious long enough, I will eventually get better at it.*

Having not long returned from a jam-packed few hours at the Day Centre, Glad is where I knew she would be: asleep in front of the news. I peer into the room and there she is, glasses slipping off the end of her nose, feet propped up on a stool. Clarence flies into the room, comes to a hovering stop in the air before her and places his hands together, eyes closed. Then with that look of concentration, he pulls his hands apart slowly to reveal a luminous... a luminous, er...

"Clarence!" I whisper loudly. "What is that?"

He shakes his head. "A lute, you appalling philistine!" Glad moves in her sleep. "Now," Clarence continues, "do shut your cake hole, there's a good girl!" And, strumming on his lute, he starts to sing.

Sleep well, my friend, sleep soundly.
On pillow dreams you lie.
As deep and dark and quiet as
The bottom of the sky.

Glad starts to move around in her sleep. For a moment I think she's going to wake up and I almost run away. She doesn't, though. Instead, her lined face (which looks as thoughtful in sleep as it does the rest of the time) seems to relax. A silent smile spreads across her features. Her shoulders drop, her head lolls gently; first to one side then the other, before rolling back altogether. Clarence doesn't say so, but I can tell he's delighted with himself. We gaze upon her slumbering form.

"How long will she stay like this?" I ask.

"Twelve hours," Clarence says, fluttering around Glad's puddingy body inspecting his handiwork.

"Why twelve hours?"

"Because, my inexhaustable inquisitor, unlike everything else in your squared-off age, magic has not yet been decimalised!" he answers sarcastically. "How should I know *why*? That's the magic of that particular song! I suppose it's because the perfect night's sleep happens to be twelve hours long. Not something I have experienced since I was in my cradle, of course, but the artiste's lot is thus. Ask anyone in the Great Dressing Room in the Sky."

"But she'll wake up at..." I glance at the carriage clock on the mantelpiece "...quarter-past five in the morning! In the middle of her living room!"

"Quite so, my dear, quite so. Refreshed and rejuvenated and with the dawning day at her disposal!" Clarence answers lightly. "Now come along. We have carousing to do."

7pm

The scene is set. There are so many candles dotted around our house it looks like a Meatloaf video. The front room is set up for auditions – my keyboard, Hol's bass and a mic she managed to "borrow" (I didn't press her to define the word). The whole lounge setup is running through Clarence. Not in a weird way. Well OK, it is weird. Clarence has transformed himself into an unbelievably gorgeous (and humungously large) amplifier. "If there is talent here tonight, my dear," he says, his voice inflected with a touch of feedback, "we are going to find it."

Dan Ashton is probably thinking about leaving his house wherever that is. I imagine him in a bedroom as cool and gadgeted-up as a Batcave. Is he thinking about me? Is he coming at all? Is anyone?

Pirate comes into my room holding a bottle of BLAST OFF! and two mugs. It tastes like paintstripper and sugar mixed together, only fizzy. Blah. I have another swig to take away the taste of the first. This process continues until my mug is empty. With nothing else to do and an hour before people start arriving, Holly suggests we have another.

8pm

Holly turns up the music (White Denim, as loud as it gets through Clarence). "Where did you get this amp, dude?" she asks me. "It's AMAZING!"

I smile mysteriously and look at myself in the front-room mirror. The hair is almost under control (I have trapped some of it under a headband) and my outfit, carefully planned for a fortnight, is working pretty well. I'm wearing leggings and a green silk top of Mum's (belted and as a dress) plus my favourite boots. Pirate did my makeup (I secretly washed some of it off). I actually think I look... *nice*. I mean good! Yeah – why not? I look good! I smile at my reflection. My smile is a bit slacker than normal and my eyes look a bit sleepy. For some reason I find this funny and laugh at myself. Holly comes into the frame beside me and starts laughing too. "Any minute now," she says, "the Broken Biscuit we've been looking for will walk through that door! Cheers!"

We hug-chink our mugs together and hug, then the chorus kicks in and we start dancing around like idiots. We don't feel like idiots though. Tonight is going to be brilliant.

8:15pm

Bing bong! That's the doorbell! Have you ever noticed how funny doorbells sound? Like this, BING BONG! Ridiculous. I dance over to let whoever it is in. I open the door and a reverse-suck (what's the word for that again? Oh yes, BLOW) a BLOW of cool air brushes my face. I'm hot. I didn't know I was hot. The breeze feels fresh like it is wafting away the fuzziness in my head. Three cups of BLAST OFF. This guava stuff is dynamite.

"Hiya! Candy, right?" A tubby girl is on the doorstep. She is wearing a massive leather coat, huge boots and what looks like stripper underwear – fishnets and a corset-y looking thing. Long, black hair sprouts out of the top of her head in two bunches. There is a tiny manboy beside her. He is wearing a coat like hers but with clothes on underneath (thank God).

"Hello!" I say, a bit louder than I mean to. "Who are you, then?"

"I'm Allanah. This is Kev." She nods towards the manboy. Kev does pointy finger-guns as if to say, "Yeah! Kev! You know me! I'm cool! Cool Kev!" Allanah is carrying a guitar case. Kev is carrying a crate of brightly-coloured bottles. I'm not sure I could have someone who does finger-guns in our band but they seem like nice people so I wave them in anyway.

Allanah and Kev are settling into the kitchen with Pirate when the bell goes again. Twice.

This time there are four people on the doorstep. They also have two plastic bags, clinking full of bottles and A LOT of music equipment.

"S'up?"

"Stain!" I cry, excitedly. "You came! Hooray!" I feel a rush of affection for Stain. The Stain-o. That's what I'm going to call him from now on. He knows Dan. You remember Dan. Do you think he's coming? I hope he comes. He's lovely.

Stain puts his fist out and we do one of those knuckle-touchy greetings. "Where's the music?" Stain asks as his three friends

(Bang Bang, Eagle Eye and DJ Total – I don't *think* they're their real names) each carry a mysterious box through the door. I point them into the living room but don't follow. I mean, I don't need to supervise *everything*, do I? They seem perfectly capable of setting up and Holly is supervising the first hour or so of auditions so that I can do hostessy stuff. I'm congratulating myself on being able to relax and enjoy what looks like it might be going to be an actual real PARTY when the door goes again. Hol slips my refreshed mug of BLAST OFF! into my hand. I take a quick swig and go to answer it. That tastes different. Maybe it's not BLAST OFF! after all…

9pm

The doorbell never stops! There are people everywhere! PEOPLE! EVERY! WHERE! In the lounge (and by 'the lounge' I mean *my* lounge. Candy Caine's lounge. Candy Caine who has, like, one alive friend under eighty. Yes THAT Candy Caine. ME! MY LOUNGE!) In MY LOUNGE there is a full-on hip hop battle kicking off. I know! Mental!

People in hoods are MCing and DJ Total (he's brilliant!) is scratching. Records! Holly is in there checking out the talent. She's sitting in the middle of a sofa full of burly lads, playing along on her bass (it's not even plugged in! What a loon!) having the time of her life. Clarence is doing his work – sending awesome sounds booming through the air. Total shouts, "This setup is SICK, man! Where did you get this amp?" We can all feel the music working. The party is taking off. It's a room of open faces – smiles and laughs and EVERYONE! TALKING! LIKE! THIS!

Someone is flipping through Mum's old records and passing them up to Total. STOP WORRYING! It's fine! She never plays them these days anyway. Suddenly the hook from *The Wow* by The Rain drops into his mix. How funny! I didn't even know she had this one! F-U-N-N-Y! Everything's funny when you think about it, though, isn't it? Here's to you, Mum! And to my Maybedaddy wherever he is! I raise my mug. Empty again? What happened?

10:15pm

BINGBONG! Silly doorbell! BINGBONG! ALL RIGHT I'M COMING! I'm sitting on the stairs talking to Ashley. Asha? Aisha? She is A-M-AZING! But she is crying. Her boyfriend dumped her? (LOSER!) Her purple glitter eye makeup has spread all over her face and she keeps saying she feels sick. There is bad stuff in her hair already. I hope that isn't... Poor Ashley/sh/isha. I throw my arm around her shoulder trying to avoid the potential vom in her tresses. But it's sort of tricksy. I mean tricky? Because my arms won't do what they're told? That's weird. I flap them a little bit to check they're working. HAHA! LIKE WINGS! They feel heavier than normal. I try to touch the end of my nose like on a cop show. Anyway turns out THAT is actually quite hard?

"DUDE! MOVE ON! HE SOUNDS LIKE A LOSER!" I am shouting everything now. So is everyone else, though. Not the people sitting on the stairs below us. They are just snogging furiously. Like, horribly. Their chins have gone red. It looks like they're eating each other.

"BUT I LOVE HIM!" Ashley/sh/isha wails. "AND HE LEFT ME! FOR THE BIKE OF DEPTFORD PARK!"

Why has he left her for a bike? Would she not let him get one? Does she have something against cyclists? That is so wrong! It's like racism but of SPORT? I am about to ask when BINGBONG! The silly SILLY doorbell goes again and I had better go and let in whoeveritis.

A little bit of cold air on my face which is so hot and sizzling-sssss like bacon in a frying pan. On the doorstep, you'll never guess? Guess! Go on! Guess! Ah you're rubbish – DAN ASHTON! I KNOW! AMAZING! He is wearing an old leather jacket and his perfect eyebrows from before. I want to touch his hair. It looks springy.

I throw my arms up in a one-woman Mexican wave and

punch the air. "DAN ASHTON! WHOOOO! I THOUGHT YOU WEREN'T COMING!"

"Candy! Hello – you look… like you're having a good time?"

"ALL TIMES ARE GOOD, DAN! ALL TIMES! COME IN!"

Dan comes into the hall, holding a six-pack of expensive beer. He is so sophisticated! He hands them to me and for some reason it makes me laugh. "HA HA! IT'S LIKE YOU'RE FROM THE PAST! YOU'RE SO HISTORICAL! LIKE A KNIGHT!"

"Oh? Er, thanks… Which way?" he asks. We have three choices – the hip hop-off in the front room, the kitchen which is full of smoke and some boy called Dean who has a ponytail playing acoustic guitar really ANNOYINGLY. (We're not going in there. He's ANNOYING – definitely not joining my band). Or upstairs.

We push past the snoggers on our way up, me in front. What will happen to their chin skin if they keep going? What if it all gets rubbed off? Will they just be skulls from the nose down? Then will their noses rub off too? So many questions… Ashley/sh/isha is sobsobsobbing now with big, shaky shoulders.

Dan stops. "What happened to her?"

I pull him up and past her by the arm of his jacket, we're not stopping for her sort. I lean in and whisper knowingly to him, "SHE'S A SPORTS RACIST."

11

Wrecked

11:25pm

I'm in my room. In my room with Dan Ashton. Away from the noise
and the people I suddenly feel soberer. Is that a word?
Soberoberoberer... Making an effort to stand up straight. it
occurs to me that there might be something more than guava
in BLAST OFF! And, when you think about it – what actually,
actually is guava anyway? Is it foreign for booze?

Another one of Pirate's brainwaves (evil genius! Love her!) was
keeping people out of the bedrooms in case the place got
trashed. Mainly Mum's. That was easy as it has an old lock on it.
The key is now cunningly strung around my neck on a ribbon. My
room (being in the attic) was harder to barricade. We settled for
piling up as much stuff as we could find on the stairs in front. This
worked (sort of. There's nobody in it when we get here) but among

the random furniture were some cases of Mum's vintage stuff which have been opened. So there are people (mainly boys! Idiots!) running around the house in 1950s dresses and hats. Every now and again I keep seeing one and thinking she has come back early. A mini front room is also under construction on the landing, using the furniture from our blockade. As we squeeze past I hear a girl say, "Look at all this stuff! It's like a scrapyard! This house is so *weird*!" and feel embarrassed. I catch Dan's eye. He heard. He smiles kindly and puts his arm around me, guiding me past them and up, up. So here we are, sitting on the floor because...

The bed seems a bit, well...it's a bed.

And the floor was where we left off last weekend at The Blue.

Dan looks up at the stars on the ceiling. "Your room is cool."

"Thanks. Except the curtains..." I smile. The duvet-of-humiliation is hidden under a load of clothes but there wasn't much I could do about them.

"I like them. Ironic," Dan says. I nod knowingly, although I'm not really sure what he means. He points up to the top-left hand corner of the room where my Muse poster was until last weekend. I haven't found anything to replace it yet. Sweet-shop-striped wallpaper pokes through the gap like embarrassing underwear. "What happened there?"

"Just… just an old picture I got rid of." I take a mini swig of the super-posh beer he has opened for me. It tastes just as disgusting as *BLAST OFF!* How can people drink this stuff?

"Fickle, eh? I'd better watch myself." He laughs, so I join in. Music from downstairs drifts up towards us – the battling MCs have made way for thrashy screamo. A super-high, operatic voice starts singing and I know it's Allanah, the girl who arrived at the party first. I'm not sure if it's Dan or the booze or the music or all three but I'm feeling really strange now. Like my brain is miles away from my body. I am definitely starting to suspect that *BLAST OFF* might contain alcohol.

"Let's have a tune." Dan goes round to the dock at the bottom of the bed and plugs in his iPhone. He fiddles around a bit and then a little acoustic song starts playing that makes my heart feels like it's made of eggshells.

"What's this?" I shuffle over on my knees to have a look. "Slow Club? Funny name for a band…"

"Er… Isn't your band called the Broken Biscuits? That's funnier. How's that going, anyway? Found any new talent tonight?"

I ponder this for a moment. Total has already told me he's not up for joining, I think. It was hard to tell. He used the phrase, "Total can't roll wit all'y'all twenny fo-sev." Which sounded like a No. There's a screech from downstairs as Allanah hits a particularly high note. I look up at Dan. "No talent yet."

"I think I might have found some."

"Really?" I'm about to ask who it is when he grabs my wrist and pulls me up on to the bed. Now, maybe you do this all the time. Maybe being pulled on to your bed by the boy of your dreams while fizz-brained on hooch is just your average Tuesday. Not me. Not even on a weekend. I have no precedent whatsoever for any of the events in my house tonight. I am seriously, seriously winging it here. But now, more than when I was watching the strangest strangers fill my house, I have suddenly become keenly aware of the fact that *I have no idea what I'm doing.* Climbing back down is just as scary as keeping going.

"Are you all right?" Dan asks. Oh God. I'm on top of him. Pulling me up here was supposed to be all sexy but because of the BLAST OFF! in my system, it was more like fishing someone from a lake unconscious.

"Sorry. Yeah, yeah, I'm OK. Sorry..." I roll over and we lie side by side. He sighs. Looks at his watch. The song changes to one that goes:

I'd swim across Lake Michigan
I'd sell my shoes

I'd give my body to be back again
In the rest of the room
To be alone with you...

Oh no! I'm messing this up! Why did I have to soberise now? We both stare at the fake sky on my ceiling. Feeling stranger than ever, I close my eyes. "I really like you, Dan."

"Yeah?" he says flatly. "Cheers."

"But I don't know what I'm doing, I mean... I'm having a really weird night."

He turns on his side to face me and I do the same. "You're fine. The night is fine. You've just had too much to drink. Don't worry about not finding anyone yet. We'll go downstairs in a bit and you can sort your band out."

"No... It's... I've got so many things to fix, Dan. The band, but not just the band! I'm trying to find my dad. My mum's marrying a total loser. And now I'm here with you! Doing... doing whatever this is that we're doing! And I'm not... I'm not this!"

For the first time ever, Dan looks ruffled. Angry even. "You're not what?"

"I'm not this cool person who has parties! And gets drunk! And lies on my bed with boys!"

Dan looks exasperated. He does that thing people do – nips

the top of his nose between his eyes.

"Candy I know you're not this person. I know you're not cool… not *this* kind of cool, I mean. You only just had those braces with the elastics that clamped your jaws together taken off."

I run my tongue over my teeth. Their three-month-smoothness is still a relative novelty after a year with a mouthful of metal.

"You're the only person from our school who has ever, to my knowledge, actually set fire to themselves."

"I have a lot of hair! Safety goggles don't keep your hair out of the way, you know! *Unsafety* goggles is what they should be called. And anyway, I was concentrating on warming the end of the test tube!"

Hang on… How does he know this stuff?

Dan's crossness has disappeared. He's smiling. His face is close enough to see all the different colours in his eyes: brown and green with tiger-stripes of gold.

"I thought you didn't remember me from school?" I say.

He goes, "I lied."

And then he kisses me.

11:35pm

What is kissing Dan Ashton like? Christmas morning when you're little. Not *the whole morning* obviously. Not chocolate for breakfast in the wrapping-paper pile while your mum drinks sherry in her dressing gown. I mean the first three seconds of Christmas morning. When you've waited for so long. When you've been so excited you feel like you might burst. You think you'll never fall asleep but by some miracle you do. Then you wake up. And just before you open your eyes you think...

It's Christmas!

It's like that. Only on repeat. I'm sorry on-the-stairs snoggers, I take it all back. Even if I spend the rest of my life with a skull chin. Even if my nose rubs off. This will have been worth it.

11:53pm

I am starting to feel a bit weird. I don't know if it's lying down or being squashed up here with Dan. Or the fact that I had some of his beer because I didn't want to seem uncool. Or maybe it's that we have been snogging each other's faces off for ages. Whatever it is, I suddenly feel boiling hot. I become aware that the room is spinning. Dan kisses me again and this time I can really taste that posh beer. In fact that's all I can taste. He puts his hand on my waist and squeezes. That's when I know I'm going to... I'm going to...

"GET OFF!" I throw him to one side in desperation and manage to get my head clear of the bed before I throw up.

Somewhere behind me I hear Dan clamber up making disgusted-sounding noises.

"Oh for... look what you've done!" he shouts. "Look!" I turn around to answer him. Bad idea. A huge wave rises up inside me. At first I think it's nausea. Wrong. It's vomit. Again.

Lots. I hear rustling and stamping as Dan grabs his belongings. He knocks the bed a couple of times and makes it even worse. I try to raise my hand to grab him, to tell him to stay, but it's no good. My body won't let me do anything else until all of this... *stuff* is out. The door slams. For a while all I can do is lie there, my head hanging over the end of the bed, eye to eye with my maths textbook which is covered in puke. Then the sick-sensation evaporates almost as quickly as it came. I suddenly feel more comfortable than I ever have in my entire life. My alarm clock beeps once. Midnight. The last thing I remember thinking is *I suppose this means I'm Cinderella again...*

BANGBANGBANGBANG!!! "CANDY! CANDY!! Are you in there?"

Holly's voice on the other side of the door. For a second I can't work out what she's doing here. Then I remember that she's here with about a hundred others and that there is actually a huge party going on in my house. Isn't there? Actually – I can't hear any music. Or people. One person in particular appears to be missing... Where is Dan? The last thing I remember he was right here. We were... Oh no. OH. NO!

I lift my head and open my eyes which are greeted by a penetrating stream of sunlight pouring in through the gap in my "ironic" curtains. It feels like a pickaxe through my head. The sun. Why is the sun in my room? Unless... Oh God! It's tomorrow! Holly knocks again. Each rap is like a nail gun being fired directly into my aching brain.

"Can! I think you'd better come out here. There's been an... um... There's a plumbing issue we need to address?"

Gingerly, tentatively, in the manner of an elderly tightrope walker, I pick my wobbly way across the bedroom to my door. I open it, revealing Pirate, her hair wrapped in a large green towel. She is swathed in a vintage kimono of Mum's worn over yesterday's clothes, accessorised by an enormous pair of shades and wellies.

"Why are you wearing wellies?" I croak. She throws an arm around my shoulders and leads me downstairs to the landing. That's when I see the water. Why is there water? We're on the third floor... Hol smiles. "So... sleep well?"

I shake my head, trying to dispel what feels like a ten-sizes-too-small crash helmet of ache clamped all around it.

"No. And I don't think passing out really counts as *sleeping*."

"Chin up," Hol says, patting me in a conciliatory fashion. "In a way this is good. It shows you have the genetic capability to party like an Oxblood. That kind of skill cannot be learned, only inherited! Try to look upon this as an experiment that yielded unexpected – but ultimately positive – results!" She leads me out on to the landing and that's when I see it. My house looks like... like... like Godzilla ate it and then sicked it up again. Weak at the knees, I grab on to Hol with one hand and the banister with the other. No matter what kind of upbeat spin Pirate attempts to put on this, this is – in every sense of the word – a disaster. If this is partying like an Oxblood, count me out.

"What... what *happened here*?" I manage to ask.

Hol grimaces and affects the clipped posh tones of an old school stiff-upper-lipped army man. "Yes. Rather a poor show, old stick. You see, after you nodded off Dan came downstairs and... well... I think he was a touch peeved that your night had been cut short and between he and his friends it sort of... um..." she waves a hand around, indicating the house and its contents (most of which look like firewood) "...kicked off."

"Dan did this?" I ask, incredulous. Pirate makes a face.

"The *cretinos* he was with did it. Then everyone else joined in. It didn't look this bad until the sun came up."

In silence, we make our way downstairs. Everyone has disappeared and the devastation is hard to describe. You know the tornado in *The Wizard of Oz*? It's like three of them have been fighting each other. And then some elephants have joined in. Exploding elephants. The walls are bare and there's furniture everywhere but none of it is where it should be. There are random misplaced objects dotted everywhere. And food, food all over the place! The contents of the fridge-freezer Mum and Ray re-stocked specially are spread all over the house, giving the place the look of a mangled all-you-can-eat buffet. A broken alarm clock, an upturned sewing box. Someone has broken the fruit bowl. Apples bob past, floating on the water pooled at our feet. As we wade through the wreckage (seriously – where is this water *coming from*?) it takes a few seconds for me to register what each room *should be* before I can even start to take in what it actually *looks like*. I don't freak out, though. Not yet. I can't. I'm too shocked.

We're standing in the kitchen mutely appraising the walls which have been rudimentarily papered with a selection of torn-out images from Mum's stash of wedding magazines (and then defaced in ways that I think I'll just leave you to imagine).

"Are you OK, dude?" Pirate asks. "You've gone all pale. Paler than normal, I mean."

"I've just got to go and... call someone," I say, my voice coming out sounding all shaky like an old lady.

With that I pelt back upstairs to my bedroom. It stinks in a way that is made no less disgusting by being entirely my fault. Holding my breath and looking up to the star-covered ceiling in a bid to avoid seeing or smelling the rapidly-drying vom puddle, I reach into the corner and grab hold of The Beast which (thank God) is still here and no more messed up than it usually is. Putting my left knee on the bed, I lean the guitar over it and hit B Major. Nothing happens.

"Clarence?" I try again. And again. "Clarence! Come on! I know you can hear me! I need you!"

Suddenly there is a flash, considerably weaker than usual, but a flash nonetheless. Clarence appears in front of me hovering midair, lacklustre and defeated-looking like a bee on the last day of summer. He groans. "Well that was *quite* the most taxing soirée I've attended since Elton's first wedding." He has moved his headband down over his eyes (presumably to block out the light) and is massaging his temples in a Marlene Dietrich-disturbed-at-home fashion. "Candypop, I appreciate that you are but a callow youth bereft of social skills or empathy but must you shout so? Some of us are trying to *sleep*."

"Sleep? Are you kidding me?" I'm really shouting now. "Have you seen what's happened to my *house*? Where *were you*? Aren't you supposed to be helping me? How can this kind of stuff happen on your watch?"

"My dear, I have no idea what you mean. Your décor and your destiny are two quite disparate matters. I am interested in the latter only. Besides, I was otherwise occupied amplifying the sonic assault you and your coterie seem to think passes for music these days." He grimaces before doing an alarmingly accurate impression of Allanah the screamy opera-goth from last night.

I grit my teeth. "Fine. You were busy. It happened. Are you going to help me now? With cleaning up?" He looks at me as if I just spoke in Cantonese. "Well?" I ask.

In films I have seen, by which I'll grant you I mainly mean *Mary Poppins*, this is the bit where Clarence would smile before gaily buzzing around the house snapping his fingers or flicking a wand or whatever the hell magical people do, restoring sanity, order and the furniture to its rightful place. He doesn't do this. Instead he lifts his headband away from his eyes, glares at me and asks in a voice dripping with sarcasm, "Do I *look* like a washerwoman?"

"What? No! Of course you don't! It's just…"

"What then? A builder? Mr Fixit?" He looks behind me, out into the waterlogged hall. "A *plumber*?"

"No! But I need you to…"

"Do you think that I have *quite* so little to do in demi-death that every little glitch, hitch and pitstop in the layby on the road to you reaching your goals must be an excuse to tax my powers? Is that all I am to you?"

"Clarence! Be reasonable! Help me! The house is a wreck – can't you fix it? You're a fairy!" I'm too hungover to watch what I'm saying but as soon as the word escapes my mouth I know what a huge mistake it was. Clarence flinches like a scalded cat.

"I have never in all my *death* been so insulted! How very *dare you*! Do your own cleaning up!" he says, and with another flash he is gone.

I'm standing there, wondering what on earth I'm going to do and where I'm going to start, when I hear a noise. Or – to be precise – a voice: Ray's. In the front room, amplified to ear-splitting proportions.

"Welcome, positivity seekers!" he booms.

For a second I freeze, thinking he's back early and then I recognize what this is: his motivational DVD for clients. I run down the sodden carpet in the hall as Ray drones on. "Congratulations on making the life-changing decision to ELECT to DIRECT! You've chosen to make changes in the adventure that is your life. I'm Ray Hoppings and this…" he leaves a dramatic pause, "…is the first day of the rest of your life! Let's *Hop To It*!"

I burst into the front room to be greeted by the sight of Pirate and MC Calum Stainforth, who is holding a mop in one hand and the DVD remote in the other.

"Sorry! It must have got wet. I can't switch the bloody thing off! I was cleaning up and I knocked it. People were watching it last night…"

Aren't they, like, normal English words? What happened to his indecipherable rap-chat?

He struggles apologetically as Ray drones on. Hol and I start looking for the plug.

"Don't touch anything electric!" Calum shouts. "The water! Some idiot put the plug in and left the bath to overfill. I turned the water off but I haven't even come close to cleaning all this up yet."

We stop immediately. Ray doesn't, unfortunately. I find myself sucked into watching him smiling in his purplest suit and shiniest tie, with a grin so big you could play his teeth like a xylophone. He is standing in front of a poster of a sunrise and a wilted fern. "Are you ready to maximalise your potentialities…?"

Suddenly there's a huge explosion, the TV goes black and what look like actual fireworks shoot out of the front of the DVD player. I look around to see Hol clutching Calum's mop, having clearly just whacked the thing with considerable force.

"Sorry," she shrugs, "his voice was doing my head in."

It's Sunday night. I can't begin to tell you how crap I feel. After a whole day of solid cleaning, Hol and Calum have had to go home to do other things. Hol, in fact, is off on a religious retreat with her family for two whole days. She pulls off her rubber gloves and deposits them straight into our latest binbag of indescribable grossness. "I think we got the worst of it sorted." She smiles, placing a hand on my shoulder. "*No te preoccupes!* I'll call you, OK?"

"OK." I smile. It isn't OK, though. Our efforts have barely touched the sides. Even Mum's room (which I'd specifically locked) ended up getting trashed. Brilliant. I guess I know what I'm going to be doing the rest of the week until she gets back. Later that night, next door in the Doily Graveyard I flop back on the bed, exhausted from all the cleaning and an hour of pretending to Glad that my life is totally fine and in no way resembles a hollow and lifeless crater left behind by an asteroid strike. Where life and hope once flourished, now every trace of both is gone. I've messed up my one chance to get the band together and my chance with Dan in the space of a single night. The nylon eiderdown underneath me crackles slightly with static as I list my miseries for the thousandth time that day. I always end on Dan. How could he trash my house and then leave? And then not call? It's all such a mess.

❋

I don't call Holly when I get up on Monday. I don't call her the day after, either. And going to school is out of the question. My phone goes, "PIRATE" flashing up on screen with that daft picture of her gurning, but I can't face it. The school secretary rings the house and I pretend to be Mum. I'm lucky that she is notorious as "a bit of a character". The rest of the time, I spend cleaning the house. I pick my way through the wreckage of the party feeling like Scarlett O'Hara at the end of *Gone With the Wind*. An ever-increasing pile of broken stuff starts to mount up on the kitchen table to be sorted out before Mum gets back. A plumber comes and gives me a seen-it-all-before look before making sure none of the pipes are broken (they're not, thank God). Then he proceeds to clean out the savings it took the last fifteen years to accumulate in my building society account.

By Tuesday night, I am thoroughly depressed. Sixteen unlistened-to messages from Holly and I haven't summoned

Clarence either. He's probably knackered. Besides what's the point? I've just blown my chance of ever getting the Broken Biscuits off the ground so there is no destiny, no music. Besides at this rate I'm going to have to pawn my guitar to replace our stupid DVD player anyway. And as far as finding Nathan Oxblood goes – how, exactly? No money, no band. No way to find him and nothing to offer him even if I could.

I'm sitting at our kitchen table in front of the pile of smashed objects that I have mentally christened *Brokecrap Mountain* when Mum calls.

"Darling! Guess what I can see?" For some reason hearing her voice makes me feel like that song the other night – as if my heart is made of eggshells. One wrong move and I'll start bawling and tell her everything. I take a deep breath, shoring myself up with sandbags of fake cheerfulness.

"Hello Mum. What can you see?"

"A mountain! The most beautiful mountain in the world!"

I stare blankly at *Brokecrap*. "That's great, Mum."

"You'd love it here, Candy. Ray and I were just saying – after the wedding we'll come back here. The three of us! What do you think?"

I think it sounds like a living nightmare. "I think it sounds… that sounds great, Mum."

"So how are you doing?" she asks.

"Great!" I fake-chirp.

"How's Glad? How's school?"

"Great!" I lie.

"Is your friend Sally with you?"

"Yes – it's great!" I haven't got the energy to correct her on Holly's name. "She's… she's just here, actually. I'd better go. We're about to… watch a film. It's starting. It's… it's great." God, this is exhausting. There's a pause on the other end of the line.

Then Mum says, "Darling if you want me to come home, you only have to say so."

I manage to squeak, "Don't be silly! Everything's great!" and say goodbye.

I hang up and throw my mobile across the room. It hits the wall and breaks in half. So this is what happens when I'm left to run my own life. Everything (and I mean *everything*) in it gets broken. What a joke – I'm supposed to be following my wildest dreams and I can't even throw a party without it ending up like this. The world feels like it's ten sizes too big. I'm lost but Mum has moved on. In three months, Maggie Caine will become Maggie Hoppings. Does that mean my mum won't exist any more? Maybe not the way she was. How am I supposed to manage without her? Exhausted, confused and utterly miserable, I curl up like an empty tube of toothpaste in my chair and finally start to cry.

I don't know how long I'm sitting there (our kitchen clock froze at 2:28 sometime in 2006) but the blue-ink evening sky is properly night-time dark when there's a knock at the door. The noise makes me jump. My eyes are still puffed up from crying like two Yorkshire puddings but I ran out of actual tears a while ago. As quietly as possible, I sneak to the door and put a pudding-eye to the spy hole. Standing on my doorstep, adjusting the angle of his cap and looking skinnier than ever in his over large hoodie, is MC Stain. He keeps slipping his huge headphones on and off nervously. What should I do? Should I let him in? He did stay most of Sunday, helping me clear up. He knocks again. Then speaks. Shouts, in fact – through the letterbox.

"Candy! Are you in there?" He continues, louder now, "Candy! It's me. Calum!"

Two huge, dark blue eyes and the tip of his cap's peak appear at the letterbox for a moment looking for me. Then his mouth again. "I… er… I brought you something, like. Thought you might need something to eat. Shall I just leave it on the doorstep?"

◎

Ten minutes later, Stain and I are downstairs in the darkened salon sat behind the till. The only light in the room is coming from the computer monitor in front of us. We are eating Glad's legendary Pineapple Upside Down Cake directly from a cake tin.

"This is really nice." I mumble through a particularly squidgy mouthful. "Thanks."

Calum smiles shyly as he taps away on the keyboard. "Dunno why she made it for me, really. All I done was fixed a couple of their old lamps up. Anyway, I couldn't eat it all myself and last time I saw your oven it was full of shoes, so I thought you might not be cooking..."

I shake my head, rueing the time I spent scrubbing the thing clean yesterday.

"Here it is. Look!" Calum says.

And yes, you would have to concede, there it is. Kylie Carey's (the most popular girl in school) Facebook page. Her picture sits in the top left-hand corner like the illuminated first letter of a medieval manuscript, dominating all below it with its beauty. Her long red ringlets tumble obediently past her shoulders. She smiles coquettishly at the camera through cupcake-colour gloss. The *Me? Ohmigod I'm, like, so not pretty!* smile of someone as certain of their beauty as their surname.

I look at Stain. The sight of Kylie has coaxed a gooey grin from him. She makes me want to puke. I will officially never understand boys. "How are you friends with her again?" I ask.

"We're cousins," he replies, unable to tear his eyes from the screen. Before adding (a bit too hastily), "*Third* cousins."

Kylie was at the party. I remember now. She was with Dan's friends. She greeted me with a hug, apparently forgetting that for the last four years our entire relationship has constituted her either blanking me or greeting my entrance at registration every morning for six months with a sarcastic, "Nice shoes! You going *bowling*?"

Post-hug, she parted the human sea like Moses, strode into the kitchen and then commanded the boys to play The Doors songs on their acoustics (they instantly complied) while she writhed unrhythmically beside the dishwasher like a work-experience lapdancer.

Anyway, according to Calum my conviction that I have ruined my life is misplaced. In fact, it couldn't be further from the truth. It seems nobody who is anybody has been talking about anything other than my party. And of course anyone who's someone has been talking about it here. Kylie has posted an album of grainy mobile phone photos from the big night. She is pulling a practised-in-the-mirror-pretty face in each that is so identical it almost looks like she's been added on afterwards like Stalin. We've just done him in history. Apparently he was always painting himself into old portraits to make himself look important. This is only one of the many things he and Kylie seem to have in common.

Anyway the album goes like this:

Kylie Carey
In these photos: **Alex Clay, Dan Ashton, Emma Rainton, Hannah Edwards, Kylie Carey, Padma Parmar...**
Sat Nite :) !!!!!!!!!!
43 new photos
14th March at 7:32pm – **Comment Like Share**

I start looking through the pictures. You couldn't really describe the camerawork as anything other than shoddy. We start out with Kylie and "mi cru! XXX" getting ready at hers, a process catalogued over fifteen fascinating shots of them posing next to a radiator. Then they're at my house. She's dancing. Hugging various people. Doing the face. Face again. Face.

Then it starts to get interesting. They're in my front room. The MC battle is going off – Stain, I mean, Calum is there – laughing and MCing, playing on what looks like a mixer. I appear for one shot playing The Beast with Hol on bass. We are laughing. A memory pops up like a bubble from underwater. I do remember that. We were playing my new song *Big Bad Dad*. Then I disappear from shot – this must have been when I was upstairs with Dan. Shot after shot of ridiculous loopy daft fun. Padma Parmar punching the air on Matt Simmons' shoulders. Steph Jackson doing a headstand. Then Dan reappears. I flush with shame as I remember how disgusted he was when I was sick. He looks a bit serious in the first couple of shots but then starts smiling. Then I get to a picture that makes me feel like throwing up all over again. Kylie Carey is sitting on his lap. Whatever – she's a total desperado, there's no way he'd fancy her. Is there? I shake off the thought as Dan disappears from shot and the fun continues, getting weirder and weirder until some dude aged about a hundred – who Stain claims nobody can remember – turns up playing a saxophone. I had thought the night went down like a fart in a spacesuit. But judging by the comments underneath it seems not. Saturday has gone down in Bishopspool history.

43 people like this
View all 125 comments
Lisa Tuncliffe Party was EPIC!!!Proppa lush babe u looked mint!!
Kylie Carey Thanx so much mi feet were killin the next day off dancin! NE1 remember how we got home in the end???

167

Hannah Edwards Er yeh! Nightbus!!!!! LOL!!!

Casey Price Gr8 pics Kylz. Did u c Dan Ashton cdnt take his eyes off u!!!

I snort in disgust when I read this. *As if.* Then I think, *Yeah – well the last time Dan saw you, you were praying to Rolf. Who's he going to find more attractive?* Then I think, *Shut up voice in my head. You are me, so that makes you a loser too.* Then carry on reading and feel a little bit better.

Alex Clay Who knew Caine was a cainer – not such a loser after all ;)

Kylie Carey She's sweet! Cnt w8 4 her nxt party!!!

Having spent three days up to the elbows in soapy water and my own tears I had very much written this weekend off as the biggest disaster since the *Titanic.* I kept thinking, *I got close enough to look destiny in the face and gave it a good slap.* This is fantastic news (apart from seeing Kylie *Scary* perched on Dan like he was an armchair). Then I remember him knowing all that geeky stuff about me. That must mean something. Mustn't it? Calum gulps down the last of his third slice of cake in half an hour. One thing I have observed about Calum Stainforth is that he never stops eating. But he seems to be a kind of portal that carries food directly into another dimension: not only is his appetite impossible to sate, he is also as thin as a rake no matter what he eats. Boys. If they weren't so bizarro I'd totally want to be one.

"I feel much better, Calum. Thanks so much for showing me," I say. He shrugs, his bony shoulders almost touching his ears.

"Everybody's talking about it, Candy. Who got down to the second round? Didn't your mate tell you? The little emo one?"

"Holly's not emo. Not any... What do you mean 'the second round'?"

"The second round of auditions! Next weekend!"

I look at my annihilated mobile.

"I was going to suggest you call her but..." Calum reaches over and cautiously removes the phone. "Gis a look..." He adopts the sceptical expression of a mechanic inspecting bumper damage. "Nasty. But if I just...'scuse me." He produces a pair of black-framed glasses and slips them on shyly, their bottle-bottom lenses making his inky blues look even more enormous. After about a minute's fiddling he presses a button and the phone lights up. He hands it back to me. "Now *that* is magic."

I smile and hit the number 1 key for voicemail.

"You have. Fifteen. New messages," says the smug robot lady.

She always sounds smug. I thought it was because she usually got to tell me I had no new messages but here I am with fifteen and she still doesn't sound any less superior. "Message. Received. Monday 15th March. At. 9:10.am."

I know who I'm going to hear next, of course. Holly. She is yelling with over excitement, her voice exploding from the earpiece. Calum pretends not to listen.

"Can! It's me! You feeling better? Hope the house is sorted. Listen, *everybody* is talking about how amazing the party was! I've got a Biscuit list as long as my arm babe – call me back. We need to talk talent! Later!"

By lunchtime the bounce in her voice was going. "Can. Me again. Where are you? Seriously dude, call me, I'm fielding calls from people who want in on the Biscuits. We need to talk about this. I can't come over, I've got church stuff – remember? We're on that contemplation course thing. I'm already contemplating running away. Ha! *Appelle moi*! Byee!"

By that night she was cross. "Candy. It's Holly. What's going on? Are you ill or something? Ring me! We've got too much happening for you to flake out on me now, man! Call ANY TIME OK? ANY TIME!"

This morning she was worried. "Hey Can, it's me. Are you cross with me or something? Have I upset you somehow? Is it about the BLAST OFF! I told you on Sunday – I had no *idea* it had booze in it! I thought it was just herbs! We've got to keep our phones off mostly but I'll try you again in a bit. Speak soon hopefully. Bye."

By lunchtime she was cross again. "Can. Holly. Listen, it's all very well for you to do this little disappearing act because you're off snogging Dan Ashton's face off or whatever but you should think about other people, OK? I'm holding the band deal together here. The whole day I've been staring into bloody candle flames and singing and all I can think about is how bloody cross I am with YOU! Then I've got to come back and start organising things. I know you're music aristocracy now that we know your Dad is Nathan Oxblood, but you don't have to act like you've got an ego like his already! I'm not your crapping PA, you know?" She sighs. "Look, I'm going to start without you because I don't really have any choice but you'd better call me… Yes Mum, I'm coming! I'M COMING! It's a personal call all right? I do have a life of my own you—" The line goes dead.

Five o' clock this afternoon. Her last message. Her voice is low and flat, full of suppressed rage. I can feel her trademark shark-eyed stare as Holly spits out her message. It is testament to Pirate's powers of petrification that as she speaks I actually look around the room to check she isn't here.

"Caine! You are in deep trouble. We drive back tonight and when I get into school tomorrow you'd better be there otherwise you and me are DONE... Mum will you GET OUT??...Yes, I KNOW it's Enlightenment Hour... I'm ON THE PHONE!!... Well maybe it's an ENLIGHTENING phone call? Did you ever think of THAT???... Right. Caine. You. Me. Tomorrow."

"Message. Ends," says smug robot lady. I gulp.

"That sounded like quite a lot of shouting," Calum says, making a grimace of sympathy.

"She'll come round. She's a bit of a shouter anyway..." I smile, unable to suppress my relief that while Pirate might kill me tomorrow at least my attempt at social suicide this weekend appears not to have worked.

I see Calum out and on the way to the front door he grabs the incinerated DVD player waiting in the hall to be binned. "You using this again?"

I examine the thing. It looks like the black-box recorder from a plane crash. "For what? Kindling?"

He smiles back, inkblot peepers creasing up under the black-rimmed glasses he's forgotten he's wearing. They suit him actually. "I might be able to use it for spare parts if it's no good to you? I, er... I like to build stuff in my spare time."

"It's all yours, dude. It's the least I can do."

Back on the doorstep he pauses for a second, looking down at the charred hardware in his hands. "So you and Dan. You... er... and..." I wait for him to finish the sentence. He doesn't.

"What about me and Dan?"

"Nothing! Just, you know, do you... know where he is?"

I frown. None of my fifteen messages were from him.

"No. Why would I?"

"You seemed... you looked... like you might be together, like. On Saturday."

"Yeah well, that was then. The party is definitely over now. I haven't heard from him and I'm not expecting to."

Calum throws me an awkward smile. If even MC Stain pities my love life, it must truly be disastrous. He taps a hand on the blown-out box he's holding and turns to leave.

"Oh. Well. If you hear from him... tell him to give us a buzz."

I wave him off into the skin-licking chill of the night. I might not have a boyfriend, but it looks like I'm one step closer to having a band. The Broken Biscuits are back on! That is, if I can persuade Holly not to hang, draw and quarter me at school tomorrow. It's not just her, though. There's someone else I need to forgive me too. I park myself on Mum's bed. Her room is more or less back to normal: Mum-normal at least (it still looks like a Victorian showgirl's dressing-up box). I sit down with The Beast and I strike the chord to summon my Godbrother. Somewhere, off in the invisible I hear his voice.

"Well, fancy that! A call from my juvenile overlord! What is it? More cleaning? Perhaps you have some gardening to do! Or a chimney I can sweep?"

"Don't be like that, Clarence!" I appeal to the empty room. "I wanted to tell you I'm sorry! Please come." There's a sudden crack and a flash and he's here again, shining at full wattage and back to his old self.

"Clarence!" I grin, pleased to see him. "You look great!"

"Well, I did manage to grab forty winks of beauty sleep," he says, fluttering over to admire himself in the wardrobe mirror before turning back on me sharply. "But never mind my restoration to perfection. You said something about being sorry?"

"I am," I say. "Truly. Mates again?"

"I suppose so!" Clarence says airily. "Not that I don't have a *thousand* of those in the ether already. I was just saying to my dear Bob…" He waits for me to ask, so I do.

"Which Bob, Clarence?"

"Marley. He's a very mellow soul. Fantastic in a crisis. Anyway I was just saying to him how lucky you are to have me! My books are full, chumwise."

"I am lucky," I say, and at the end of the longest few days of my life despite everything, I really feel it. A smile spreads across my face that reaches all the way down to my toes and, as the whole town sleeps outside and an ice-cream moon peeks in through the window, I tell Clarence everything. I might have messed things up with Dan but in Broken Biscuitland, things are looking up. Clarence chuckles as I reach the end of my tale.

"A tangled love life, coupled with a promising rock career and a hangover? Maybe you are an Oxblood after all!"

12

Queen Candy and the Court of the Insane

We're side-by-side as usual, waiting for Mrs Francis to come in for registration but today I don't dare meet Holly's gaze. Talk about a shark-eyed stare. She looks like Jaws when he's in the middle of eating a boat.

"Look, I'm sorry Hol. I know you were sorting band stuff out but I was fixing the damage from Saturday! I spent two hours on Monday trying to find the bathroom door. Someone took it off its hinges and dumped it in the back lane. We were both doing our bit in different ways!"

She pouts, then softens. It seems that three solid days' cleaning is enough of a penance for Pirate. I am forgiven. Which is just as well, really. I need someone sane on my side to notice how mental everyone is being today.

"Have you noticed how mental everyone is being today?"

Holly asks. Which is exactly why she's my friend.

"Yeah it's weird!" I nod, waving back to a random group of smiling girls I don't recognise as they walk past the classroom door. "It's like everyone, like..."

"...*Likes* us!"

"I know! Mad or what?"

"*Demente!*" Pirate shakes her head. "Someone actually *opened the door* for me when I came in this morning. I mean *the right way*. Not, like, into my face." Her phone buzzes. Laughing, she shows me the message. "Oh of course! I forgot! Um... I think this might explain things."

She holds it up, revealing a text from none other than Calum's third cousin, Kylie Carey: "Cnt W8 4 Sat. So glad I'm down 2 the final 6! KCX"

"The final six?" I give Pirate a look that, if it were an acronym, would be WTF? She nods sagely.

"Big *X Factor* fan. Like you said, you have to put the concept into terms that people understand."

"Right... And what instrument does she play? You should have seen her dancing! She's got about as much rhythm as an octopus in an electric chair." The image pops into my head again, Kylie on Dan's lap, him grinning, her doing her stupid lemon-sucking face. The lemon-sucker. Then I remember throwing up again. This is ridiculous. I've gone from green-around-the-gills to green-eyed monster in the space of a few days. It must be Like. I am *in Like* with Dan Ashton and it has sent me mental.

"She, um…" Pirate shuffles in her seat a bit. "The thing is, Can, she's really actually quite good? And I sort of couldn't say no to her. I got carried away. And it would have been awkward at school. And then I was cross with you so…" She trails off. I'm sensing something bad.

"What does she play?"

"She plays guitar. And sings."

"HOLLY!" I bang my hand on the desk as I shout, drawing stares from everyone in earshot. But whereas these would usually be followed by paper-throwing and name-calling all I get by way of reproach is a single look of vague curiosity from Simon Harchester. "Holly what were you *thinking*? I'm our guitarist! And our singer! We don't need another one!"

"Well – it's not like there's a law against it or anything…" she mumbles. I throw her a look and she starts again. "Dude, I'm sorry! She's probably going to be rubbish! It was most likely just an in-the-moment thing. She can come and audition. Epic fail. Leave. Everyone's happy."

"Duh! Except her! She'll turn the entire school against us!"

Holly looks around us as she considers this, then gives my

hair a ruffle before hopping up to sit on the desk. "Which will be nothing more than a return to the *status quo*, my frizzy friend. Now why don't we enjoy being queens for a day?" She pats the desk beside her and, grumbling, I hop up.

This is (for some reason) the way only popular people are allowed to sit. Of course everybody instantly notices. As they turn to look at us a murmur of silent assent works its way round the classroom like an invisible Mexican wave. If when I'm old I ever forget, please use this as an example to remind me: school is so unbelievably massively unspeakably weird.

Temporarily installed on her new throne, Holly starts dispensing nods, winks, waves and in one case, a small salute to her subjects below. "Lap it up my friend!" she instructs me through the corner of her smile. "While it lasts!"

Popularity is a strange sensation. Even though we know everyone only likes us because Kylie Carey has issued a decree obliging them to not because they actually do, it still feels nice. Being liked is like ice-cream. It doesn't really matter who you get it from, it's still delicious.

By Friday night I'm fairly certain I can tell you exactly what it's like to be in the biggest band in the world. Because in our school; our world, the biggest band are the Broken Biscuits. Everybody's talking about the auditions tomorrow when – it's widely assumed – Kylie Carey will be installed as my co-singer guitarist and a future music sensation. Pirate and I are keeping mum. Speaking of which, she's due back tomorrow morning. The house is almost back to normal and most of the kitchen table is visible again, *Brokecrap Mountain*'s consistent parts having been repaired, recycled or dispensed with. I'm hoping her compulsive hoarding will mask the fact that things have gone missing until... er, until I leave home, actually.

Clarence and I are upstairs in my room with the window open so I can hear the rain outside (it's my best thing). I'm writing a song which is (for now) called *Friends in High Places*. I know, I know. Working title.

I strum The Beast without having to think much about what to do next, sliding a bar chord shape up and down its slender neck as I sing along under my breath:

I've got friends in high places
They're showing their faces
In the kind of places
They shouldn't be seen.
They're hanging with weirdos
Their heroes are zeros

Not our kind of people

Do you know what I mean?

The Beast has become an extension of me these past few weeks. I'm writing songs every night and lots in the daytime too. I'm keeping a notepad to jot ideas down as they come to me. Even Clarence is impressed at how quickly I'm getting the hang of playing. "Destiny, my dear Candypop – providence! I only ever knew one person who forged such a bond with the apparatus with which they might realise their creative impulse..." he pauses, arching an eyebrow for added drama, "*moi*. When I was alive my instrument and I were quite inseparable."

I try and fail to suppress a snigger at how unintentionally rude this sounds. Clarence rolls his eyes. For a little while, neither of us says anything. I pluck randomly at The Beast's strings and think about the song and... Nathan. I stop playing. My Fairy Godbrother has been dressing up to amuse himself and – at this present moment – is wearing one of my best charity shop scarves across his nose, like a belly-dancer's veil. Noticing me looking, he stops undulating across the dressing-table and says, "Yes?"

"What do you think it's like Clarence? Being a rock star, I mean? You must have met a few." I cast my eyes heavenward. "You know – up there..."

"Well, generally speaking, it does mirror your experience over the past few days, on a grand scale. Albeit with the usual additions of a crippling drug habit, money problems and an insane spouse."

"Yeah, I don't fancy those bits of the job much," I mull, trying to strum my way to the other side of the bridge I've just written.

"A cliché is a one-size-fits-all garment, my darling. And they are never flattering. If you take my advice on anything let it be this: in fate, as in fashion, bespoke is always best."

"Since Dan still hasn't called I suppose I don't need to worry about that anyway. I'm miles from getting a boyfriend. Sane, insane or of any other variety," I sigh. Clarence smiles at me wearily. Over the past few days I have agonised over the Dan Situation with him a lot. And Pirate. I sense that they are both on the verge of telling me to shut up. I'm about to ask another question when the doorbell goes.

Looking out of my bedroom window I follow the raindrops down to the street, three floors below. It's Calum! Or Stain. Or whoever he's being today.

Calum hesitates on the doorstep. "Hiya." He says it like it's an apology.

"Hey Calum! What are you... do you, er... want to come in?"

Deep inside his hood, a bent-fender smile. "Nah. I'm not

stopping. Just on my way past. Brought you this." He lifts up a plastic bag from his side and hands it to me.

I take it and brush the rain off. From inside I pull out... our DVD player. Is it? Or is it a new one?

"Calum! How... how did you..."

He shrugs. "I like fixing things. This model's pretty crap, like. De-chipped it for you, though. You can watch region ones now."

Calum shifts from foot to foot in the rain, soggy clothes hanging off his skinny frame like washing left on the line in a storm. How far has he come to get here anyway?

"I don't know what to say. Thanks so much. You sure you don't want to—"

He cuts me off before I can finish which is lucky, really. I mean, what could I actually have said to him at 10 o' clock on a Friday night?

"Nah. On my way out. See ya." With that, he lopes off into the rain and my skin is officially saved.

The next morning, Mum arrives back shiny-eyed and full of the joys of nature. And *love*. Sorry, just sicked up in my mouth a bit there (turns out I tend to do that when things get romantic). I tell you what, though, it's kind of hard to see her this happy and not feel slightly heart-warm. Or maybe it's heartburn. Or just relief that

– so far – she hasn't noticed anything's amiss in our rave-blitzed house. We still haven't got any spoons, for example. Why would they take our spoons?

"Oh darling, it was wonderful!" she trills, dumping her bags on the bed and looking as wistful and rosy-cheeked as Julie Andrews in *The Sound of Music*. Not that Julie Andrews ever wore leopard print. Certainly not before 10am. "The second-hand shops over there are amazing!" she enthuses, raking through her bag, scattering a selection of recently acquired bric-a-brac across the bed in the process. "I got you a little present!" She then produces what I must admit is a deeply cool fake fur cape. It will probably get me beaten up. But it's love at first sight.

I wrap it round me and then wrap myself round her for a massive bear hug. Sometimes (especially when you haven't seen her for a week) my mum is awesome. She leans back and holds my face in her hands, scanning it like I'm an ancient treasure, covered in hieroglyphics she's trying to decode.

"I missed you so much, sweetheart! Have you had something to eat?"

"Yup. Toast," I say through the squishing. She pecks me on the forehead.

"All right then. I might fly downstairs and have something. I was so desperate to get back to you we missed breakfast this morning. Although Mrs Walker from the B&B made Ray a sandwich for the car. She was very taken with him!"

Glad to have him out of her house probably, I think darkly. "We haven't got much food left, Mum, only the last of the bits you bought."

"Don't worry, darling, I'll just have some cereal," she says, disappearing down the stairs. "Um… OK then. I'm off to Holly's!" I shout, leaping up to grab my bag and making a sharp exit before she works out she's going to have to eat it with a fork.

13

The Broken Biscuits Come Together

So here we are. Pursuing the rock 'n ' roll dream. I won't lie to you – this isn't how I pictured it. Standing outside Holly's parents' church on the stroke of a cold wet March midday, waiting for our potential bandmates (Hol keeps calling them "the unbaked Biscuits") to arrive. There was no way I was going to have another one of these things at my house so welcome to our second-choice venue for Operation Awesome, Phase Two.

We (me, Pirate and Clarence) shelter in the porch of the brand-new bright-bricked building, watching the spring rain pitter-patter on to the perfect tarmac of the deserted car park. Clarence (for reasons best known to himself) has decided to come disguised as an old-fashioned Polaroid camera, complete with a strap that allows him to be slung casually around my neck. And when I say "casually" clearly I mean "embarrassingly". I think he's doing it to mess with my head: everyone else can see him, but I *almost* wish they couldn't.

"That thing is coolio. It looks really new! Must have never been used. Your mam bring it back from the Lakes as well?" Pirate says, dragging on her nicotine inhaler. Like it has anything in it and she isn't just doing it for effect. But since I'm not only wearing a vintage camera like a necklace but also my new fur cape, who am I to judge? My outfit is the ultimate glasshouse.

"Yeah. Who are we expecting first?"

"Darren Shears. Drums." She exhales. "I'll go and check we're all set in there."

Since the only religious practise I was brought up with was skincare-based, I can't say I have much experience of what a church should look like. Wouldn't have thought it would be like this, though. It's fresh and new but strangely clinical. I suppose if I was going to start going to church, I'd like it to be somewhere a bit more intense. Somewhere I might either go blind from a retina-scorching peek at Nirvana or get assailed by a vengeful skeleton. Coming here would be more like going to Sainsburys with a shopping list that just says "God".

As soon as Pirate has disappeared, I lift Clarence up so that to a casual observer I might appear to be examining his workings whereas in reality I am going to tell him off. "Clarence.

Dude. Seriously! Is it too much to ask that you come as something useful?"

SNAP!

There is a flash. I am momentarily blinded. He's taken a picture of me. "*Au contraire,* my dear! Today I have come as something *indispensible*." A little square of plasticy photograph paper slides out of a slot at the base of his form.

I squint at it warily, my eyesight returning in blobs. "Can I touch this? I mean, it hasn't come out of the equivalent of anywhere gross?"

"You are so depressingly *literal*!" he groans. "Just take it out!"

I do, making a mental note to wash my hands as soon as possible, just in case. The photograph in my hands is of me. Upside down and angry with the top of my head cut off. Not my best look. But here's the weird bit. All over me and around me is a cloud.

"Not a bad spectrum," says Clarence as if this were a run-of-the-mill compliment.

"What am I looking at exactly?" I ask, although I think I know.

"Your music," Clarence says smugly, "made visible. Since I am untroubled by the limitations of earthly flesh, mine is perceptible already. You may have noticed it before." He puffs himself up as much as possible for an ancient camera and I look back at the photograph. There are colours all over me. Less than there are within Clarence's pearlescent whiteness, but quite a few.

"Is it like an aura?" I ask.

"Well I'd rather not put it like that, since that's only a few steps away from a fringed waistcoat and a mood ring but... sort of, yes. It was Andy's idea!" he explains as I stare deep into the glittering tones of my double chin.

"Andy?"

"Warhol. Strictly speaking, he isn't in with our lot but he drops in – very much a kindred spirit. He was terribly fond of Polaroids in life, you know. Awfully revealing. This will make choosing your collaborators a breeze!"

Just then a big, family-sized people-carrier pulls into the car park, driven by a large man who looks a bit like he might be made out of Play-Doh, wearing a black short-sleeved shirt, open with a Led Zeppelin T-shirt on underneath. In the back is a slightly smaller but otherwise identical (and identically dressed) version of him. He winds the window down. "WHOO! Caine! You got kit in there?"

"Yup. We're all sorted."

"ROCK AND ROLL! I'll just get me gloves. Bye, Da."

Darren Shears clambers out of the Renault Espace as gracefully as a cow alighting a helicopter. He's wearing a carefully tied red bandana and fingerless black leather gloves. As he approaches me he reaches his arm over his head and to his back like he's going to scratch an itch, and produces the biggest pair of drumsticks I have ever seen which (God help us) must have been secreted in his bum crack. He starts spinning them wildly. I wince.

"WHOO!" he shouts in my face.

"Hello Darren," I say.

"ROCK AND ROLL!"

"Hey Darren," says Pirate, reappearing from inside.

"WHOO!" bellows Darren. "COME ON GIRLIES! LET'S DO THIS THING!"

Inside the church's function room we quickly discover that while Darren Shears might have the social skills of a human-sized spider, he also has the dexterity. The boy is all over the drumkit! Unbelievable! Using the Rodgers' family band drums (more accustomed to sedate versions of *Our God Reigns*) we belt out a song I wrote the other week called, *Bang Bang Bang*. This is the song we are using as our litmus test of today's candidates. As the title suggests, it's a pretty daft song, really. And LOUD. It's the kind of thing people can put their own stamp on a bit. Darren's drumming gives it a kind of intricate oomph. Like machine-gun fire making a pretty pattern in a sheet of metal.

The song goes like this:

Get up girls and get up boys
Bang bang bang!
Hey what's that noise?
Bang bang bang!
We'll wake you up
Bang bang bang!
And shake you up
And hammer-hammer, hammer-hammer, hammer-hammer,
bang bang bang!

Like I said. Daft. After Darren's paradiddled his way through that we take a snap on Clarence. Darren's aura is somewhat unsurprisingly Spinal Tap-esque. That is – none more black.

The rest of the day is a finger-stinging ear-pounding head-throbbing jam-fest. Apart from the bit where Pirate's dad Alan, pops in with sandwiches and crisps. "How's your group going, Berry?" he asks (Berry is Hol's nickname in the family. Like Holly berry? As in the tree fruit, not the actress).

Hol grunts a reply, "S'right." And he takes back the Tupperware, stacking it up against his *Bird World* fleece. He's big on birds, is Alan. "He's so embarrassing," Hol mutters darkly as Mr

Rodgers busts out some more Tupperware. (Homemade flapjacks – result!) "I wish I had cool parents like you."

"We haven't made much of a start on finding BioDad *yet*," I say through a mouthful of floury bap. "And as it stands, I've actually only got one parent. But if by cool you mean 'more issues than the *Daily Mirror*' then, yeah, my mum's cool."

Hol and I are at somewhat of an impassé over parent-envy. While we love our respective 'rents, I do often think a swap would work better for all concerned. Like, when I was a kid I always wanted parents who had a full complement of the correct picnicware, and Holly would really appreciate a mum who knows all the words to Green Day's *Basket Case*.

Hayley Jackson, who's a keys player's up next. She's all right – nothing to write home about. Then Martin Everetts, a long-haired guitarist who turns up with no eyebrows and a large penis drawn on his face in permanent marker. "Fell asleep at my mate's," he mumbles. "Tossers."

Understandably, Martin is cagey about getting his photo taken but since they apparently YouTubed the entire process last night and it's had several hundred hits already, decides he's got nothing to lose. He comes out mainly red. Hmm. To be fair he still plays pretty well: having a bald forehead and face genitals might affect some people's performance.

Our penultimate auditionee is Spooky Li on drums. Her real name is Suki but nobody calls her that. Spooky is so unbelievably tiny that I feel like I should offer her a leg up on to the drum stool. There's no way she's going to be able to play those things, she looks like a four-year-old trying on her mum's shoes. I give Pirate a look that suggests I know that she has just chosen Spooky because of her legendarily awesome hair and fashion styling but which also indicates that this is something I do not entirely disapprove of. Spooky's ensemble today is a triumph. It consists of what appears to be three different outfits, layered together – the kind of look that, attempted by the average person, might draw concerned stares, if not professional mental health intervention. Her glossy bobbed hair is jet black and poker-straight on top, purple underneath. At the party last week it was all black with white dots sprayed on it like a domino.

We start to play and Spooky listens for a bit, her shiny head bobbing along in time, twitching the sticks in her hands, feeling out a little plan. To be honest, before she even starts playing I know that we have found our drummer. Then she leaps in with a silly skippy beat that sort of speeds up and slows down without ever actually falling out of time. She makes the song sound a bit like it's being played on a wonky old record player but in a really, really good way. She's so in our band. Not that we tell her that. We snap her (she's comes out with tiny rainbow triangles all over her face, especially around her eyes) and then take a break outside. The rain has worn itself out at last and everybody is out and about while it's dry.

Only Kylie Carey left to go. She's definitely going to be late. Partly to keep us waiting to show that (while it's an audition) she's in charge and partly because people like her always have more than one place to be at the weekend. Hol and me sit on the church's front step splitting a bottle of coke and play her favourite game – Twin Me. You take turns matching passersby to their celebrity twins. If you draw a blank on anyone you have to do a forfeit. Hol's aptitude for this game approaches *Rain Man* levels. She takes a chug on the bottle.

"Three o'clock. David Hasselhoff."

Sure enough, seconds later an extremely short fat David Hasselhoff walks past. A woman with long mousy hair and three little kids (one of whom she's shouting at and lifting off his feet by the arm) pushes a pram towards us.

"Er… Jennifer Aniston?"

"I'll give you that. Probably shouldn't. Ooh! Jordan and Alex!" A muscly orange couple in flammable-looking velour tracksuits and shades stroll past us towards *Bodyworxx*, the gym next door to the church. The lady's hair extensions are thicker than her legs. Damn, Hol's good at this.

The game goes on for a while. We spot Al Pacino, Geri Halliwell, Philip Schofield and an extremely down-at-heel Lady GaGa. I can't really concentrate, though, because a thought's stuck in my head, so eventually I just say it out loud.

"Do you think I look like Nathan Oxblood? Like, would you Twin Me with him?"

Hol scrutinises my face. "Dunno. A bit I guess. You're very like your mum, you know. Apart from..."

"My eyes?"

"*Exactement*. It was the first thing I thought of when you told me. I mean, it's a mad colour. Unusual. Proper shouty green like..." Hol scrunches her face up, searching for the right comparison "...an Amazonian tree frog."

"Wow. Cheers," I reply.

I finish the last of the coke and start tapping the bottle on my knee idly, mind wandering. How the flip am I going to find Nathan Oxblood exactly? As well as my nocturnal music lessons, Clarence and I have been devoting quite a bit of sneaking-time to going online after hours in the salon and looking for stuff on him. The odds of me making contact couldn't be worse. He lives in a secluded mansion in Los Angeles where he apparently spends most of his time looking for aliens via his specially built observatory. He's only done one interview since 2002 and that was to announce that The Rain were breaking up. Apparently they all hate each other so much that the guitarist (Nate's childhood best friend) now has a tattoo that reads, "Blood is thicker than water and Oxblood is thicker than anything" in Latin; presumably so that if he meets any ancient Romans they can have a good laugh about it.

"Hey up – Miley Cyrus." Pirate says suddenly. "Oh *Sheize*! And the dude off *Twilight*."

I look up. Coming towards us across the car park are Kylie Carey and... Dan. She's with Dan! He's carrying her guitar case for her, his expression as indecipherable as ever. Kylie puts her hand on his shoulder like an astronaut knocking a flag into the moon. He hangs back and she trots towards us, her TopShop shoe-boots scrickk-scrickking on the tarmac. Kylie does little jazz hands accompanied by a fake squeal of excitement, then hugs me and Pirate in turn. One of those no-body-contact ones; like we're competition winners who have by dint of amazing good fortune got the chance to meet her. Over her shoulder, my eyes meet Dan's for the first time, but after a split-second he looks away.

"Afternoon ladies!" she yips. Kylie's got one of those put-on puppy-voices. *Squeak squeak squeak*, trying to make herself sound cute and helpless. It makes me want to smash her on the head like I'm playing Whack-a-Mole. I breathe in hard, yank my mouth into a smile and say, "Great to see you, Kylie! Come on in. Hey Dan." Dan dips his head to acknowledge me and looks away.

"You two know each other?" Kylie asks me incredulously. She turns to Dan, "You didn't tell me that babe!" Kylie rolls her eyes and giggles, adorably. SMASH SMASH SMASH! "We're still finding out so much about each other. I suppose it's natural, though, isn't it?"

Dan at least has the decency to look embarrassed.

"We've only been together a month," Kylie leans in, giving Dan a squeeze, her head against his chest momentarily. "You've got… little friends all over the place, haven't you? Now – shall we get in there and get cracking?"

Together?

Hol shows Kylie through the door, they brush past me but I can't move. My feet are rooted to the spot. My body feels like it's been turned into concrete. Dan hangs back. I look up and meet his eyes. This time he doesn't look away.

"A *month*?"

I don't know whether I'm asking him or just saying it out loud.

"Don't, Candy." He shakes his head, half-smiling.

"What do you mean 'Don't'? Don't 'Don't' me!" I shout under my breath, fully aware of how ridiculous I sound but unable to stop. He rolls his eyes and huffs exasperatedly.

"What do you want me to tell you? After the way you flaked out on me at the party, I wouldn't have thought you were bothered. You threw up all over my stuff and didn't even apologise!"

"I did what?"

"You puked into my bag. Don't pretend you don't remember, Candy. You wrecked my iPhone, my wages were in there… everything!"

He shoots me a look and flounces after Kylie. Oh dear. I changed his contract to Vomaphone. I guess that explains why he didn't call.

◌

Even worse than the discovery that the boy of my dreams had to carry the contents of my stomach home all over his belongings, is what I find out next: Holly was right. Kylie is good. Her voice is breathy and pretty and while it still makes me want to stamp on her until she's powder, that's not *actually* her fault. Or Dan's. If anyone's to blame here, it's me. Apparently, Kylie's uncle owns the guitar shop in town and has been teaching her to play for years. He also gifted her a guitar that is the polar opposite of The Beast. A brand-new black-bodied Fender Strat. The paint job is factory-fresh and glitters like a clear night sky.

I look down at the instrument in my hands as she plays, laying confident little flourishes over my strumming. I'm so fond of The Beast these days I can't really bring myself to slag it off but from the outside – from Dan's perspective, I mean – it must look bad. Like she's driving a Ferrari, while I'm in a rusty third-hand Skoda. I'm mulling on this when I notice what appears to be a new sticker on The Beast curving around its side. It says in fancy lettering *The Show Must Go On*. Maybe Holly put it there. *She's right*, I think. Dan hates me but the show must go on. I've got to get on with doing what's right for the Broken Biscuits. Whatever else, Kylie looks great and sounds even better – she's perfect for us.

We come to the end of the song and I smile, first at Holly, then Kylie. "That was really good. You're dead talented."

"Mad isn't it?" she grins.

"Can I take your picture?" I ask, holding Clarence's viewfinder up to my eye.

"Course!" she squeaks, immediately squeezing her face into the lemony pout I spent an hour looking at on Facebook this week. "Come here babe!" She grabs Dan and pulls him into the shot. I press the button. SNAP! It feels like shooting myself. I throw the photo into my guitar case before the picture even appears.

"Well, we must dash, girls. Dan's coming for dinner at ours tonight, aren't you babe? Knowing my stepdad it'll be like *Meet the*... What's that film called again?"

"Fokkers," Hol says grimly, levelling a look of loyal concern in my direction.

Kylie hugs me again, with all the sincerity of Miss World embracing her arch-rival.

"So great to see you – hopefully speak soon, yeah?"

We bid them both goodbye. Dan doesn't say anything but as he holds the door open for Kylie to go through, he looks at me again. Straight at me. I stand looking at the doorway for a bit, as if he might change his mind at the last minute and come back and run over and kiss me again and make it all right like at the end of a film.

"You OK?" Pirate asks, punching me on the shoulder.

"'Course!" I lie and start packing up a bit too forcefully.

"I know you like him, you know. You can say it. You asked him to the party after all and..."

"Whatever. He's OK and all that but I'm not that bothered. The main thing is the band, Hol. The only thing in fact. Let's just concentrate on that."

I'm ferreting around behind an amplifier, winding leads into figures of eight over the heel of my hand and my elbow (a roadie trick Clarence showed me using a shoelace) when I hear the door open again. My heart jumps into my mouth. I literally drop everything and leap to my feet. He's come back! He's changed his mind! He's...

"Stain!" Hol shouts cheerfully. "*Que Pasa*, dude! What the effingtons are you doing here?"

"All right!" Calum says bashfully and I genuinely think I might start crying. "Don't wanna interrupt, like, but... I thought..."

We both wait for him to complete his sentence. He doesn't. Sensing that I am too crippled by disappointment to do so, Pirate takes the reins of conversation. "Stain, are you here to audition?"

Calum gives a *hyuck-hyuck* chuckle in the affirmative, then disappears out the door and re-emerges carrying a huge black box.

"I thought you might wanna see what I can do with this?" He opens the flight case and produces a mysterious-looking computery box with about fifty knobs sticking out.

Hol points and frowns. "Whassat?"

"Mixer," Calum says quietly, swiftly hooking it into a laptop and a battered keyboard.

Curiosity overrides my disappointment and I move in for a closer look. "It's a funny looking thing, though, Calum. I don't know much about mixers but I've never seen one that looked quite so... er... like that."

"Yeah," he grins. "Built it. Got a studio setup coming together in my room now."

Then he starts up the music, a track he has built too. It's a scrapbook landscape of borrowed noises, full of strange sounds that bump up against each other but somehow manage to fit together, like wave-peaks in the same sea. Calum starts playing a simple tune over the top with his right hand on the keyboard, twisting and distorting the sound through the mixer with his left. I lift Clarence up.

SNAP!

Looks like our band is going to be a five-piece.

Later that night, Clarence and I retrieve all five snapshots of the Broken Biscuits and place them side-by-side on my bed for analysis. I'm first: chopped-off and gurning but sparkling and rainbowy all over, a lot like Clarence.

"Your first pap shot!" he sighs. "Straight to the *Heat* magazine circle of shame for *you*. Next time my darling, please try to remember: either a pout or a huge laugh. Nothing in between is worth printing."

Next is Hol, who I snapped while she was playing. Her music

sits in her chest, a glowing ball surrounded by different-coloured rings. It kind of looks like she just swallowed Saturn. Clarence taps the picture. "Self-contained, this one. It's all internalised but definitely there – kept close to her heart."

Then it's Spooky's eye-triangles. "Fascinating!" he muses. "Triangles, of course, are a symbol of creativity: of creation itself, in fact. They're around the eyes – she's very visual about her music, almost synesthete." I shoot him a confused look. "She might even *see* music," he explains. "And notice how the triangles are all pointing upwards? Success, Candy! This girl is good."

I feel simultaneously inferior and a bit bad that I mainly chose Spooky because of her awesome styling. "Her hair's great too, though?" I venture.

Clarence nods gravely. "Never underestimate the power of good hair. Many of history's most memorable hairstyles were an inch away from the brain of a genius. Just ask John Lennon. Or Einstein."

Calum is in the middle of playing in his shot too. His eyes are closed. One hand is on the keyboard, the other on the mixer. They are both lit up with colour – each finger is a different shade. The brightness spreads out so that from a distance it looks like he's wearing rainbow boxing gloves. "Let me guess," I say. "He's the practical type."

"Indeed," Clarence nods. "He's a maker, a do-er. Mostly. But look – he traces a shimmering finger up to Calum's face. It's around here, too: in his speech."

I look at the picture. Sure enough, there's a glow around Calum's mouth and back into his throat. I try to equate this with the oratorical skills he has exhibited to me previously. Let's face it, he makes Paris Hilton sound like Barack Obama. "There's no doubt he's a nice guy and stuff, Clarence but... Are you on glue? There's no music in the way Calum talks."

Clarence picks up the photograph. "That depends on whether you believe – as I do, Candy – that music is truth."

Finally we move on to Kylie. Just like Clarence and I, her music is spread all over her. My eyes flick between the picture of her (looking perfect, obviously) and me (looking like an angry melting waxwork). If she gets to look that much better than me, surely I must have more colours than her? I don't, though. At least I don't think I do. It's too close to call. Feeling grumpy, I settle for asking Clarence a question. "What does it mean when the colours are all over like that?"

"Kylie is like us. A feeler."

"Blah. Sounds creepy," I say.

He rolls his eyes. "What it means is music is like your skin, it covers you from top to toe. Every experience you take in comes

204

to you through it; and everything you put back out into the world has music in it too."

I feel momentarily awesome again, until I remember that he's also describing my nemesis; who is (in this shot and probably at this actual moment) wrapped around the boy of my dreams. Ah, Dan. Actually: Dan? Now that I'm looking at him properly, Dan looks like… that can't be right. Clarence notices me noticing and goes quiet.

"That's weird," I say. "Can you only do one person at a time then?" I turn to face Clarence. He purses his lips, scratches the back of his head and looks away.

"Is that why Dan looks like this?" I pick up the photograph and hold it up to him. Clarence hovers for a moment as if he's trying to work out what to say. Eventually he decides.

"No."

I wait for him to add something else but he doesn't. "Expand, Clarence! What do you mean 'no'?"

I look back at the photograph. It's not unlike the picture of Mum and Nathan actually, only the roles are reversed. Kylie is the aggressive one wrapped around Dan, giving the camera (me, I suppose, since I took it) a warning glare, while he is handsome and engaged elsewhere looking out of shot. But while she's the same pearlised, every-colour white that I am in my picture, Dan is... completely normal. No rainbows, no triangles, no glowing fingers... Nothing.

"I don't understand, Clarence. Where are his colours? Why has Dan got no music on him?"

My Godbrother shrugs his shoulders. "That, my dear, is the million-dollar question."

14
This Just In

So we are the Broken Biscuits: Me, Pirate, Spooky, Kylie and Calum. Over the next few weeks we start rehearsing in earnest. Glad has lent us the function room in the Day Centre. Every night after school, every weekend, we're there practising, kicking into shape every new song I turn up with. He won't admit it but Clarence is really proud. For my part, I have relaxed the rules about his public appearances and have allowed him to accompany me to our practice sessions in fairy form. I've almost learned not to look as he zips around as we play, literally glowing with pride. He let slip the other day that watching us makes him feel alive again, and I know what he means. I feel the same and I'm not even dead. Our rehearsals have become the coolest after-school hangout in town. I act like it's all completely normal but let's face it, it's not: The same people who used to point and laugh at my clothes are now asking me where I got them.

Kylie's the reason for it, of course. I thought asking my arch-nemesis to join the band would be a nightmare but it turns out that her becoming a Biscuit has changed most things for the better. It takes less getting used to than I thought to have another guitarist in the band, and she actually adds a lot with her knack for coming up with backing vocals.

The online stuff has gone really nuts too. Now Clarence and me spend most of our after-hours sessions on the salon computer. Half our time is spent following the conspiracy theories, gossip and out-and-out crazy jibber-jabber about what Nathan Oxblood gets up to these days, and trying to come up with ways we might be able to get to him. Short of figuring out how to stow away on the next flight to L. A. we're no closer to solving that one. The rest of our time is keeping the band's fanbase happy. That's a big job – online and in real life, Hol and I have been given the keys to Popularity City. For the first time we're going places with people who aren't each other: the fair, the park, shopping, actual real-life parties. Hol loves it but I'm not so sure.

"They don't really like us for US, though Hol. They like us because of Kylie," I say while we are packing up one evening.

She shrugs. "It's the adulation of the unthinking masses,

dude!" she says, dragging on her empty inhalator. "They don't need to like us for US. You want to follow in BioDad's footsteps and be a rock star? This is the job! People who don't know you randomly love or hate you. *C'est la vie*. Enjoy it for what it is. Stop over-thinking."

Hol's right. Apart from bumping into Dan (or "Yoko" as she insists on calling him) every five minutes, life is pretty sweet. He still hasn't spoken to me properly. I still haven't worked out what's going on with the photo. My latest theory is that I took it when I was heartbroken and somehow blocked his music coming through on film. It's on my windowsill with the others. There's a little crease running down the centre where I fold Kylie out of the picture and put it next to mine so it looks like we're together.

As for things with Mum, they're ticking along. Just. I haven't been home much these past few weeks other than for bed and breakfast. She keeps trying to tempt me to stay in for a "girls night". What's the point? All she does is talk about the wedding. They've set the date. Our dresses have arrived. Mine hangs on the outside of my wardrobe door, glowing radioactively through its plastic garment bag. It feels like my funeral outfit. June 26th. Ten weeks 'til life as I know it ends for good. Hanging around there is pointless. All it does is remind me: home is just another house.

Our house is still where I sleep, though, and that's exactly what I'm doing when my phone goes off at 5:27am one Wednesday morning. My eyes refuse to open so I feel wildly around on my bedside table in the darkness for my mobile, sending everything else on it clattering to the floor. It takes three agonisingly loud bars of *I Want Candy* by Bow Wow Wow before I get to it.

"Wha?" I croak down the line. Oh no, hang on, that's my iPod. Another blast of 80s post-punk later I have the phone. I have also managed to partially open an eye. "Hellowhoozit?" I mumble, mouth still half asleep.

"Dude – are you *watching this*?" Holly squeals. I pull the phone away from my ear to check the time.

"It's half-past *five*, Holly. In the morning. I was watching the back of my eyelids! What are you doing up?"

"Skyping Bruno," she says as if getting up in the middle of the night to make secret web calls to the Brazilian boyfriend you have never met is an everyday activity. "Don't change the subject. Put Sky News on."

"Why? What's happened?" I ask, rolling out of bed and wobbling down the stairs like a zombie. Holly's reply is an evil-genius laugh so loud I have to move the phone away from my ear. She calms herself down enough to answer me properly, just as I flick the TV on and see for myself.

"Your Dad's on telly."

It's so early that it isn't even the normal news dude yet. It's a dough-faced desperado whose ringed eyes and haunted expression indicate that being in a suit and tie before 6am reading the news to precisely nobody was never part of his plan. "...The time is five-thirty here on Sky News and our top story this morning. Music fans worldwide are waking up to the news that controversial British rock band The Rain are set to reunite..." he keeps talking as footage of Nathan flashes up – the video for *Super Silly Us*, The Rain's final release. Despite being the most expensive video ever made at the time, the single bombed (not surprisingly – it was rubbish). News Dude continues "...The Rain, seen here in 2002, split acrimoniously later that same year in an onstage fracas that led to numerous arrests. Singer Nathaniel Oxblood, who now lives reclusively in the United States, held a press conference with the rest of the group near his California home last night. He told Sky News they were excited about the reunion and their festival plans for the summer..."

And there he is, all of a sudden: Nathan as he is right now. He looks good. Great, actually! Fit, tanned and smiling, if a little jumpy. I suppose it's understandable. There are hundreds of microphones and cameras trained on him as he sits at a long flower-strewn table in a posh-looking hotel with the rest of the band. Illuminated by firecracker flashes from the bank of photographers in front of him, he starts to speak. Softly and slowly at first, like someone who knows the world is hanging on his every word.

"Fame has been a hard road for us, you know, as individuals and as a group. Sure, in the past we've had our differences but ultimately these guys…" He places a silver-ringed hand on the shoulder of JJ Jameson next to him. Even through JJ's thick leather jacket I'm sure I see him flinch, although, obscured by his enormous shades his face doesn't show it. Nathan continues, his voice rising to an emphatic crescendo, "The Rain is a special project and we're excited about creating again. For us that's what it's all about. We were never a critics' band – it's all about the fans! And the shows! There has been a drought, people. It's time to bring back The Rain!"

There's a hubbub of approval from the crowd and hands immediately shoot into the air. Nathan points at a young girl with long blonde hair who doesn't look much older than me. "Yes?"

"Sophie Churchill, *NME*. Yeah, is there any truth in the rumour that you're going to be headlining Glastonbury Festival this year?" she asks.

Nathan makes a face. "Sophie, Sophie, Sophie! What are you doing to me?" Sophie giggles. Everyone laughs and Sophie looks like she might actually titter herself to death. "As for Glastonbury," he continues laconically, "I'm sworn to secrecy. Ask me no questions and I'll tell you no porky pies." Suddenly the camera cuts back to News Dude in the studio and I realise I'm holding the phone. Pirate is still on the other end of the line.

"Well? What do you think?" she says excitedly.

"You're right about the eyes." I yawn. "Total tree frog." I move a terrifying-looking contraption that I happen to know is a new electric anti-flab massager Mum's trying out for the salon and plonk myself down on the sofa.

"Not about his eyes, dofus! I mean about Glastonbury! This is our way in!"

"To Nathan? How exactly, Hol?"

"Duh? He's playing Glastonbury Festival? We should, like, go? And find him?" she says.

Hol always makes every sentence into a question? When she's being sarcastic? Like this? As if she's talking to a three-year-old? It's really annoying? I decide not to rise to it, adopting my most reasonable tone. "All right, early riser. Don't get carried away. He didn't actually confirm they were doing it."

"Upppffgh!" Hol splutters. "Of *course* he confirmed it! He just didn't say it in so many words. If he is your dad I hope you inherited your Mum's ability to keep secrets. He's frubbish at it!"

"Hol, listen. Even if you're right, Glastonbury is the biggest music festival in the entire world. The tickets are a fortune and even if we could afford them, they sold out months ago! It's also in Somerset which is, like, a million miles away!"

"It's not a million." Hol pouts down the line sulkily. "It's two hundred and seventy-nine. I just looked it up."

"What so we just *turn up* and chance it? Did you also look up how much security they have? The place is like Alcatraz, Hol! Anyway, Nathan is one of the biggest stars in the world. He's not going to be pitching a tent and roughing it with the plebs, is he? He'll be backstage in the VIP area!"

Holly doesn't reply, except by emanating extremely powerful sulkiness. Eventually I cave in. "What? What do you want me to say?"

"I just don't get why you're being so negative about this!" she whines. "This is your big chance! I thought you wanted to find Nathan."

"I do!" I protest. "I really do! I just can't imagine how we're going to get there. You might as well have rung me to say he's playing a gig on the moon!"

"Well," says Hol. "Luckily for you, your bandmate is a genius. I know where we can get a rocket!"

I slump deeper into the sofa cushions. "Holly, it's not even dawn yet. It's too early for metaphors. What on earth are you on about?"

"Just say it," she says, her voice full of mischief.

"Say what?"

"Say that if I can find a way to get us into Glastonbury, you'll do whatever it takes to get there."

I open my eyes again. "Are you serious?"

"I'm serious, dude. *Rhythm is a Dancer* serious. Now swear it. Swear on The Beast."

A little rush of adrenalin surges through me, forcing me back to my feet. She's serious. I raise my right hand and close my eyes, picturing my guitar – in all its scruffy glory. "I swear."

"YES!" Hol shouts before remembering herself and whispering, "Caine. If I'm right about this, we are going to Glastonbury! Naturally this means I won't be at school today."

"Naturally!" I echo sarcastically. "Er, why exactly?"

"I'm going on mission," Pirate replies gravely "Meet you for rehearsals at seventeen hundred hours." It's always a bad sign when she starts using army talk. Unreasonable behaviour generally follows.

"In civilian English please, Hol. Why aren't you coming to

school?" She isn't listening, though.

"Lots to do, soldier! See you tonight. Over and out." The line goes dead and I'm left alone in our living room as the sun creeps up outside, wondering what on earth life will throw at me next. The morning sky is pink and gold and the clouds are lined with silver, just like in the saying.

I mute the TV (Nathan's face over and over on the rolling news) and stick Mum's old copy of *The Wow* by The Rain on the stereo. Comparing my face to his, I pout like Nathan at the mirror. Our eyes are already identical. Once I contort my lips into the famous Oxblood 'dog's bum', the resemblance is uncanny. The chorus kicks in and I can't help it: I start pogo-ing around the room in my PJs.

Don't try to hypnotise
Disguise the supersize
Lies behind your eyes now!
Surprised you recognise
Something you can't deny
Hits you between the eyes
POW!
You and me we're The Wow!

At three forty-five, having phoned Mum to make my excuses at home, I arrive at the Day Centre. Clarence is fluttering idly around the blossoming flower garden. I, on the other hand, am pacing and fidgeting like a maniac. Partly it's excitement. But I suspect it may also have something to do with the four cans of *Slam Dunk!!* energy drink I downed at school this afternoon. Having got up earlier than I ever have in my entire life, by lunchtime today I was exhausted. Before the world as I know it went nuts, this would have merely meant I crashed out on the sofa by teatime. Not now that I'm popular. Within ten minutes of moaning about how tired I was Leo Armstrong (off-duty blazer-wearer, head of the school computer club and unofficial King of the Nerds) had arrived to present me with a bag full of cans of *Slam Dunk!!* Apparently it's big among the computer and science fraternity ("If you're hitting the wall, this will help you smash straight through it," he intoned. "Thanks to these I did six hours on *Urban Dead* last night and still got into school on time."). I checked them for booze. Negative. There must be something mad in them, though, because right now I feel like a bottle of coke that's been thrown down a flight of stairs. My heart is fluttering like a hummingbird and I have to keep fighting the urge to break into a run. I'm about to burst through the Day Centre's front door when it opens from the inside out. Glad's mate Ernie's knees emerge before the rest of him, covered by a tartan blanket and sitting in his wheelchair.

"Oops! Ernie! Sorry!" I say, stopping myself from careering into him just in time. He smiles and waves away my apology. Then I notice the catchers-mitt hands pushing his wheelchair. The rest of Calum follows them through the doorway. He sees me and blushes. The tips of his ears (for once not covered by a baseball cap) turn a furious fuschia.

"Hey!" I smile. "What are you doing here so early?"

Calum stares mutely at Ernie's flat cap. A shrill Scots voice coming from inside the Day Centre answers on his behalf. "You might be better asking what he *isn't* doing here, lassie."

Glad emerges into the gentle spring sunlight clutching a pair of pliers which she points in Calum's direction. "This young man has been fixing us up in here for a good while now. He's a marvel with the electrics!"

Calum's pink ears turn beetroot as Ernie's frail voice fought its way out from deep within his wrappings. "Reminds me of the lads in the DAF," he says, taking a long and difficult breath. "Boy could find his way round a Tomahawk engine, I'll bet." His voice trails off into a wheeze.

I try to catch Calum's eye but he's having none of it. Wonder if he knows what a Tomahawk is. I don't but it must be good if

Ernie's comparing Calum to his Desert Air Force pals. Unable to keep still, I hop from foot to foot as Calum pushes Ernie past us.

"Coach is waiting," he mumbles, making for the parked-up council minibus.

Glad and I watch them go. "Such a good boy," she says after him. "He was a worry to his grandad for a while but he's come into his own now."

"You mean at school and stuff?" I ask; hopping and mentally replaying the legendary moment Calum released the hounds into his exam.

"Yes. Wilf was very disappointed with his results. He was so gifted. But – I don't know if he mentioned it – his dad had left. It was a hard time for him. Luckily he's got a strong grandad and mum. He's come through the other side."

"That's a lovely story," I say, quicker than expected, unable to fight the urge to hop from foot to foot. Glad gives me a hard stare. Four is definitely too many *Slam Dunk!!*s.

"What on earth is the matter with you today, lassie?"

"Nothing!" I yelp. "I'm just excited! We're expecting news from Holly."

She eyes me warily as Calum rejoins us, having deposited Ernie safely in the minibus. "Anythin' else you want doing, Mrs Appleyard?" he asks softly.

"No, dear. You two go on and get on with your group." Glad smiles indulgently at Calum. "I'm sure you have plenty to chat about."

I follow Calum inside. His lopes are so long I have to do little skips to keep up, allowing me to unleash some of my skittish energy. We arrive at the Function Room, which is still set up for the 2pm line dancing class. By which I mean someone has accidentally left a Billy Ray Cyrus CD playing on rotation and there are Stetsons everywhere. Calum and I start piling the hats up to the tune of *Achy Breaky Heart*, me at double-speed.

"How long have you been helping out here, then?" I ask him, selecting a particularly fine blue headpiece and donning it at a rakish angle.

"Since I got excluded," Calum shrugs. "Go to college as well. Maths and electronics."

"You're a bit of a brainiac on the sly, aren't you?" I chuckle, attempting my own version of the cowboy footwork that made Miley Cyrus's dad famous.

Calum smiles sheepishly and I plonk the next Stetson in the pile on his head. He blushes but laughs, bobbing awkwardly in time to the music as we deposit the rest of them in the cupboard and start unpacking our gear.

We're set up and still mucking about (playing along with the

CD tragically enough – both giggling) when Hol bursts through the door. Understandably, when she sees us she stops dead in her tracks. Calum whips off his Stetson and hides it behind his back. I pull mine over my eyes, with *if I can't see you, you can't see me* toddler logic.

"Dudes! WTF?"

Calum turns pink again and dives for the off-switch. Hol doesn't seem to want an explanation, though (just as well, really – can there ever be an excuse for jamming with Cyrus?) Hol is full to the brim with another purpose. She seems... different. It's not the way she looks. She flounces into the silent room as cockily ever in her black skinnies and biro-ed Converse, blonde hair dragged across one smoke-ringed eye: Alice in Emoland. Today, though, her smirk is cheekier; her eyes are twinklier; her flounce is bouncier. Holly is beaming. Glowing. Emanating. She's radiating a contentment I have seen before. Holly is basking in the afterglow of a dubious victory. Nervous, excited and still caffeinated to the eyeballs I ask, "Well?"

She's about to answer when Spooky and Kylie walk in behind her. Holly spins around. "Afternoon girls! Just in time." Then from her cavernous yellow pleather bag she produces five brightly coloured pieces of paper, spread out in her hand like a fan. "I was just about to ask these here cowboys whether they fancied coming with me to Glastonbury this year. I've got five tickets and they're all VIP."

It's as if she's just whipped out five million-pound notes. Everyone lunges, snatches then pores over the spoils.

"OH MY GOD!" shrieks Kylie. "Where did you get these?"

Calum shakes his head in disbelief, smiling from ear to ear. Spooky's jaw is somewhere near her knees. "Are these *real*?" she asks.

Hol nods. Spooky closes her eyes, actually kisses the paper. Hol stalks over and, with a triumphant flourish, hands the last one to me.

It's so colourful it almost looks like Clarence made it from music. There are holograms. I've read about those – they stop people making forgeries. It's bright and beautiful like currency from a foreign land. I take back what I said about these being million-pound notes. They are worth more than that: five tickets to Glastonbury. Somewhere in our not-too-distant futures, five doors swing open on to everything any of us could ever want. Each of us gawp and giggle, imagining our various dreams coming true. For me there is only one. I'm going to find Nathan Oxblood. I can hear Clarence fluttering beside me, examining the ticket in my hands and "Ooohing" excitedly, but when I eventually tear my eyes away from it, it's to look at Holly.

"Hol – how...?" I can't even finish my sentence. Removing my hat and placing it on her own head, she throws her arm around my shoulder and pulls me into a half-headlock hug. "*Mon Ami!* Have I ever let you down? Let's just say I know a bloke who knows a bloke." I lift my head and meet her gaze. Something in her look tells me not to ask any more questions. I don't. Pirate has performed a feat of magic as amazing as any of my Godbrother's. I'm not going to break the spell by trying to work out how. Standing up, she addresses the room.

"They're artist tickets – that means backstage access and backstage camping, food and drink, the lot! The only requirement is..." and here Hol's smirk cracks into a full-on grin, "we have to play a set."

There's a general gasp of amazement and a couple of squeals. I look down at the ticket in my hand. There's a picture of the Pyramid Stage, just like in my dream. Underneath it says *Glastonbury, Wednesday 23rd – Sunday 27th June*. The same weekend as Mum and Ray's wedding. How many miles did Pirate say Bishopspool was from Glastonbury? 300'ish... It's too much to take in. I run my hand through my thicket of hair which, as always, springs straight back up again. "So let me get this straight. If we do this, not only do we get to *go* to Glastonbury Festival; we get to *play* Glastonbury Festival as well?"

Hol eyes me from beneath the brim of her Stetson. "Yup. You swore, remember?" She says it like an accusation, knowing it's a choice between letting the band down or Mum.

I think of the open door again. Through it I see myself up onstage, looking out across a cheering sea of people. One of them is Nathan. I think of the picture of him and Mum. I imagine Mum in her wedding car driving off into her new life with Ray, waving goodbye to me through the back window. I think of the orange bridesmaid's dress: glowing out of its dust cover in my empty bedroom like an old streetlight in a neglected part of town. The others have gathered around Pirate expectantly, apparently waiting for my say so. I take a deep breath.

"Let's do it," I say and everybody screams. Suddenly I'm at the bottom of a people-pile: a huge, cheering, sea monster of a hug. Somewhere I can't see, Calum pipes up, "I might be able to get us a van, like." And we all start laughing. Somewhere else I can't see, I hear Clarence laughing too.

15
Finding the Wow

We did our best rehearsal ever that afternoon. People from school (and from Not School) started turning up until the place was wall-to-wall. Most of the audience I recognise, but some are new: friends of friends from a town or two over who have come to check us out. They're all the kind of people I used to wish I could be friends with. Fun people. People whose ease with everything – dress, conversation, laughter – is the opposite of my own. They're still not my friends, of course. Not really. They're something better: fans. I would never say it out loud, for fear of sounding like (as Calum would put it) a total and utter BELL but after all those years being the odd sock at the bottom of life's laundry pile, it feels good. After a month of hanging out while we play they know the lyrics to our songs almost as well as I do. They have started joining in and singing along, started filming when we play their favourites, shouting out their names when we don't.

"Do *Astronaut*! ASTRONAUUUT!"

"Candy! Kylie! *Every Colour You*!"

That afternoon it's as obvious to everyone else in the room as it is to us: the Broken Biscuits are ready. We played out of our skins. Bashing our way through two new songs and eight we knew already which brings our total set to ten. Over and over, ironing out some kinks and knocking others in, we play. Lighting fires and breathing life, making the scribbles from my quiet bedroom into sound, using everything Clarence has taught me and feeling surer than ever that this is the thing I was born to do.

I don't know if it was euphoria, too little sleep and too much caffeine, the music or actual magic, but The Beast felt more alive than ever before. Its battered red body shone, peeling red paint glowing deeply as slick and vital as blood. I hit chord after chord without once having to think about what to play next, lost inside my songs. Looking down at its body I could have sworn I saw scratches disappearing, gouges and knocks getting shallower like a dried-up riverbed in a flood. When I packed The Beast into its case that night, the badge where the volume knob should be said "PHO…GENIUS".

I drop into the corner shop on the way home and that's when I see the magazine. After The Rain's appearance on Sky News a media frenzy has kicked off around them. Nathan has declined to do any interviews, though. Until now. *Hiya!* magazine must have stumped up some serious cash.

"Thirty page EXCLUSIVE!" screams the headline, "At home with the reformed Wild Child Nathan Oxblood and his model wife Jasmine Hudson!"

I buy a copy, run all the way home, brush off Mum's request to watch *Muriel's Wedding* on DVD (*again*) and head down to the salon on the pretence of using the computer. I lock myself in a switched-off spray-tan booth for extra security and start to read.

The article had obviously been a massive scoop. The journo was so unbelievably grateful to get it the sycophancy practically ran off the page and congealed in my lap. I flick past glossy photos of Nathan and Jasmine at home (wearing incongruous eveningwear in their kitchen! Lounging in velour in the cinema room! Laughing by the pool! On a tree-swing in the orchard...) This is what it says:

Legendary rocker Nathan Oxblood memorably sang *"You, me and us/ It's a blast like from a blunderbuss,"* in The Rain's hit song *U+ME=US* and has revealed to *Hiya!* exclusively this week, that

the inspiration for the megahit was his wife of fifteen years, model and designer Jasmine Hudson. "When I met Jas I was a mess," he confessed this week. "She sorted me out – got me chanting, changed my headspace, changed my life. I owe her a lot."

Reclining in the 'rumpus room' of his Los Angeles home, The Rain singer (37) looks surprisingly at ease considering tabloid speculation about his lifestyle. "They call me a recluse – let them!" laughs the former wild man. "If you're not falling out of Bungalow 8 and pulling a different bird every night the tabloids think you're Howard Hughes! Onstage I'm Nathan Oxblood – and I can kick it to any crowd in the world! Offstage, I'm just an ordinary bloke, a family man who likes my privacy."

Privacy is certainly one thing the rocker and his other half won't find hard to come by in the secluded and sprawling Los Angeles estate they call home, one of eight such dwellings around the world. Asked what he has been up to since the notoriously acrimonious split of his band on a Hamburg stadium stage back in 2002, Nathan shrugs, "Being Nathan Oxblood takes a lot of work. There's an artistic side – a creative side I need to nurture – but also my physical and spiritual self, both of which I discipline with various practices like Bikram and Kunta kinte yoga. Dog-walking. That and the legal stuff takes a lot of time."

The "legal stuff" includes a record 118 lawsuits which

members of The Rain brought against one another over the intervening years, now all dropped or settled out of court. When asked about it, Nathan is philosophical.

"It was what we had to do at the time, you know. Part of the process of loving each other deeply as we do now was hating each other just as deeply. It was like poker – I'll see your lawsuit and raise you… In the end it was ridiculous. I think JJ [Jameson – The Rain's guitarist] sued me for defamation eighteen times based retrospectively on lyrics I'd written while I was in the band. Eventually it got so daft we had to start talking. That was the first step and now the band are back together for our upcoming tour which we couldn't be more excited about."

Nathan describes his wife Jasmine – Wonderbra girl-turned dinnerware designer – as "My soul mate. We do everything together from dawn till dusk. It may be unusual but it works for us." It's a sentiment Jasmine (34) echoes. "People say you shouldn't be with your man all the time but I just can't get enough of Nathan! People are constantly asking us if we just met because we're like newlyweds." She giggles, sipping a bellini by her cosy inglenook fireplace, before taking *Hiya!* on a guided tour of the Oxblood family home that the couple share with their two children and eleven dogs…

It's nothing I didn't already know. Not really. I knew that the same year made my way into the world he was walking up the altar to marry Jasmine Hudson. And that my half-sister Ottoline was born that Christmas. I have a brother too. It's strange to see them like this – page after page of their perfect shiny life together. They don't look like anything's missing or anybody. How would someone like me fit into a family like that? I open the tanning booth, walk out into the empty salon and come face to face with myself in the mirror. My face is shiny and my hair (as always) is practically on its end. I'm in a tattered old T-shirt and braces with a skirt I nicked from Pirate. I look ridiculous: the opposite of Ottoline who's already an It Girl. She's got a handbag named after her and everything. Can you learn that kind of perfect or is it like gymnastics – the kind of thing you've got to start doing as soon as you're out of nappies? Come to think of it, I bet Ottoline never wore nappies. She's so perfect she's probably never done a poo in her life...

❊

The next eight weeks are nothing but practise. Bit by bit our set gets tighter and scratch by scratch The Beast's wounds seem to heal. I have the dream again: I'm on the Pyramid Stage at Glastonbury. The crowd below me, lights crackling like the sky in a storm. Hol starts playing the wrong notes. I wake up wondering whether it really was a dream or a premonition. And if it was – was it good or bad? Tonight, though, I can't sleep at all. It's almost midnight and Clarence and I are in the back yard staring at stars, listening to a band named after a galaxy. The night air is damp and misty, full of the sea as usual but the chill has gone. Tomorrow is Monday. The longest day of the year. The first day of the week my mum gets married. Four more before me and my band run away to the biggest music festival on the planet.

The CD skips – the fault of the old paint-splattered machine we've brought out from the kitchen. I give it a hefty whack and the track rights itself. Pinprick dots of blue, red, yellow and (genuinely hideous) purple paint leave little indentations in the side of my hand. There are more than ever now that Mum has decided to re-paint the house. The weekend before her wedding. Typical.

Mum's never been big on cleaning. She prefers what I call binge decorating. Once every six months or so when the house starts looking too much like a junk shop, she suddenly decides to strip it all out and paint. The little bumps of emulsion tiered up over one another on our old CD-radio chronicle every stage of our history, each one a testament to her totally inappropriate approach to interiors (we had – for one extremely memorable year – a bronze lounge).

With Ray about to move in and the wedding almost upon her,

Mum has got the urge once more, although this time she has decided "to tone things down a bit". As of this weekend, most of the house is a colour called Dove Grey. Mum thinks it's "chic". I think it's the colour of old bones. Or maybe an eraser: rubbing out the evidence of our old loud life and replacing it with dusty, quiet blankness.

"What do you think, darling?" she asked yesterday afternoon, after a final zig-zag of the roller on the kitchen ceiling. "Just right for a fresh start?"

"It's perfect." I agreed, staring up at the glistening film of white and wondering for the millionth time between two months ago and today what on earth is going to happen this weekend. I keep trying to imagine it but everything beyond Friday night (when I will slip out of our back door and into the van with the rest of the band) is a blank.

Mum and Ray were supposed to have all the painting finished by yesterday, but even with the awesomely excellent organisational expertise that Ray couldn't stop showing off about, the job still isn't finished and our yard looks like a rag and bone man's. I'm reclining on a refugee rocking chair surrounded by the rest of our downstairs. Clarence is sitting on an empty paint can and drumming along to the music on another. I search the sky for shooting stars. *If I see one*, I think to myself, *it means everything is going to be OK.*

My room is the only one in the house that isn't being painted. Partly because it's taken me two whole years to create my star ceiling and collage walls and I'm not ripping all that down on a Mum-whim, partly because Mum needs somewhere to put her wedding stuff. There is tons of it. All of it is white and gold and the centrepiece is Mum's vast dress. The place is like a transvestite Santa's Grotto. No wonder I can't sleep. After two hours lying on my bed without so much as a wink of the stuff, I slipped an old hoodie on over my PJs, used The Beast to summon Clarence for a bit of company and came down here.

At our rehearsal today, Calum showed us the keys to the van he's borrowing this weekend. "It's a mate's, but she's in Ibiza for the summer so she doesn't need it," he explains.

Calum's going to drive us to the festival. Ideas are becoming actions. Sleeves are being rolled up and bullets are being bitten. My turn is coming.

"They love improvisational drumming at Glastonbury, you know," Clarence remarks, pounding the paint can. Its hollow *boing* sounds like an Indian drum. "Up at the Stone Circle at the top of the festival site. They drum all night until the sun comes up. Terribly pagan. Some of the clothes are atrocious but one can't disregard the potency of the experience."

I sit up a bit, fighting the lateness of the hour and the gloomy anxiety that always accompanies it these days. When the sun is out and I'm with the Biscuits, it's easy to be as excited and gung-ho as them about what we're planning. We all laugh when Kylie's talking about telling each of her divorced parents (who hate and refuse to speak to each other) that she's at the other's house for the weekend. When Calum's helping Spooky create plausible leaflets for an imaginary "Hair Show" in Manchester that she'll be attending. But when it's dark and I'm home and Mum's upstairs dreaming about her wedding it's much harder – knowing that when she wakes up that morning, I'll already be gone...

I shudder involuntarily. *Get over yourself!* I think. Who says I'm so important anyway? Who says I have the power to ruin the wedding? She knows I don't like Ray and she's still marrying him. If I mattered that much none of this would be happening at all. I keep looking but the sky doesn't give me any answers. There are no shooting stars tonight.

Clarence is saying something but I'm so deep in thought I can't tell what. I think I hear him call my name a couple of times. When a third attempt to get my attention fails, he picks up the empty paint can and throws it at my head. It catches me at an unfortunate angle, whacking into my eyebrow like a hammer.

"WHAT DID YOU DO THAT FOR?" I yell.

"My darling, I was acting quite out of concern," Clarence replies. "You were unreachable. Entranced. I feared I may never again regain you. Sore?" He turns out his lip in unconvincing sympathy.

"YES IT'S FLIPPING SORE! YOU JUST HIT ME IN THE FACE WITH A LUMP OF METAL!"

"There, there dear, do try to stop short of hysteria. Most unbecoming offstage," he says, fluttering up to my face. I move my hand away and he touches my tender eyebrow with his pale hand. There's a burst of music and colours explode through the vision in my right eye. It lasts a split second then disappears, along with the pain.

I jump up and start pacing the yard huffily. "You are unbelievable, Clarence! You're my Godbrother! You're supposed to be *helping* me!"

"Forgive me, Candypop, do," Clarence appeals. "But after all, you summoned me. And now that I'm here, you're distant. You know it is my task to encourage you to seize the moment! Fate beckons. The time of action is at hand. And yet I can feel you are conflicted. It's frustrating and..." He hesitates, reluctant to commit the thought to words, "... frankly my dear, it's rather... boring." He flits over to the CD player and pulls out the one that's playing, throwing it carelessly behind him.

Just to put this into context, boring is the worst thing

Clarence could ever call you. It is his ring-off hang-up conversation-over non-come-back-fromable insult. If Clarence had written the Ten Commandments the list would have been much shorter. "Thou shalt not bore" would have been pretty much it with a possible addendum about wearing flares. I swing round to face him, my cheeks hot with anger. He pretends not to notice. Placing a hand into the open CD player, he swirls it around as if he's stirring a pot of soup. A sparkling disc of light appears. As soon as I speak my voice starts to wobble. "Boring? I'm being boring, am I? Because I've got a conscience?"

"Yes," he answers. Clarence closes the CD player and hits play. Immediately, the machine whirs into life. "This is about following your wildest dreams, Candypop. Your wildest! Destiny is for the brave. History remembers the trailblazers – the leaders. And *upstairs*..." He casts his eyes heavenward (although by now I know that's not where heaven is), "is full of them. People who didn't worry about the judgement of others: people I have had the pleasure of getting to know intimately. Jimi, Jim, Janis, John Lennon, Joe Strummer..."

I sniff back a wet-sounding breath. "Well I'm sorry I'm such a let-down. Maybe it's because my name doesn't begin with a J?"

"Don't be ridiculous, Candy. How about a few others? Bob Marley, Freddie Mercury, Keith Moon, Kurt Cobain, Johnny Cash..."

"Begins with J." I interject sulkily. Clarence rolls his eyes and places one hand on his hip.

"And there are still a few here on earth. How about *Nathan Oxblood*? No 'J' there. And never a second thought about following his artistic calling."

I consider this. After all the reading I've been doing, I know better than anyone that Nathan has a reputation for getting rid of people who don't agree with him. The dismissals are often controversial but always final. Managers, record producers, labels and band members have all been jetisoned over the years when their opinion about what to do next conflicted with his. Reading story after story has got me worried: was Mum the first casualty of this tactic? Maybe Nathan got rid of her because she got in the way. Or I did. In which case – why would he want anything to do with me now? The closer I get to finding Nathan, the less sure I am of what will happen when I do.

"My point, my little Candypop, is this," Clarence continues. "If you are going to be a musician then you must focus. Go to Glastonbury. Play your show. Find your father. Make your dream happen! To hell with what anybody else thinks. Jiminy Cricket didn't sell any records and he certainly didn't get invited to any parties."

I stop pacing and sit down on a box. Something

fragile-sounding inside breaks. The music from the CD player swirls around us: shimmering guitar chords combined with the kind of utterly over-the-top and completely unapologetic synthesizer-use that only happened in the 80s. There are no vocals – it's instrumental. There's something familiar about the song. My sleepy, fed-up brain aches trying to place it, and to make sense of Clarence's latest pearl of wisdom.

"So you're saying I need to be selfish?"

"Yes."

"But wouldn't that make me a horrible person?" I ask incredulously.

Clarence is irritated. "According to whom? As opposed to what? Nice? You'd rather be *nice*?" He says it like being nice would be even worse than being boring. Unsure of anything other than that the truth – which is "Yes" – would be an unacceptable answer, I stare at the ground.

Clarence fixes me with a glare of pouty disapproval. This has the odd effect of making him look even more beautiful than usual, probably because it's exactly the kind of expression you might see on the cover of an intimidatingly trendy fashion magazine.

"I'm sorry, Clarence," I mumble. "It's easy for you. You're not a natural worrier. I can't help it! I've always thought about other people. Maybe I am nice. And boring... Maybe I'm not cut out to be a rock star. Maybe I'm going to disappoint Nathan. I wish you could do all this stuff for me, Clarence. It's hard."

He flutters closer so that we're eye to eye. His glow pulses in time with the music, shining even more brightly than usual. In fact, I can see my reflection in him. Clarence's exterior mirrors me: My furrowed brow and firework hair topping a tattered old hoodie and polka-dot pyjamas. He gives me a glum upside-down sympathy-smile and touches his hand on my shoulder for a moment. As he does so, I feel a sadness that spreads right down into my bones.

"You are forgetting why I was sent here in the first place!"

"I know, I know. To be my mentor. To guide me..." I mumble.

"Before that. The reason I was sent to do those things is that we are twin souls! Our music matches. You think we are different. We are not. What you want, I wanted. I never got it, of course, what with being so unrelentingly tiresomely *dead*!"

"We are different, Clarence!" I raise my voice over the crescendo. "Look at me!" I point at myself, indicating not only the appalling pyjamas but also my general lack of rock n roll mettle.

Clarence laughs bitterly. "Do you think I was always so decisive? So wise? Such a pioneer?!"

"So full of yourself?" I add, but my voice is lost in the music around us.

"What?"

"Nothing. Carry on." Clarence is getting emotional now. He adopts his onstage voice which is quavering slightly as if he is addressing a crowd.

"As I was saying – I am not in death as I was in life. Much has changed. This music – have you heard it before?"

"Yes – it's driving me mad! I can't remember where!"

"You haven't heard it before. You think you have because you're the only other person who could have written it. It's mine. Me, I mean. With my band." He presses his knuckles against his lips as if he's trying to control himself.

"Oh!" I don't really know what else to say.

"My first record. I was supposed to go in and do the vocals the next day. I mean the next day that never came. I could have finished it! Posthumous fame could have been mine! I could have died having left my legacy for the world to find, like Van Gogh! If only I hadn't waited!" And with that, Clarence B Major starts to cry.

"What happened? What were you waiting for?"

I'm not sure if he can hear me, though, because Clarence is becoming hysterical. Great big sobs rack his body, his breath shudders like a car failing to start. "I didn't want to record it without the rest of the band!" he splutters. "We were in it together.

You'd think we were Musketeers – not a bloody... bloody... hairspray rock band from Croydon!" He dissolves into a fit of wailing.

For the first time ever, I hug him. It's weird. I can't really feel him but at the same time I can. I can't tell where I end and he begins. It's like hugging your own leg. "There, there," I mutter over and over again while he tries to speak.

"I could have... I could... I could have *been someone*! Waaaahhh!"

I pat Clarence.

"Don't let it happen to you, Candy. Just as you are the only one who can dream your dreams, you are the only one who can make them happen. You're worried about your mother but she will understand eventually. She lost her dreams too."

We stay like this for a long time, the song swirling around us as beautiful and incomplete as a winter tree. Then and there I know two things. The first is that I am going to finish Clarence's song. The second is that this weekend I am running away to that festival as fast as my legs can carry me and I'm not looking back.

16
G-Day

From the moment I wake up on Friday morning, my heart feels like a kick drum in my chest.

BOOM BOOM BOOM!

Down the stairs to breakfast. The whole house is grey now. The furniture has been rearranged. All traces of me have been tidied up and washed away except in my little cupboardy bedroom. What would it be like to never come back? What if this is the last time I ever see that banister; that picture? My granny and grandad have arrived from the Costa Brava for the wedding. As small, tanned and wrinkled as a couple of prunes. We have not seen them for years but nothing has changed since we did. Grandad is still (as far as we can tell) mute; Granny is still horrible. We eat an awkward breakfast at which the main topic of conversation is my unfortunate height.

"She's just like you were. Terrible for a girl to be tall. I was always glad I was petite," says Grandma. "You want to watch she doesn't get a stoop. Sit up straight, Candace!"

Mum glares at her with ice-eyes. "Her name is Candy."

"I always preferred Candace."

⚬

BOOM BOOM BOOM!

There it is again. On the way to school; then there all day. Double maths and English lit and hanging round the back in netball, rolling up the sleeves of my T-shirt, trying not to get involved (or mud on it because it's the new Frankie and the Heartstrings one I had to save up for). Unusually, Pirate and I don't talk much today. We're side by side in solemn silence, two soldiers in a battle line getting ready to charge.

BOOM BOOM BOOM!

Back home and Ray and Glad come over for tea, much to Granny's annoyance. The relationship between Granny and Glad is a bit like the one between scientist and lab rat. It's a cocktail of barely-concealed resentment (Granny), lofty curiosity (Glad), simmering rage (Granny) and detached amusement (Glad). Since she doesn't dare say anything about Glad coming over, Granny settles for complaining about Ray instead. "It's bad luck to see each other so close to the wedding!"

"We're not traditional like that, Mum." Mum speaks with studied calm but shoves the lasagne into the oven with more force than usual randomly switching on all the knobs. "Besides, we might have done it earlier but you and Dad 'couldn't get away for longer than the weekend', remember?"

Granny ignores the question, looking Mum's outfit up and down – a 1970s maxi-dress in bottle-green crêpe (it's always been one of my favourites). Zebra-striped shoes.

"Well you can tell you're not *traditional* by taking one look at you, Margaret. I hope you'll be wearing something… appropriate tomorrow," she carps.

It's all she does. Bloop, bloop, bloop – burping out insults and grumps like a goldfish bringing up bubbles. I sit at the table and stare deep into the fruit bowl, imagining smashing every item in it over Granny's stupid head. The melon is particularly satisfying.

BOOM BOOM BOOM!

Unsurprisingly (to me – Mum seems amazed) Grandma and Grandda love Ray. He charms them at dinner with thrilling tales of life at the sharp-end of life coaching. One of his clients has recently decided to buy a caravan in Alnwick, where she will pursue her love of watercolour painting at the weekends. Glad sits opposite making polite conversation. She's excellent at it, even though I know it's something she hates. Granny seems to be trying to goad Glad by putting on a particularly peacockish display of idiocy. She gives us her views on Jamie Oliver, Mum's waistline and the population of Britain (which are pretty much that the aforementioned things are a bit too big already and shouldn't increase any further). She gets the Prime Minister's name wrong three times, in three different ways. She tells me not to bother doing any GCSEs as they're "a waste of time for girls". Glad doesn't rise to any of it.

It's only when Granny tells me that the idea of starting a band is "ridiculous" that Glad says softly, "You remember what Oscar Wilde said about ridicule, Sylvia?"

Granny answers this by throwing out a blank and slightly fearful look from within the folds of her forty-a-day suntan.

Glad smiles. "'Ridicule is the tribute paid to the genius by the mediocrities'. Come on, Candy. I'll help you with the washing up."

We're gone before Granny can unpick the insult.

BOOM BOOM BOOM!

It's ten o'clock. Everybody has gone home or gone to sleep, except me and Mum. She is currently sitting on my bed in her dressing gown, veil and wedding shoes. For the last twenty minutes she has been claiming she's about to go and get some 'beauty sleep'.

"You don't need it, Mum," I say, truthfully. "You're going to look beautiful tomorrow."

She gives a squeal of excitement before pulling me in for a massive cuddle. I breathe in her smell for bravery (van at 11pm) and marvel. Mum lost everything through having me. Started again in a new town. She's been poor and heartbroken (often at the same time). She's got a human lemon for a mother. And to top it all she's marrying the Most-Boring-Man-in-the-World™ tomorrow. If I was her, I'd be screaming into my pillow. And yet... she's excited.

"Mum?"

"Mmm hmm?"

"How did you manage to grow up so cheerful when Granny's such a... so..."

Images of my mum's mum dressed up as various sci-fi baddies, bloodthirsty queens and dictators flash through my mind.

"Negative?" Mum suggests.

"Er... Understatement! I was going to say evil."

She giggles, then tuts. "Candy! She can't help it, you know. She's frustrated. Frustrated and disappointed."

"By, like, her life?" I ask.

Mum strokes my hair and screws her face up. "No, by mine.

She always wanted more for me."

A momentary flush of guilt runs through me like cold water. "She didn't want you to have me?"

Mum shakes her head and hugs me even closer. "Actually Candy, she did. 'A baby is the greatest gift life can ever give you,' were her words when I told her. I rang her from the payphone at King's Cross. Didn't tell her where I was, of course. I hoped she'd tell me to get the train home." Mum closes her eyes for a moment and I know that she is there again, all those years ago. "She didn't. 'You've made your bed down there, now you'd better lie on it.' It was everything else I decided to do that Mum had a problem with, Candy. Moving here. The business. Men. Not you. Your Gran loves you. She just isn't very…" She reaches for the right words. "She just isn't very good at loving people." She shrugs and kisses me on the head. I hug her back extra hard, an advance apology for tomorrow.

."Then how come you are?"

She thinks about this for a minute and smiles. "I've had a lot of practice."

BOOM BOOM BOOM BOOM!

When Mum goes to bed, I pull out my rucksack and guitar case. I shove my bridesmaid's dress into my bag (my plan involves making Mum think I'll meet her at the church, so I can't leave it here for her to find) and, after waiting ten long minutes, I slip out of my bedroom door, quick and quiet like a burglar. I pad past her room and down the stairs, jumping past the creaks like I'm playing a scale on a keyboard. I head towards the kitchen, leaving my grandparents' identical snores behind me. From the front-room behind me (where they are housed on the sofabed) their sleep-sounds ebb and flow, overlapping like waves on a tropical beach. Kind of. Then it's out of the back door and into the yard, the night, the world.

Parked up in the back lane with its engine purring (I am not making this up) is a giant Dalmatian. By which I mean a white van with black spots, a red collar, enormous black ears and a tail. The soft sound of a song by The Drums emanates from its interior. On the side it says, "*THE POOCH PARLOUR! MOBILE DOG GROOMING*". Then added underneath in slightly less professional hand, *"WE ALSO DO CATS!"*

Travelling incognito, then.

Zzzzzzzip!

The van door closes behind me and I am bathed in orange light. I am the last one in. As you can probably imagine, the interior is deeply weird. The standard seating has been removed and replaced with caravan-style benches. The back of the van has been screened off into what I can only describe as a 'doggy shower'. There are huge bottles of dog shampoo, aprons and rubber gloves everywhere.

Kylie, Spooky, Pirate and Dan (who has volunteered to share the driving if we sneak him in) are all sitting inside, their eyes aglow with the same mix of nervous excitement that is currently coursing through my veins like a sugar rush. Calum turns round to greet me from the driving seat, shoots me a sheepish smile and says, "The van's my friend Diane's. She's an animal beautician."

I nod and do "really?" eyebrows, as if Calum's explanation makes the fact that we are running away in the middle of the night inside a giant dog sound entirely reasonable.

"I... er didn't know you could get animal beauticians," is all I can think to say. Calum faces front and we set off. I sit down next to Pirate. She is wearing a battered leather jacket over a stripy knitted dress and big boots. For some reason, she also has an old-man style pipe in her mouth. She removes it and fixes me with a deadpan expression.

"Dude, this vehicle is more than *un poco loco*. I mean, who gets their *cat* groomed?"

"You're smoking a pipe now?"

"Bubbles," she responds, placing the shiny mahogany creation back between her lips and puffing a few out by way of a demonstration. "Thought it would look good onstage."

I shake my head. "You look like Popeye. Especially when you talk out of the side of your mouth like that." I turn to greet the others, who are (like Pirate) all dressed in what they think constitutes festival-wear. Spooky is wearing a ripped multicoloured jumpsuit with a dress over the top and a vest on top of that. Her fringe has been dyed green. Kylie's Barbie-perfect fezzie look is her tumbling red ringlets, a tiny T-shirt and endless legs which look like flower-stems growing out of her designer wellies and disappearing into her denim shorts that stop almost as soon as they start. Dan is wearing his usual picked-up-from-the-floor crumpled cool. He looks positively edible.

"Hey all," I say, studiously not looking at him. Even though he not only hates me but is also dating my bandmate and arch-nemesis, sitting in an enclosed space with him is a bit like being in the back of your maths lesson and suddenly being seized by an almost irresistible urge to swear at the top of your voice. I have to consciously stop myself from jumping across from my seat to his and kissing him on the mouth.

He hates you. He hates you. He hates you. I repeat to myself. I place a hand in the pocket of my jacket and produce Clarence. With fewer opportunities to get away from everyone so that I can summon him, so much to think about and so many distractions around already at a place like Glastonbury, Clarence has agreed to come with us as an object everyone can see, rather than himself. My fairy Godbrother is now a small ornate compass on a chain around my neck. The added genius of this is that we won't get separated and he can still help us on our adventure: instead of the traditional North East South West markers, his say MUSIC, LOVE, FATE, TROUBLE. His rainbow-coloured arrow in neon-bright colours spins wildly around the face. Calum takes the exit for the A1 and a few seconds later it settles on MUSIC. Too right – Glastonbury here we come!

TAP TAP TAP!

Something hits me on the forehead three times. I open my eyelids a crack and discover that I am nose-to-nose (and indeed eyeball-to-eyeball) with a very small, very wizened and impossibly ancient hippy with a huge beard. He has just tapped me on the forehead with what would appear to be some kind of staff and is now staring at me. Hard. Imagine Gandalf doing an impression of Janis Joplin. That's him.

For a moment I think he is inside the van with us, then I realise that he is outside and I have fallen asleep with my face pressed up against the window which he is tapping. I am drooling. I unpeel my forehead from the glass and wipe my chops in one movement, turning to my left and Pirate – still asleep next to me with a straw hat over her face. Suddenly, from underneath it, she speaks. "Don't worry. He can't see in. The windows are tinted. He's been there ages." She makes no other movement so after a while, I clamber sleepily over her and out into the body of the van, stretching and trying to catch sight of the clock on the dashboard. Everyone else is still out for the count; everyone apart from Calum. He's in the drivers' seat, with his arms crossed over the steering wheel and his hood up.

"How you doing, Cal? What time is it? Are we nearly there yet?" I ask the back of his head as I clamber up behind him.

Calum turns to me, to reveal that he is – in fact – Dan.

"Hey," he says.

"Oh!" I say. "Hey. Sorry – I thought you were…" I look down to avoid meeting his eyes. That's when I catch sight of Calum, curled up on the passenger seat, hood up, cap on, knees touching his forehead. He looks more like a pile of washing than a person. Dan nods towards his friend.

"He needed a break. Said I'd take over a couple of hours ago."

He turns right round to face me. I can't avoid him now. He looks just like he did in my bedroom: late-night eyes, creasing at the corners. He rubs them then runs his hand up through his mess of hair. "It's almost six. And yes, we're nearly there." He laughs ironically at my childish question.

Oh God – how embarrassing! I think to myself. *"Are we there yet?" What am I – five?* I turn, about to head back to my seat when he squints up at me through his eyelashes and says, "I'm shattered, man... Come and help me stay awake?"

I look around the bus partly to check this is, you know, *actually happening* (he hates me, doesn't he?!), partly to make sure Kylie is asleep (she is. I note – with some satisfaction – that she is snoring). Then I climb over the back of the seat in as un-knicker-flashing a fashion as possible, careful not to wake Calum. Sliding between the two of them, my eyes adjust to the watery morning light and the hour, and I start to take in our surroundings properly. They are a bit odd.

"So it's six am?" I ask. "And we're... are we in a traffic jam? In the middle of the countryside?"

"Yep." Dan laughs, nodding through the windscreen. In front of us, snaking out of view and occupying every inch of the leafy winding country lane ahead, are a queue of what look like fallen-down skyscrapers. Tourbuses. Tons of them! Black and gleaming, polished to within an inch of their lives. Dan turns his hand out with a flourish. "The Rain are loading in."

I gasp. There must be at least eight of them. My mouth hangs open in awe like in a cartoon. The huge vehicles snake away out of sight like a giant black sea-monster. Our little dog-van, the buses and creepy Gandalf-hippy are the only things to be seen for miles around. The numberplate of the bus in front is R4IN N8N. As in: *Rain Nathan*?

"What's in all of them?" I whisper, as if the buses themselves might hear me.

He shrugs. "Amps, instruments, entourage… A band that big has a lot of stuff. And if you believe the legends, they probably have a separate tourbus for all the groupies." He chuckles to himself. Staring into the impenetrable back window of the bus in front, I involuntarily picture Mum behind it – one of a crowd – sitting silently, looking like she did in the photo of her and Nathan. I wonder if there's a tourbus for 'love-children' (as Glad refers to kids like me when we crop up in *Corrie*). How many of us are there? Maybe so many we wouldn't all fit on a bus. My stomach flips over like a pancake. I feel sick.

"You all right?" Dan asks. I drag my gaze from the bus in front back to him. He's staring straight at me. *What is this?* I think. *First he asks me to come and sit with him, now he's all bothered whether I'm all right or not. Anyone would think he wanted to talk to me… Bloody hell! He wants to talk to me!*

I give him a small test-the-water smile. He returns it and something quivers in my chest. For a second, I think it's my heart but then I realise – it's *on* my chest. It's Clarence, still in compass form. I pick him up. His arrow is spinning. As I take hold of him, it starts to settle... FATE. I follow its elegant point back up to Dan's face.

"What's the matter?" he asks.

"Nothing. Just..." Unsure how to end the sentence, I start another one instead, "Dan, I'm sorry. About the party. I didn't plan it – getting drunk, I mean. Obviously I didn't plan the other bit..."

Dan snorts, knitting his eyebrows together sarcastically. "The bit where you kissed me? Or the bit where you lost your lunch all over my stuff?"

For a second I think he's still angry, but then he cracks a smile.

"The lunch-losing." I grimace.

He nods then turns, levelling his gaze straight at me. How can eyes be brown and bright simultaneously? I feel like a deer caught in his headlights. "What about the other bit?" he asks.

"I... it... I didn't plan that either," I stammer. "It was nice, though."

Dan smiles and moves a little closer. The springs in the front seat are past their best and the closer we get, the more we roll together into a single well of broken springs and leather. It's not the comfiest I've ever been, but I'm not complaining. I shuffle towards him, avoiding a particularly pointy spring in the bum.

Then he says, "I've been thinking about this a lot and... I'm sorry as well. About Kylie. It isn't how it seems."

There's a quiver in my chest but this time it's not the compass. I take a deep breath. "How is it, then?"

"We weren't together when me and you..." He looks over to his snoring girlfriend momentarily, then lowers his voice and leans in a bit. I do the same. We're so close I can feel his breath on my face as he speaks. "She said we were but we weren't. Not properly. I let you think it cos I was angry. I wanted to upset you... I'm sorry."

Dan smiles, and his whole face lights up. It's the opposite of the Polaroid I took through Clarence – and now I know why. Being hurt, being angry with me must have stopped his music coming out. I bury my head in my hands and groan – as quietly as possible.

"Oh *God*! I'm such a *loseoid*!"

He laughs and takes one hand off the steering wheel to grab my wrist, pulling a hand away from my face. I catch his eye and I know he is remembering pulling me up on to my bed that night.

"You're not a loseoid." He smiles. "You're..." and then he drops my hands and brushes my fringe out of my eyes, although it wasn't really in them. "You're a very interesting girl, Candy Caine." At this point a sensible person would be leaning their face towards his and making sure they looked as gorgeous as possible.

Instead I say, "Dan, you have no idea how complicated my life is right now. How weird. I mean, I'd love to tell you but... I wouldn't know where to start."

Which makes him lean back a bit. *Why did you do that? You are such an idiot!!* I think. But his chocolate-sauce eyes never stop looking at me. The dog-van rumbles silently, through the open window of the van I hear birds tweeting. I have just had long enough to think, *What the flip are you doing, you loon?* when he says, "I like weird. Weird is good. Most of the best things in life are a little bit off the map. Things only get interesting when you start colouring outside the lines, Candy." I drop my gaze and watch his hand as he tentatively reaches down and strokes a couple of fingers over my knee. They come to rest halfway up my leg. Then he leans in close and whispers, hot and fast in my ear, "And like I said, you're a very interesting girl. That's why you're here." It's that feeling again. Like every atom in my body is on its end. His nose brushes the side of my neck and I think I might faint.

"I... I..." I'm trying to work out whether he means 'here' as in 'in a dog-van running away from your mum's wedding to Glastonbury', or 'here' as in 'in the front seat of said dog-van, contemplating copping off with your frenemy-slash-bandmate's boyfriend' when something stops me in my tracks.

"Dan... Oh! Dan! Dan! *Dan!!*"

At first he thinks I'm overcome with pleasure like an olde-style damsel, and starts nuzzling me even more fervently. And it's really nice. I mean *really nice.* But I'm not overcome with pleasure. You see, while Dan has been whispering in my ear I've been staring out of the windscreen. Probably not what you're supposed to do in these situations, but I'm not going to look at Calum, am I? (Sick!) Or in the rear-view mirror, where I have a perfect view of Kylie snoring? (Double sick! Especially since I sort of did look at her a bit...) Anyway, I've been staring at The Rain's tourbus. And unless I'm mistaken, its roof has just started to come off.

I grab Dan's hand (which has probably already gone as far up my thigh as it's wise for it to go right now) and when he extracts himself from my neck enough to give me a "What's the problem?" look, I turn his face so that he can see as well. Then frozen in silent amazement, the pair of us watch the vast vehicle in front of us open itself up from the inside out like something out of *Transformers.*

Section by section half the roof slides open from the middle to the back, creating a sort of open-air terrace. Frustratingly, we're behind it so our view is blocked by the retracted sections.

Then out of the top, a head appears.

It belongs to an absolutely teeny-tiny (I mean *indescribably miniscule*), orange-hued woman. At least I think it's a woman. It's so small it could actually just be a really massive doll: Earth's Biggest Barbie™. She certainly looks Barbie-ish: ski-jump nose, almond eyes, dentist-sign smile; all framed by a disproportionate amount of tumbling blonde hair.

"Is that a lady?" I think out loud in Dan's general direction.

"I er... I think so. Judging by her... er... yes," he whispers, transfixed, unconsciously making the international sign language for *humungously massive boobs*. Not that I need the actions to know what he means. From our perspective, Barbielady's head and shoulders appear to be floating on two giant skin-balloons, approximately the same size as her bonce.

"Are those real??" I whisper.

"Who cares?"

Barbielady speaks. Surprisingly, her accent is broad cockney and her voice (loud enough to project itself through Dan's open window and into our dog-van) is nails-down-a-blackboard screechy. Like a very angry crow.

"NAAAAYYFFFUNNN!"

After yelling into the depths of the bus she waits for a reply, looking cross in a tight-faced kind of way.

"NAAAAAAAAAAAAYYYYYFFFUUUUUNNNN!"

A few seconds later, another head emerges. Taller this time and with hair matted at the back like it was just on a pillow. Even from the back I know it's him. The mid-life-crisis haircut with a few too many layers and a bit too much product, the tight black vest revealing tanned yoga arms and tattoos (each bearing the trend of its time: a Celtic band here, a smattering of Chinese characters there, some later block-ink and Maori-style stuff...) And of course by now I know who she is. She doesn't look anything like her pictures. Dan says her name first, though. Shouts it, in fact.

"Bloody hell! That's Jasmine Hudson! And Nathan! Nathan bloody Oxblood!"

His cry wakes the rest of the van from its slumber. One by one the rest of the band come back to life around us, gathering in the Dalmatian's nose, jostling for a better look at the sight ahead. I feel Kylie giving me a hard stare when she realises I've been sitting next to Dan, but I don't take my eyes off Nathan Oxblood the whole time.

That *Hiya!* piece the other week described Nathan and Jasmine as "blissfully happy – one of the few showbiz marriages to last the distance." Which is strange. Because from where we're sitting it's quite clear that they hate each other's guts.

We can't hear him but occasional phrases of hers make it through the window. We drink them in thirstily from the front seat – you could hear a pin drop in the dog-van.

"Was she? WAS SHE?"

"...do I want to be in the middle of bloody *nowhere* for?"

"...it's a *two-way bloody street, mate!*" and finally (and most unconvincingly) "I AM CALM!!!"

After this last one, Nathan moved straight towards us and I got a good look at his face for the first time. He looks thinner than on telly, a bit worn out and obviously miserable. His tree-frog eyes are hidden behind shades. We finally hear him speak (he says, "Keep your BLOODY VOICE DOWN!") then he slams a button we can't see and they disappear from view behind the closing roof. As soon as it shuts, the Broken Biscuits break into spontaneous whoops and screeching. Sighting a proper actual Rock Legend before we even get on site! Amazing! Hol laughs along, but gives me a sly that-must-have-been-weird squeeze on the shoulder when no one else is looking. Then Nathan's bus shudders to life and we're off again, climbing uphill along the tiny lane behind their gargantuan transport.

I check Clarence. His arrow spins round once before decisively pointing back at FATE.

After a while we turn a corner. The hedgerows that have been lining the little track up to now fall away suddenly and for the first time we see it. Glastonbury Festival itself…

It's enormous – bigger than I'd ever have dreamed. Field upon field of blue canvas – thousands and thousands of tents that together look like a bubbling sea. Lorries, buses, caravans, fairground rides (some still with their lights on from last night). There are flags and banners everywhere in a hundred colours. Rising out of the middle of it all like the head of a giant spear is the Pyramid Stage. Now that *is* like I dreamed. The field around it is tentless and green. The stage itself is smooth and silvery-white and perfect. It almost looks like an ancient monument – like Stonehenge down the road – the thing that everyone here has come to see, to pray to. I think of Nathan. Tonight everyone here will be staring at him on that stage. They want a spectacle, a miracle. They want him to give them the time of their lives. And at that moment – even with his robot bus and his eight houses – I don't envy him one bit.

Eventually we come to a farm gate, *The* farm gate in fact: Worthy Farm. Glastonbury takes place on a real live dairy farm. Clarence claims he rode one of the cows back to his tent after watching The Smiths play in 1984. ("It was majestic! There was a photograph in *Sounds* magazine and everything!")

Dan shouts, "PASSES OUT, PEOPLE!" and the bus in front is

waved through. The ground is dry and as The Rain's fleet of tourbuses pull off the road, they send up huge clouds of dust. Before Nathan's transport disappears out of view, I grab a discarded pen from among the dashboard detritus in front of me and scrawl something on the back of my hand. R41N N8N. His numberplate.

17

Inge Rhabarbermarmalade

"Nice ride!" laughs the guy on the gate. "You do know we don't have a canine field?"

Gate Guy doesn't look much older than us but has the air of officialdom. Perhaps it's the clipboard or maybe it's his high-vis tabard which is decorated with a colourful array of backstage passes. When he catches me looking he puffs out his chest, a proud war veteran marching in his medals.

"I'll handle this!" Pirate pushes past me and (much to Kylie's wordless annoyance) leans over Dan's lap to poke her head out of the window. She is wearing her butterfly shades and hat which contrast weirdly with the pipe once again poking out of the side of her mouth like... well, like *an actual pirate,* I suppose. When she starts talking it is in the weirdest accent I have ever heard: clipped and angry like a broken robot.

"*Nein* caaaniine field!" she barks tersely. "We here to play, *ja*? Band, *ja*?" Then she removes a few folded sheets of A4 from a pocket inside her jacket and hands them over with a flourish. "*Sound of Glastonbury 2010 winner.*" She removes her pipe and taps the mouth-end on what must be the relevant part of the letter for emphasis. "Says here – *understandein*? 'Rhiannon's Chalice'? Park stage! We hurry now, yes? *Beeilen sie sich!*"

Something about Pirate's tone makes Gate Guy swing into action. He hands her back the letter, takes our tickets and scuttles off to a nearby portacabin. "*Schnell! Schnell!*" she calls after him before sliding back between me and Dan, chuckling. "Chop chop!" she says to herself, then (to us) a cheerful "Budge up!" forcing me to squish right up to Calum. She puts her pipe back in her mouth and starts bubbling away contentedly.

I turn to Calum and make the international sign language shrug for "What the... ?" but his dumbfounded expression says it all. In fact the whole band – every member of 'Rhiannon's Chalice' – looks as confused as I feel.

"Holly... what the hell is going on?" I ask calmly, quietly; my gaze trained on the portacabin door. Whatever Holly's done, there's no going back now. We're too close. There is silence for a moment.

Then she says, "*Scheizen.*" She grimaces. "Sorry dudes. I

forgot I hadn't filled you in on the details. Got a bit carried away. I've never had *documentation* before." Even now she can't resist waving the letter around. I snatch it from her and start speed-reading.

"Told us what, exactly?" Spooky's muffled shout comes from the back of the van where she is secreted inside a box labelled *COCOMUTT DOG SHAMPOO* (since she's the smallest it was decided she should hide instead of Dan). The box features a disturbing image of a Labrador wearing a cocounut bra and flower garland so delighted with his glossy coat that he is doing what looks like the hula on a tropical beach. Hol goes quiet again and resumes bubble-blowing; albeit with a grave expression on her face.

"I'll tell you what she hasn't told us, Spook," I say, passing the letter back to the rest of the band. "She's only gone and picked up a bunch of tickets some other band have won. The slot we're playing is theirs! *Rhiannon's Chalice*, whoever they are! She's pretending we won a competition to get to play! What were you thinking, Hol?"

She grimaces."Can! You make it sound so *naughty*! Trust me, I've been through this over and over! (a) It's a completely brilliant plan, water tight. And (b) from a moral standpoint the pros outweigh the cons. We need this!" She slides her shades down to the end of her nose and eyes me over the top. "And none of us need it more than *you*."

Dan punches the steering wheel with rage, catching the horn by accident. It gives a pathetic little beep and everybody shushes him in unison. He looks incredulous. "Don't *ssshhhh* me, you idiots! Don't you see there is *no way* this is going to work! The other band must have told the organisers their tickets have gone missing. We're probably about to get arrested! That's why he's taking so long!"

Inside her box, Spooky gasps. Calum throws his head back and covers his eyes with his hand. Kylie squeals with rage, sounding like a boiling kettle. "Oh for... I bought this outfit *specially* Rodgers! I am *not* dressed for prison! If this weekend gets messed up I'm going to *kill you*! Do you understand? *KILL YOU!*"

There's a flash of luminous yellow in the portacabin doorway and Gate Guy almost reappears but someone inside calls him back. I whisper angrily at double-speed, "Howthehelldidyoueverimaginewe'dgetawaywiththis???"

Hol smiles and tucks her pipe between her teeth. "People, people! Trust me! Recon, dudes – I did my recon. Just let me do the talking. PS If anyone asks, you're all German and you don't speak any English. 'K?"

Before we can process this, Gate Guy emerges and strides towards us purposefully. He leans into the window taking up slightly more room than necessary, as if to prove a point. Hol leans back across Dan's lap, all smiles.

"There seems to be a problem with your paperwork, Miss... What was it again?"

"Inge, *dahling*! Inge Rhabarbermarmalade!" She says it quickly and he doesn't quite catch it. All the same he gives her a quizzical look.

"Well, er... Inge. It seems you haven't called ahead to register your tickets."

Hol makes a pouty yet confused face. The kind an Olsen Twin might make if you asked whether she fancied a bag of chips.

"YOU HAVE TO REGISTER THE TICKETS?" Gate Guy shouts as if louder-than-usual English would be easier to understand. "VALIDATE? YES?"

Hol pouts harder. "I see this problem, *ja*? Reason we come early is for... for make ticket good, *ja*?" Gate Guy looks back at the portacabin.

"It isn't just up to me. My supervisor would go spare if I let you in with these..."

Pirate removes her sunglasses. With her baby-blues revealed and sparkling at full wattage it's all but over for Gate Guy. She bats her lashes at him. "He here now? I speak with him?"

"No..." GG mumbles, staring into the limpid pools of Hol's irises. "He's not in yet."

She laughs (a bit cruelly, I can't help thinking – the poor sap). Hol places a hand on GG's beefy forearm. "My band new in this country but very good. You should check us out. We very good at keeping secrets also. You fix this – maybe we hang out after show? I not tell your boss you do for me."

Twenty minutes later, 'Rhiannon's Chalice' are cooking a victory breakfast on their drummer's portable barbecue. We are in the backstage camping enclosure. Around us are the most luxurious set of tents you have ever seen in your life. Zebra-print, cowhide, organic cotton tipis... Artfully discarded boots are lined up outside each little domicile. A couple of the magazine-spread campfires are still smouldering in the early morning sunshine. The tent next to us has a little washing line, to which expensive-looking kaftans and bikini-tops are pegged. Somewhere a radio plays a folk song. It's like the world's most glamorous refugee camp.

We all have multiple laminates and lots of small pieces of paper (all of which it's apparently essential that we don't lose and none of which I remember the location of three seconds after I get them). Gate Guy ("Stu" apparently) has even thrown in an extra set just in case, so Spooky is sorted. She emerges from her box accompanied by a lingering smell of coconuts but otherwise unscathed. Spooky, Kylie and Dan each have these amazing tents that automatically pop up into position as soon as you take them out of the bag. Calum will be sleeping in the dog-van "to keep an eye on it". Hol's tent (like mine) is older and a bit ropey but (unlike mine) has been a constant companion during her very outward-bound-type childhood. She could put the thing up in her sleep. I'm still struggling with my groundsheet as the others sit in their various doorways on stools and cushions (Kylie's tent and accessories are all Cath Kidston), laughing and speaking fake German as they grill tomatoes, mushrooms and bacon.

My tent was a promotional giveaway with *Mountain Lichen Facial Rejuvenator*, a face cream Mum sold (not very many pots of) for a bit. As I'm getting it out of the bag it occurs to me I probably should have checked it actually has all the relevant parts *before* we left Bishopspool. And the material looks really thin. I hope it doesn't rain. Not that Glastonbury is notorious for rain or anything... I unfurl the snot-green body of the tent. Printed on the side it says "Celebrate the wisdom of lichen". I'm about to start swearing when a hand appears in front of my face clutching a bacon butty.

"All right?"

Calum smiles. I smile back and take the sandwich. Then, without either of us saying anything else, he puts my tent up for me. I pretend to help for a bit but eventually stop and just lie on my sleeping bag studying Clarence as Calum works away around me. Clarence's arrow tick-tocks back and forth between MUSIC and TROUBLE stopping momentarily on each word before flicking back the other way.

I take out my mobile and check the time. 7:30. Time to send the text. I spent ages writing it last night – all I have to do is press send... there.

Mum – sounds weird but there's something I hav 2 do B4 the wedding. Go 2 church w/out me. M fine! Will xplain later. Love u XXX

I'm aiming for reassuring (don't panic! I have not been child-snatched!) and true (I *will* explain later – just a lot later than she thinks...) I'm hoping that they all get to the church and then decide they might as well just crack on without me, since they know I'm OK. Mum will be cross. But cross is OK. Cross and married is ideal. What I can't have is worried, freaking out, calling the police and them or her turning up here before I get to do what I came here for. I check that the text has been sent one last time and then turn off my phone. I close my eyes and feel Clarence's arrow going *tick-tock, tick-tock* against one side of my ribs while what feels like a huge balloon of nerves, guilt, excitement and general *weirdness* inflates on the other. It's been building up throughout this extremely odd morning and I'm wondering how much room my lungs have left when Calum says, "Candy?"

"Mmm hmm?" My eyes are still closed but I can hear him shuffling awkwardly.

"Why have you come here?" he asks. I open my eyes to see him examining the promotional mallet he used to put the tent up with, in great detail.

"Um… because we're playing at twelve thirty?" I answer.

"No. That's why the rest of us are here. I mean why have *you* come here? It can't just be to play a gig. It's… it's your mum's wedding today. Glad has been talking about it for months. She's always saying how close you and your mum are. Why would you…" He tries and fails to think of a nicer way to put it. "Why would you run off on a day like this? This isn't you. There must be another reason."

The question punctures the weirdness-balloon like a perfectly aimed arrow and the strange and scary mixture of feelings explodes all at once. My face feels hot and my eyes start to sting. I cover them with the crook of my arm. "Why does there have to be another reason? Why can't it be an act of wild and impulsive teenage rebellion?" I bite back, defensively.

Calum thinks for a minute, then answers softly, "Because you're *you*, Candy. That's not really your style, is it?"

"Oh?" I ask. "And how would you know exactly? Because you know me so well, of course? Because we're *so* close?" I try to pitch my voice at 'unbothered' but hit 'shrill and emotional' instead.

Calum goes quiet. "I s'pose not..." he mumbles, adding, "It's just..." before trailing off into silence.

"Just what, Calum? Hmm?" I sit up on my elbows to say. My voice is coming out too fast and I sound angry which is not actually how I feel. Not with Calum anyway, who is looking at me like a puppy I just kicked. It's hardly his fault that my life feels like an out-of-control rollercoaster. Unfortunately for him, though, he's trying to engage me in a reasonable conversation in the middle of the ride. It's just impossible. All sorts of things are flashing through my mind. Has he said something to Glad? She's so sharp she'll be on to us in a flash if he has... They could be on their way here now. Could be about to stop me getting to Nathan! Does he know about Nathan? How? Did Pirate say something?

Calum rubs the back of his head with his hand and scrunches his face up. "I'm sorry. It's none of my business. I should go." He starts to crawl away. Backwards. As exits go it's a bit undignified but that's tents for you.

"Calum, wait..." I sit up and reach out to him. He shuffles back in a fraction. "I'm sorry. I'm having a really weird day. You're right. It's not just the gig. I mean – I really want to play – but there's something else. Some*one* else I'm here for."

Calum's open face clouds over. "I knew it," he says almost under his breath.

"You're right about Mum, too," I add, swallowing the lump that is rising in my throat. "I feel really crap about leaving her. The wedding and everything... I don't want to hurt her but this is my one chance. I would have been there otherwise. Even if she is marrying a total..." I search for the right word, tilting my head back like I'm keeping it above water, trying to stop the pooling tears underneath my eyes from rolling down my cheeks.

There's a silence. Well, not really a *silence* as such, they're awkward. There's a quiet. I breathe in deeply and lasso my emotions back in a bit. "I'm not a bad person, Cal. Am I?" I put my hand on Clarence again and feel his steady *tick-tock* between MUSIC and TROUBLE. "I'm following my heart. My fate. Isn't that what you're supposed to do?" I look up at Calum.

Suddenly his answer seems really important. He shakes his head. "You're not a bad person, Candy. You're the best. He's lucky to have you." A sad smile. "I just... I'm just... surprised, I suppose."

Nathan. He knows about Nathan. *Please don't have told Glad!* I think. It must show on my face because he holds his hands up and says, "I haven't said a word to anyone. You need to work it out between the two of you."

"Did Holly tell you?"

Calum shakes his head. "Nah. Figured it out myself." He shrugs. "The shop, then the party and then... well, this morning... I wasn't asleep as long as you thought I was." He starts shuffling backwards again. "I never really got the Kylie thing. She's all right but you... Anyway, you two look good together. I just wanted to be sure because if I'd been wrong... Never mind. I'd better get on. See you later."

And then Calum's gone and I'm alone in the tent I didn't even thank him for building and I realise two things. The first is that he thinks I'm here because of Dan. And the second is that it appears that Calum might... sort of... love me?

By midday professionalism, a passion for making music and sheer dedication to the cause of rocking and/or rolling has eclipsed the fact that not only am I skipping out on my mum's wedding to stalk the man I believe to be my father, I also appear have got myself involved in a love triangle. Well not a *triangle*, exactly... there are four of us. Can you have a love square?

Calum – who isn't exactly a chatterbox at the best of times – has gone extra-ultra-super quiet. *Charlie Chaplin* quiet. Dan, on the other hand, appears to have had a massive testosterone injection. He's swaggering around like a one-man action movie. Lugging amps with added manly noises, plugging stuff in decisively. He's got no idea what he's doing, mind you. It takes me about twenty minutes to untangle all the leads he's connected and hook them up the right way. He is trying, though. And he does look gorgeous while he's doing it. He rolls an amplifier into position on our stage and wipes some non-existent sweat from his brow before grabbing The Beast's case and handing it over to me with a surreptitious wink. "Here you go, Miss Caine!"

I move to take it but he doesn't let go of the handle, so our hands clamp together. He grins mischievously. "It should be good today. You lot are *on fire* at the moment..." He pulls the case towards himself slightly, taking me with it and adds in a whisper, "... Especially you. You're hot. Very... very... hot."

It's the kind of *fromage*-on-toast line that (coming from anyone else) would have me claiming lactose intolerance and making a swift exit. But as he says it he lets go of the case and kind of traces his finger up the inside of my forearm as he moves his hand away and honestly… well… He's right. I am hot. It's boiling. So boiling that Dan proceeds to take his top off. Oh. My. God.

I plonk the case down and take a minute to get my breath back. The view is unbelievable. Not Dan. OK, not *just* Dan… We're playing on a little old-fashioned bandstand in the Park Field, right at the top of the site and from here, you can see everything.

The Park is one of a dozen different fields and areas that sprawl out into the surrounding area outside of the main stages. Each area has a different vibe and is almost a festival all of its own.

There's Trash City – an area full of circus freaks and huge scrap-metal sculptures that have been known to literally breathe fire (apparently it doesn't really get going there until 2am). Then there's the Field of Avalon (where the proper old-school hippies all congregate. Clarence claims there are people who have been there since the very first festival. "They probably still think it's 1970 and that T. Rex are headlining!" he said archly as I packed to leave. "Shame they aren't. Even though Marc Bolan's been dead thirty years he could still teach your errant father a thing or five.") There's also the Kidz Field, the Theatre and Circus Field, The Dance Village (all of which more or less do what they say on the tin) and tons of others. And growing out of the middle of everything dominating the lot is the Pyramid Stage. Ten hours until The Rain.

And despite all the jokes people have been making, it looks like they are the only 'rain' that's coming to the festival this year. I stand with the scorching midday sun on my back looking out, trying vainly to take it all in. I want to remember this forever but it's like my eyes aren't big enough. Just looking at it all makes my brain feel like it's overflowing. With everyone up and about, the site looks ten times bigger than it did as we drove up.

Everyone is dressed up (either as something or as themselves – it's hard to say which is freakier). Everyone is going somewhere. Everyone is excited. There is more to look at, more to be amazed by, more that I need a second to stop and figure out. Right here now in front of me there is just… *more* than ever before in my whole life.

At 12:30, I poke my head out from behind the backstage curtain to find that an audience – if you can really call them that – has gathered to watch us. Or at least to watch the band the blackboard with today's stage times on it incorrectly proclaims 'Rhianna's Chalice'. We're the first band of the day which appears to have an upside (there is less other stuff on so a crowd has gathered to hear us) and a downside (most of said crowd are sitting or in some cases *lying* down. Several people have picnics. It's not exactly "GOOD EVENING GLASTONBERRY!") All the same, I'm a bit nervous. Good-nervous: rolling-down-a-hill, about-to-kiss-a-boy, out-after-dark nervous. Hol and I are in a tiny dark and sweltering curtained-off backstage section, tuning up while the others take a last-minute 'comfort break'. Not that there is anything remotely comfortable about the toilet situation at this event. When she went for her first wee in a portaloo, Kylie came out crying.

We're dressed for the stage. It wasn't easy getting changed in a tent but hopefully it was worth it. My outfit was selected via a series of arguments with Clarence over the course of last week. Not having had a pulse of his own since 1986, Clarence's finger isn't exactly on fashion's. But between us we settled on a look which he describes as "early Madonna with a post-pop twist" and I think of as "Zombie Spice Girl" (in a good way). I'm in a green leopard-print dress paired with several necklaces (plus Clarence still flitting between MUSIC and TROUBLE) and my battered old black boots My hair is in messy plaits and there is sparkling gold glitter on my eyes. Some of it is *in* my eyes actually. I keep catching sparkles in my peripheral vision and thinking Clarence is up to his tricks again. Contrasted with the Beast's russet gorgeousness my look is amazing, even if I do say so myself.

The Beast is unrecognisable from the smashed-up wreck that brought Clarence into my life four months ago. It is a glistening and glossy cherry-red chunk of perfection. The gouges and scratches have all healed themselves up and the body is as smooth and shiny as a racing car. Most of the stickers (that even lighter fluid wouldn't get rid of at first) have peeled away of their own accord and the few that are left have a kind of lived-in artful look. The badge replacing the volume knob says a whole word now. Well, it's not *actually* a word but at least it says *something*: "PHOTOGENIUS". Still haven't worked that one out. What I do know – what I can feel as it hangs around my neck – is that The Beast is where it has always wanted to be, doing what it was always meant to do. And so am I.

Pirate looks awesome. She's in one of her Dad's old bird T-shirts featuring a nest of baby eagles (or, as she corrected me earlier, "An aerie of eaglets, dude. Get it right.") It sounds geeky but paired with her little skirt, a glittery scarf, strappy sandals and her shades it totally works. I'm still not convinced by the pipe but I'm letting it go. A look of concentration grips Hol's face as she tweaks her E string. She catches my eye and grins.

"D'you see the blackboard, Can? It's a sign!"

I look up from my guitar tuning long enough to throw her a sceptical look. "Well *Duh...*"

"No, I mean it's a *sign*, sign! Like, we aren't Rhianna's Chalice but neither are *Rhiannon's* Chalice! Our name isn't up there but neither is theirs. Rhianna's Chalice don't exist. So we're like, not *not* the band who should be playing here. It's divine intervention. Or destiny. Or something..."

"It's a spelling mistake, Holly."

She pulls a face that reminds me of Clarence. "Candy, you're so depressingly—"

"Literal. Yes, I know." I smile. "People are always telling me that. Anyway how did you know the real Rhiannon's Chalice wouldn't turn up demanding their rightful place on the stage?"

"Like I said. Recon. I looked them up."

"You mean their MySpace?" I ask.

"Nope. I mean I *actually* looked them up. They're German eco-goths who live on a commune near Whitby."

"Eco-goths? Is that even a thing? And if they're German why do they live in Whitby?"

"Vampire country, innit?" she says, although as far as I can tell that explains precisely nothing. "I went to their caravan park thingy. No internet, no phones. No telly. Depressingly twentieth century. Although if you think that's depressing you should have heard the music. Yeuch! *Dong dong dong dong dooooonnnnggg.* It was like Joy Division on downers. *Long*

Division." She chuckles to herself and, after a final tweak of her tuning peg, she cradles her pipe in a thoughtful, Sherlock Holmes fashion as she continues her explanation. "One of my cousins is a postman up that way. Once I found out where they lived it was a relatively simple matter to intercept the letter that got us in here and replace it with a 'So sorry there's been a terrible mistake, you can't play this year blah blah blah' forgery of my own construction."

I ponder this feeling guilty and turn my bottom lip out. "Poor Rhiannon's Chalice."

Pirate places a hand on my shoulder. "Dude. Seriously. We did Glastonbury Festival a favour. Saved them from a musical ordeal they may otherwise never have recovered from. I don't know how they won the competition but it must have been a fix. Far better that this fine *fiesta* enjoys the *oeuvre* of 'Rhianna's Chalice'. And anyway there's another reason we're here, remember? Even bigger than the Biscuits. We're *on mission*! *Operation Who's-the-Daddy*!" She punches me on the shoulder. Quite hard. I wish she wouldn't keep calling it that.

Suddenly an extremely butch middle-aged lady in an oversize leather waistcoat (for which there can surely be neither necessity nor excuse) appears with Spooky, Kylie and Calum trailing behind her.

"Which one of you is Rhianna?" she asks. I shrug and look at Holly who then points at me. "Righto," nods waistcoat lady. She starts making ushering movements in my direction. "Hurry up, love. You're on."

18
Like No Business I Know

The dusty tang of hot felt hits the back of my nose as the thick black curtain – baking hot after hours in the sun – is whipped away. We are plunged from the hot and shady backstage into the dazzling noon glare, the ultimate spotlight. Blinded, I raise my hand to shade my face and step towards the microphone as the rest of the band take their places.

NNNNEEEOOOWWWWWWOOOOOOOOOOHHHHH!!!!!!!!

The Beast bursts into screaming feedback. The crowd below do a horrified gasp and cover their ears in unison.

"Oh… crap! Sorry!" I mumble, just off-mic. "Left my channel-switcher on the wrong…" I click my foot pedal off and the noise abates immediately. That's not how I meant to start this. A bubble of nerves floats up from the pit of my stomach towards my throat which tightens in response. I look to my left. Holly is unreadable:

mouth set to hold her pipe, the rest of her face is hidden behind her butterfly-lenses.

"Good afternoon, Glastonbury!" My voice comes out a bit strangulated and weird. The sound of it stops me in my tracks. I look out at the crowd. Everybody is just sitting there. Most of them look a bit cross. Some people aren't even facing the stage. One guy is lying down fast asleep with a newspaper over his face. Ice-cold panic pours over me like a bucket of water. Somebody shouts, "Get on with it!"

"I... We..." I stammer into the mic. *Oh God!* I think. *I'm losing it! I'm freaking out! Not now! I can't lose it now! And I KNOW I'm losing it which makes it even harder to get it back!* Three seconds of silence and the voice in the crowd pipes up again. "Come on girls! We haven't got all day!"

It feels like I'm standing on the edge of a cliff. My heart pounds. Panic snakes up my leg like ivy, pulling me closer to the brink and I start glancing around wildly: face after face, unimpressed and unfriendly. The sun beats down. I feel like an egg in a frying pan. I catch sight of Dan at the back of the crowd. He's talking to a girl who's dressed as a fairy. A fairy in a bikini. I'm about to fall off the edge (which would presumably involve jumping offstage and running away) when...

Calum.

I see Calum. He smiles and gives me a goofy little *Let's get on with it then, shall we?* shrug. And for some reason that makes me think that I am sort of all right. That in fact, everything is going to be all right. I clear my throat and my voice comes out just like I want it to.

"Good afternoon, Glastonbury! We've got something a little bit different for you now. In a change to the programme we bring you something of a surprise. Something even better than advertised! We've come all the way from Bishopspool to be here! We are THE BROKEN BISCUITS!"

Spooky lifts her sticks over her head. *Click-click-three-four...* and we smash into our biggest, loudest, most stupidly catchy song yet:

Get up girls and get up boys
Bang bang bang!
Hey what's that noise?
Bang bang bang!
We'll wake you up
Bang bang bang!
And shake you up
And hammer-hammer, hammer-hammer, hammer-hammer,
bang bang bang!

Holly flips her head from side to side as she plays, her blonde bob flipping around in the opposite direction. Kylie stamps her heel in time with her guitar playing as her lead part comes in. Behind me, Spooky keeps time with an ease and awesome power you'd expect to belong to someone twice her age and three times her size. I glance at Calum again. He's lost inside his hood, nodding along and firing off the beats and samples that make our band sound different. I don't mean the kind of different that relies on other stuff. That kind of different is really more 'unusual' or 'not the same as everything else'. We're the kind of different that is unlike *any*thing else: a one-off in our own right. We're properly genuinely actually unique.

Out in the crowd, heads start to dip in time. Brows un-knit themselves. During the first chorus people start to sway along a bit. By the second a few hands are in the air – people raising their plastic pint glasses to us, reaching out to the sun. The bikini-fairy Dan was talking to is right in front of the stage now too, doing interpretive dancing. Whether she's interpreting our music or a song we can't hear that's being beamed down from an intergalactic dimension, I'm not sure. At this distance it is immediately obvious that she's absolutely spannered. She's waving her hands in front of her face. She's so hypnotised by the amazingness of her own fingers that her jaw has gone all slack and she's actually started to drool. Nice. I'm glad Clarence isn't available for comment: He's outraged enough already about people giving fairies a bad name...

At the end of the song we get a massive cheer and I know it's going to be a good show. Before anyone else, I turn to Calum. I can tell from the look on his face that he thinks so too. I check Clarence and his delight is immediately apparent. His white face is flashing in every shade of neon. His arrow is fixed firmly on MUSIC.

And that's it! We're off. Over the course of the next six songs we make about 150 people fall in love with our music. They dance! They cheer! We field three marriage proposals from the audience (one each for me, Kylie and Hol – she accepts hers, the minx.) And everyone is horrified when bikini-fairy attempts a lone stage-dive on to a patch of ground that contains no actual audience members. Ow. We're about to go into our last song and it seems like we only just got started. When I'm talking to the audience now it feels like I know them.

"Thanks everyone. You've been amazing! Listen, this is a first for us. Our first Glastonbury. Our first festival. Technically this is our first ever gig!" This gets tons of cheers. "We've gone to great lengths to get here today. So thanks for sharing it with us. We're going to do a new song for you now. Well, they're all new to you, of course. This one's new to us as well. I wrote it about a party I had that went wrong." This gets even more cheers (evidently I'm not the only one). At the back of the crowd I spot Dan standing on his own. Everyone strikes up and he's looking right at me, smiling a big half-a-watermelon smile. "This is called Party Crasher." And I start to sing over the then unfinished song Clarence played me in our little back yard in Bishopspool a few days ago.

It should have been so good, it should have been fun
I threw a party and said everyone could come.
To dance and kick it, to hang out at my place.
How could I know it would blow up in my face?
I took a risk with a boy that I knew
I said I liked him. He said he liked me too
But before we could get up to much more
The Party Crasher broke us up! 2-3-4!

It's my party! So just leave me alone,
It's my party! And I wanna go home,
It's my party! But it isn't much fun.
It's my party! Tell me: why did I come?

My party crashed to the floor, what to do?
My life is trashed and my boy has gone too!
No idea what I can do to fix that
So I'll keep partying until he comes back!

At the end of the song there is stamping, cheering and chants of "WE WANT MORE! WE WANT MORE!" It doesn't matter that the chants were just one drunk guy who seems to think we're called the Dunkin Biscuits ("Dunkin Biscuits! WHOoO! MooOOOooore!") It was everything we wanted and more. It made it all worthwhile: driving 300 miles through the night in a dog-van. Sleeping under inadequate promotional canvas. The lingering smell of *Cocomutt Dog Shampoo* around our drummer. It may not be the Pyramid Stage and we may not be The Rain – yet – but today we took The Park New Bands bandstand. Hol removes her pipe for a moment and breathes in the fetid air of the backstage enclosure.

"*Veni, vidi, vici,* my friends!" she sighs contentedly. We're back behind the felt curtain in the darkened sweatbox of success, dispensing liberal hugs and high-fives and congratulating each other on the fact that, put simply, in words of one syllable: we rule. Then Calum and I are face to face. It is a moment that should very obviously involve a friendly congratulatory hug. Nothing could be more natural, more innocent. Our eyes meet and we both stop dead as the locker-room-style victory celebrations continue around us.

"Hey!" I offer, as faux-normally as possible.

"Hey." He looks at his shoes.

"That was great! Well done!" Calum shakes his head.

"No – well done you. You were amazing, Candy. Born to do it." He looks at me. Deep quiet dark blue eyes (*honest eyes*, I think, and remember Clarence saying "Music is truth"). He smiles but there is sadness in it.

"Like I said before. You're the best."

"Shall we... er...?" I open my arms out, international sign language for "shall we hug it out, then or what?"

We do but I can't pretend it isn't deeply and cripplingly awkward. Like two shop dummies who don't really get on. It seems that I have ruined what was turning out to be a really interesting friendship without doing anything at all. How on earth did I manage that? I open an eye and over Cal's shoulder, spot Dan advancing with what Glad would probably call "a roguish look" in his eye.

"Scuse me, Stain-o!" he moves Calum out of the way without any apparent effort and grabs me around the waist. "Mind if I borrow the girl of the hour?"

"Oh. Ok... Of course," Calum says and without going

anywhere, he somehow disappears again. Dan checks over his shoulder – presumably to make sure that Kylie is otherwise occupied and takes my hand.

Dan pulls me behind a stack of amplifiers waiting to be loaded on for the next band on the bill and I try not to think about how this is a really enclosed space and that I am a bit hot after the gig. Sweaty even. We're close: really close. Tucked in beside the curtain that leads onstage, my back is against the amps and my front is against him. The only thing in the way is my guitar, which I'm holding between us with one hand like a shield. Because with everything else that's going on this weekend this is definitely not a good idea. Rationally speaking, that's obvious.

Unfortunately, when it comes to Dan Ashton, I cease to function rationally. When I'm this close to him. When I can smell him. Not in a gross way. Dan Ashton has the perfect smell: really clean boy with a tiny bit of whatever-that-is (Calvin Klein?) going on underneath. I try not to think about him taking his top off earlier. Then he smiles at me and lifts my guitar off, strap and all and leans it on the amp beside us. There's nothing between us now. He checks once more that no one's looking and then pulls me closer so that his face right up to mine, his messy hair falls into my eyes. I give in and close them and the rest of the world is gone. He says, "That was so cool. That last song, especially. Did you write that about me?"

"Yeah," I sigh. Although actually, I didn't. I wrote it about myself. You can't really say that though, can you? Not in a moment like this when the lips of your dreams are brushing your cheek as they ask.

"I really liked it. I really like you." His voice is urgent now and one of his hands has found its way to the small of my back. "I've been thinking about you all day... about earlier. I haven't been able to stop thinking about it. We got interrupted when we were in the middle of saying something. What was it again?" His other hand reaches up into my hair and tilts my head back. Somewhere from the bottom of an unfathomably deep well far away a little voice cries "Trouble!" but I can hardly hear it. I open my eyes a fraction in time to see Dan smile a one-side-of-the-mouth smile. For a fraction of a second I think of the photograph of Mum and Nathan. I hear Clarence's voice, "Like a fox that's broken into a henhouse." Then Dan's lips are on mine and I don't hear anything but my heart pounding inside my chest.

Trouble...

Trouble!

TROUBLE!!

Only it isn't inside my chest. It's *on* my chest. It's Clarence – leaping around like a break-dancing eel. I shove Dan off with all the elegance of a plumber yanking a plunger from a blocked U-bend.

"What?" he asks quite reasonably. I hold up a hand both to shut him up and make sure he doesn't go anywhere. With the other I grab Clarence. He is shaking, his entire compassy person flashing neon red like an angry tropical fish. I slip the ribbon he's looped into off my neck and hold him steady with two hands. His arrow is pointing to the word over and over: TROUBLE! TROUBLE! TROUBLE!

I look up at Dan. For once his question-mark expression is more bemusement than amusement. "What?" he asks again. "What is that?" he takes Clarence from me for a closer look. "What is this thing anyway?"

That's when Pirate appears. And by appears I mean runs past us clutching her bass and screaming at the top of her lungs: "CAANNDDDYYYYY!!! RUUNNN! RUN FOR YOUR LIFFE!! THE JIG IS UPP!! SAVE YOURSEELFFF!!!"

Hot on her heels is a diminutive lady dressed head to toe in black wearing a rough-looking cloak. Her raven hair is swept up into two complicated-looking Danish pastry-type things.

Instinctively and immediately I know that she is one of Rhiannon's Chalice. For all I know she might even be Rhiannon herself. I gasp and turn to Dan.

"What should I *do*? Are there any more of them?"

"Don't panic," he says with admirable calm. His head disappears around the corner of the amp-stack for a second and re-appears looking distinctly freaked out. "OK. Maybe you should panic. There are loads of them. That guy off the gate."

"Stu is there?"

"Yes, Stu. And... and..." He looks nauseous.

"And what??"

"And the Eavises are with them. Michael Eavis and his daughter... um... Emily, I think?"

"You mean the people who run the festival?"

"Yes. That's them all right." Dan checks again.

"So they'll probably chuck us out. They're nice, though, right? Maybe I can talk them round?" I ask, nervously trying to recall any useful Michael Eavis facts that Pirate and I unearthed in our pre-Glastonbury research. I can't. Most of our research admittedly, was beard-based (he has an amazing beard. Look it up.) Dan runs his hand through his hair nervously.

"It's not just the Eavises, though, Candy. It's the police. Pirate's right. You're going to have to make a break for it." *Make a break*

for it? Where will I go? They must know where we're camped –
our van is hardly difficult to miss... The weird-bubble re-inflates
inside my chest and my breath gets short. I feel like I'm five and
lost in a shopping centre. I can't do this alone. I look back at Dan.
He's still holding me in his strong arms.

"Come with me?"

He smiles kindly. Then says, "Nah. Sorry. They don't know I'm
with you lot, see? There's no point *all* of us getting in trouble, is
there? Meet you later, though, yeah?"

And with that he's gone. In the split-second it takes him to
disappear I learn why falling in Like really is falling: it hurts when
you land. I thought Dan's inscrutable exterior hinted at hidden
depths but it's the opposite – he's a no-good coward with all the
depth of a puddle. I feel wounded, lost and stupid all at once.
Before I can work out which is worst, an extremely stern face
appears where Dan was moments ago. It's a policeman. He just
about gets out an "Oi!" before I spin around and, slipping through
a gap in the curtain behind me, run for my life.

After the first ten seconds of running I remember: my bag! I've
left my bag! On the floor in the tent. Money, phone... After the first
minute's running I remember: The Beast! I've left The Beast. I lift
my hand up to grab Clarence, hanging on the string around my
neck to see if he can help. That's when I stop dead.

Oh no!

Dan still has Clarence. I look back at the bandstand where we were playing. I start to run back. Then three policeman and a police lady come marching out from the curtained-off backstage area. It looks like they're with the rest of Rhiannon's Chalice (either that or they're going to a medieval funeral afterwards). I stop dead, rabbit-in-the-headlights-style. Then one of the members of Rhiannon's Chalice shouts, "*Schau mal! Schau mal!*"

Oh crap. He's pointing at me.

And I'm running again. Hard and fast and this time I don't stop. Not until my legs are about to give way underneath me. Not until I'm totally lost. I'm alone and I'm really in trouble. Moving away from the main drag where the hordes of people milling about seem to have increased, and round to the side of a Water Aid tent, I sink down on to my knees, swallowing huge gulps of air and attempting not to look completely insane.

After a long time my breath settles back down to normal. The burst of adrenalin that got me here has worn off and I feel eerily calm. Probably because I've got no other options left. *So that's it, then,* I think. *Can't go back to the van. No phone. No money. No idea where anyone else is. No Clarence. There's only one place left.* I straighten myself up and take a deep fortifying breath. It smells of hot earth and chemical toilets.

OK, I think, *this is it. Last chance. Looks like it's just me on Operation Who's-the-Daddy.* I look out at the site in front of me, at the huge silver edifice dominating everything else. The Pyramid Stage. Parked behind it are a fleet of tourbuses. One of them – the one I'm going to find – has registration plates that read R41N N8N.

19
R41N N8N

So here I am. Hidden behind the same random Land Rover I've been standing behind for an hour, opposite Nathan Oxblood's tourbus. It's only now I'm in front of the thing that I realise finding it was the easy part. It feels like I'm standing in front of a tank, planning to pick the lock with a pin. The bus's gleaming black windows stare out indifferently as impenetrable as a pair of rock-star shades. Is he even in there? Is he alone? And if he is there and if he is alone... how the flip am I supposed to get in? Several people have come and gone during the time I've been standing here. There was a delivery of what looked to be Japanese food. A lady in a kaftan with a pocket-sized dog. A guy in one of those white coats that nurses wear. There is a bank of paparazzi camped out just over there with their lenses constantly trained on the bus. Nobody I recognise, though. No

Jasmine and definitely no Nathan.

I have never worried about this part of the plan before – Pirate was supposed to be coming with me. And as you have already seen, Pirate's gift for blagging approaches a kind of genius. She says she's got *cojones*, whatever that is. I haven't got *cojones* (at least I don't think I have).

But it's almost half past two. Pirate isn't here and I don't have time to any get braver. I'm just going to have to get on with it. For some reason I think of Glad. What would she do in my shoes? Asking myself this unlikely question leads me to march up to the door on the side of the bus with my head held high and knock three times. Nobody comes, so after a minute I knock again. A couple of the photographers fire off lazy disinterested shots of me, checking back the digital images on the backs of their cameras afterwards. I stare at the door, attempting to maintain a confident and business-like air despite the fact that I have absolutely no idea who's going to open it or what I'm going to say to them when they do. I get ready to come face to face with Nathan's PA. Or is it PR? Manager? Handler? Personal trainer? Organic chef? The door swings open.

"Yeah?"

I don't say anything. Try to. Can't.

"Yes?"

Same again. He rolls his eyes and lowers his voice.

"Hel-lo? Anybody in there?" Nathan Oxblood looks at me over the top of his sunglasses, his green eyes flashing like fireflies and snaps his fingers in front of my face. He clocks the photographers behind me. As soon as he appeared their shutters went into overdrive. I daren't look – the sound is bad enough. Like insane crocodiles eating a wildebeest. Smiling in their direction he leans towards me and lowers his voice to a gravelly, East End rumble. He smells of cigarettes. "Listen darlin', it's sweet of you to call round but I'm busy right now so – without wishing to be unkind – do you p'raps fancy either speaking up or getting lost?"

"Sorry... I didn't think it would be you," I manage.

Nathan's expression softens into something approaching weary resignation. He reaches one hand behind his ear and the other into the back pocket of his tattered jeans, simultaneously producing a roll-up cigarette and a silver lighter.

"Well, unfortunately for me, it is." He lights up, looking into the bank of photographers like a mirror, lifting his chin so his head's at the angle you always see in pictures. "Call this the bloody countryside... Piccadilly bloody Circus, more like. Man can't get a minute to himself... Come on, then. What is it? Autograph? Demo? Oh fu— No singing, all right? You can come in but no singing. Five minutes, right? FIVE." He holds a hand up in front of my face, his fingers spread. He checks his watch. It looks expensive, especially next to the other things on his wrist: a manky old leather cuff and a few bits of what looks like string full of knots. Nathan takes a couple of heavy pulls on his cigarette and throws the rest into the grass below. He pushes the door open as wide as it will go and gives me a tooth-bearing smile before saying (with more than a little sarcasm), "Do come in."

I step up, bending down to go underneath his arm as I enter. I hear him make a sudden movement accompanied by a shout of "UP YOURS PAPPANAZIS!" Then the door bangs shut and we are plunged into almost total darkness. Behind me the sound of a lock.

"So... What's your name?"

"Candy Caine."

"Candy. Nice name. Sweet! Hahaha..." Nathan laughs at his own joke as he leads me up a set of stairs and presses a button on the wall next to him. The lights come up enough that I can see our surroundings. We're in a giant lounge that runs the full length of the upstairs of Nathan's bus. At one end (where he is) there is a bar. And by bar I mean an all-out fully-stocked Tom-Cruise-in-*Cocktail* BAR. It even has a dance floor in front with a pole in it. I silently hope it's some kind of tribute to our nation's great firefighters as Nathan crouches down behind the bar and whistles. "Beer for me... coke for Candy. You sure you don't want anything stronger?"

"No!" I say a bit too quickly before catching myself. The image of the vomaphone is still fresh in my mind. And my stomach which flips over like a pancake at the thought of downing anything alcoholic. "I mean no – thanks."

He rakes around for a bit before emerging with a Stella Artois in one hand and a can of Coke in the other and makes for the couch I'm perching on. In the seating area right in the middle of the bus, is a contraption called an 'iRide' which appears to be an electronic horse-riding simulator. It's deeply creepy and frankly it's freaking me out. I try not to look, focusing on the other end of the bus instead. In stark contrast to the bar it houses what looks like a shrine. A mat, statues, mini-waterfall, incense... the works. There are little stones all round it and photographs. As a whole, the interior resembles a kind of Buddhist *Stringfellows*.

Nathan cracks open the drinks and slinks down to an almost horizontal position on the couch opposite me.

"So, *Candy*." (He says my name in a tone that acknowledges what a thrill it must be to have him remember it.) "You came all the way from Newcastle to see us, did you?"

"Bishopspool," I say. "Not Newcastle. Near there, though." I nurse my can feeling a pang of guilt as I picture home. Mum must be worried. Nathan raises his bottle of beer in an air-toast.

"A long way, anyway. Very good of you. Cheers." Now that we're inside, some of the gruffness in his manner has dissipated and he seems more relaxed. His accent is softer too; his vowels seem to have relocated themselves nearer to Sussex than Essex. "And you're playing too, you said?"

"We played already. Up at the Park."

"And? How was it?"

"Well, it went a bit wrong towards the end but other than that..." I think back. "Other than that it was great, actually! It was our first show, though, so I don't have much to compare it to. We liked it." I manage a nervous smile.

Nathan chugs his beer and hooks his arm over the back of the couch. "Not a bad first gig! Bloody dump the first place I played... Had a residency there. Drains were always blocked and it was always bloody flooding. I remember sound-checking once while they were literally hosing crap off the walls. Tiny little place, just off Upper Street..." He cups his chin and asks (himself rather than me), "What was it called, again?"

"The Hangman," I answer without thinking. "When you were in Bodywork." Nathan's green eyes widen momentarily taken aback, then almost close themselves, his face settling into the same vulpine look of satisfaction it has in the photograph in my pocket.

"The Hangman! Of course. Long time ago. And Bodywork – what a name! What was I thinking, *Candy*?" He pauses long enough to flash me an L. A. perfect smile. I can't help thinking I liked his original teeth better. "Took us a while to get out of that *hole*. Did the job, though. Got me a few contacts. By the time I met my present colleagues," he raises a conspiratorial eyebrow, "I already had my sights set higher. Our first show was opening up for the biggest band in London. They only lasted about five minutes. Bet you can't tell me who that was!" He gives me a mischievous look and takes a swig of his beer. I smile back and roll my eyes.

"Easy! You were supporting The Weekenders at the Hundred Club. May '92. Although you weren't called The Rain yet. You were 'A Real Rain' after a line from the film *Taxi Driver*? I haven't seen it but I'm glad you changed it. If you ask me 'A Real Rain' was almost as bad as 'Bodywork'. You became The Rain just before you signed to Reckless Records."

There's a pause as he stares at me and for a moment I think I've been a bit too cheeky, then Nathan throws his head back and lets out a huge laugh.

"Well, well, well," he says. " You do know your stuff, don't you?

Unexpected. Very unexpected."

I'm surprised he's impressed to be honest. These particular facts are mere drops in the ocean of knowledge I have acquired about Nathan over the last few months. A *Rain*drop, if you will. I know every detail about him – his geography, his biography, his discography. I have viewed his appalling *Casualty* cameo as 'Male Crash Victim' on YouTube approximately one hundred times. There is, of course, one piece of knowledge I'm still looking for. The one that brought me here.

"So how is it that a young thing like you seems to know so much about a washed-up old rocker like me?" He laughs and throws his hand out, indicating our palatial surroundings (in case I don't get that he's joking).

I'm about to answer when the bus starts to wobble. Something is moving around downstairs. By the sounds of it, something huge. In fact it's coming up the stairs. Nathan plonks his beer down on the table crossly and says, "Oh for f— Jugs is up. Candy, I apologise for what is about to happen in advance."

The lurching of the bus reaches a crescendo and we both stare at the doorway at the top of the stairs. Suddenly it is filled to the very brim with a huge hairy furry... is that... a bear?

The bear clears its throat, takes a giant step towards me, puts out its paw for me to shake and says in a surprisingly soft voice, "Well well! Company! Hello. I'm Norman, but everybody calls me Jugs. I'm Nathan's manager. What are we drinking then?"

Jugs cracks open a beer and plonks himself on the sofa. "Oxo been telling you all about himself, has he? Did he tell you the one about the time we got banned from The Oscars?" Jugs throws half a can of beer down his neck, then comes back up for air. To release it, in fact. "Pardon me!" he grins, before proceeding to attempt to talk me to death. Nathan seems in no particular hurry to get rid of him. Conversation between them is a mixture of light bickering, in-jokes and shorthand (who's "the guy with the leg" who helped Jugs hide Jarvis Cocker in a broom cupboard after he mooned at The Brits?) They laugh about Nathan's ongoing feud with TV chef Gordon Ramsay which recently involved Nathan placing a £3000 Pizza Hut delivery to Ramsay's most famous restaurant). Clearly Nathan thinks drinking in all this gossip must be a thrill, but I didn't come here for this. Jugs seems nice enough – he even sort of reminds me of Santa (if the man in red liked rock n roll and pies that little bit more) but I came here to find my dad. I sip my coke and listen politely, wondering how on earth I am going to get rid of this guy and get to the point with Nathan. Jugs, who has regaled us for a full twenty minutes about playing golf with Alice

Cooper, appears to be coming to a punchline of sorts when there is a sudden blast of the Led Zeppelin classic *Rock n Roll*.

"Oops! Phone – sorry!" Jugs says, leaping up to extract it from the pocket of his shorts. The bus lurches with such force that Nathan almost falls off his seat. After a few seconds' pause, Jugs's face acquires a look of concern. "He's done *what*? Well who let him up there? Well *WHO GAVE HIM THE BLOODY WATERMELONS, ADRIAN?*" He breaks off the conversation for a moment to address us. "I'm sorry – I'm going to have to go. Nate, looks like Sticks has had one of his incidents again. I'm gonna sort it." He winks at us both and makes an exit that must be around a five on the Richter scale. Nathan and I are alone on the bus once again.

Nathan stretches a bit, taking the opportunity to rearrange himself from the casual pose he had slipped into while Jugs was here and into one befitting a professional Rock God. He smiles wolfishly. "So, sweet little Candy... Caine, was it?"

I nod.

"I think we were discussing how exactly it is that one so delightfully young and full of life has come to be such an expert on yours truly?"

"Well, I..." I clear my throat. "Obviously I know your music. I've grown up with it. You know, The Rain have been huge, like, forever!" I put my hand in my pocket on the picture. For luck. "But it's also because… er… because of my mum."

Nathan's smile evaporates. He thinks for a moment and then says, "You must have a pretty cool mum."

"Yeah," I nod. "She is cool. Bonkers but cool."

The corners of his mouth creep back up a little. "How old's your mum, then?"

"Thirty-five."

"Thirty-five! Wow! She must have had you *young*! So your Mum is only a couple of years older than me." He looks at me sideways (we both know he's really thirty-seven). His perfect smile returns to full wattage.

"Yeah." I nod. "She was pretty young."

"Well – that's up north for you I guess. Fancy another?" He glances at my drink, hopping up to replace his own.

"Um… got any water?" I shift around in my seat uneasily. How on earth am I going to, like, actually *ask him*? Do I keep on talking about Mum? *Yeah, she is great! You may remember doing the bad naughty with her in the early nineties! Guess what? I'm the result! Hello Dad!* Do I quiz him, Columbo-style *So! Mr Oxblood, you're a successful businessman. Exactly how extensive is your portfolio? Does it include any businesses I would be familiar with? Something in my area – a beauty salon perhaps?*

Nathan retrieves another beer from the fridge behind the bar. I look at the shrine again. The photographs above it all seem to be of Nathan's family. Him, Jasmine and the kids: their terrifyingly beautiful but stony-faced daughter Otto and their son Justice (I thought that was a concept rather than a name but there you go). There are lots of tropical-paradise-type shots of them larking about on beaches and in swimming pools. I think about the last time me and Mum went on holiday. A cheapo fortnight in the Costa Brava, staying on my grandparents' sofa bed. It sounds like it should have been hell but it was actually really brilliant. A sudden memory pops into my head of Mum dancing to a live band in a Spanish restaurant. We had snuck out of the patio-door window and off the balcony when Granny and Granda had gone to bed. The thought of Mum trying to navigate the railings in her enormous espadrille wedges, maxi-dress and gigantic sun hat after winching me down makes me smile.

"Enjoying yourself?" Nathan has reappeared by my side on the couch with another beer for him, a bottle of water for me and his mega-watt smile turned up to eleven.

"I suppose so," I say. "I'm a bit nervous, though."

"Candy, Candy, Candy! That's to be expected. You're meeting someone you've looked up at on your bedroom wall for years live in the flesh! It's a nerve-racking moment!"

I nod in agreement (although I've actually never had a picture of Nathan on my wall). "It's not just that, though. I came here to ask you about something."

The corners of Nathan's grin drop fractionally. Time to do what I came here to do. I reach into my pocket and produce the folded piece of A4. "I came about this." I hand him the same print-out I've been carrying around since that afternoon Clarence and I spent in The Blue, months ago. As he unfolds it disinterestedly, I think how mad it is. At last I'm here, with the person in it.

Nathan looks at the picture. Then he *really* looks at it. His mouth opens but the only thing that comes out is a little gasp of air.

"That's you," I say helpfully pointing.

"And that's..."

"...Maggie," he finishes the sentence for me. Almost. I do the rest.

"My mum."

From an expression of bemusement, Nathan's face scrunches up in confusion. He looks back at the photograph as if he expects it to say something; for Mum's head to pop up so she can explain herself.

"Maggie's your... This Maggie? Your..." he tails off, staring at the thing like it's a magic-eye painting.

"Mum. Yeah. I was born eight months after this picture was taken." Nathan's head jerks back up and he stares straight at me. I can almost see the sums flashing up on the back of his eyes as he does the maths.

"So you're... Oh my God. You..." He covers his mouth with his hand. All the colour drains from his face like they say happens in books. I've never seen it in real life before, though. I nod.

"Oh my God," he says again and looks a bit nauseous. I offer him my bottle of water. He waves it away and looks at me: green eyes into green eyes. I notice him noticing them for the first time. *See?* I think, *total tree frog.*

Then he swears. A lot.

"I'm sorry, Nathan," I say, softly. "I had to come here. She won't give me any straight answers about this. About anything. I needed to see you. To find out for myself. So that I'd know. Look at me." He lifts his head a bit, his face still a mask of shock. "Look at me, Nathan. Look at us. We're identical."

"Pfff! Identical! Not bloody identical enough! You know I thought you came here to—" He leaps up from the sofa. "I'm sorry. Sorry – I can't do this without a drink." Shuddering, he stamps over to the bar and grabs a bottle of Jack Daniels.

Without even looking for a glass, he takes three huge swigs then slams it down on the bar.

He won't look at me now. Or he can't. He's staring straight ahead, eyes fixed in the middle-distance, his real gaze travelling further back. Reaching places and people who don't exist any more. At least not the way they were then. He stays like that for what feels like a long time. Then he takes a glass and pours himself a whiskey rather than swigging it from the bottle. Quite a large whiskey but then he is a professional Rock God. I hope this means he is over the initial shock. Turning to me at last, he speaks. Controlled, considered even. But only just. There is something else now, something underneath: anger.

"If you're making this up…"

I shake my head, start to protest my innocence.

He raises his hand to stop me. "If you are… If you're working for some sordid little tabloid after a story, I'll… you'll live to regret it."

"I'm not! Why would I?" I protest dumbly. Because of course it sounds dumb. I would have everything to gain from this and nothing to lose. He doesn't know how far I've gone to get here. What I've risked, who I've hurt. Crying will probably make him angrier but I don't think I can help it.

"I'm not from a paper. I don't want anything from you." He

looks at me sceptically. "I don't!" I can't stop them coming so I lower my head and cover my eyes, letting the tears fall like quiet raindrops on to my knees.

"Don't, Candy," Nathan says but not angrily. He scrabbles round for something then hands me a napkin. Although that description doesn't really do it justice. It features a giant picture of a skull with roses for eyes that appear to be on fire. I must look confused because Nathan says, "One of Jasmine's. Her new collection is themed around the Mexican Day of the Dead."

"Oh. Right." I mop my eyes and sniff. "I'm sorry," I say. "This must be a shock."

Nathan lets out a spluttery laugh. "You could say that, yes. It wasn't exactly in my plans when I got up this morning, that's for sure. But… Maggie, you know? *Maggie…*" He shakes his head. "I haven't seen your mum for a long time, Candy. A *long* time. I never understood why. Always wondered… And now I know." Nathan looks at me, then lies back and makes a long loud noise that sounds like he's deflating. We sit like that for a bit, him looking at me, thinking. Then he says quietly, "Where is she?"

I'm not sure I understand the question. I mean Nathan Oxblood probably has more than one Love Child. But he clearly remembers Mum. Why would he *not* remember where he left her? She isn't a pair of car keys he plonked down on a coffee table absentmindedly. He set her up! Bought her the salon! Made sure the two of us would be all right! How could he forget all that? My face wrinkles up in confusion.

"Where is she?" I echo "Er... try the last place you looked? Bishopspool of course! The same place you bought her the salon! The same salon. We live above it!"

He looks at me, his face a total blank.

"Oh!" I think aloud. "Maybe you just gave her the money. Maybe you just gave her the cash and she bought it herself."

Nathan shakes his head. "Cash? I didn't give Maggie any cash, Candy."

This is the part of the story I was surest of. Homeless pregnant young women don't just go around buying houses and businesses. I recite it to him as if I'm correcting a small child. "When you found out she was having your baby you gave her the money to buy the salon. To see her right – to see both of us right!" It's only when I hear it said out loud that I realise I don't actually *know* that. Not for sure. Nathan swallows.

"You think... You think I'm your father?"

"Well *duh*!" I'm perplexed, almost irritated. "Isn't that what we've been discussing this whole time?"

Nathan shakes his head holding his hands up, pushing me away. "No! No. I'm sorry." He looks like someone complaining they're too full for dessert. But I'm not offering him a knickerbocker glory. I'm his long-lost daughter. According to the chat shows I grew up watching, this is the point at which we would traditionally start weeping and run into each others' arms.

"What do you mean you're sorry?"

"I mean, I'm sorry – I'm not your father, Candy."

20
Jugs and Melons

"Let me get this straight. You're saying without any doubt whatsoever present in your mind that there is no conceivable way on earth you could be my dad."

He shakes his head again. "No. I'm not."

"You mean you and my mum never…"

"NO! No. No of course not! Never!"

I don't understand. He's been getting misty-eyed for about the last twenty minutes here. They clearly had a thing going on… But they didn't… He can't be my… Which means… The pieces of the puzzle whirl around my head like a shaken-up snowglobe. My head starts to hurt again. The facts start to settle, to crystallise. As far as I can tell, they are as follows:

1. Nathan is not my Dad

2. I still don't know who is

3. I have ruined my life to get here

4. It was all for nothing

I'm standing in front of a stranger. It's as if someone's just grabbed the whole bus and spun it like a roulette wheel. I can't go back home and I can't go forward into the life I'd dreamed up for myself because it doesn't exist. I'm nothing to him and he has no reason not to chuck me out of here to... to what? Get arrested? Hitch my way home thumbing lifts from potential axe murderers? Have I even got a home? Mum's made her fair share of mistakes in her time – I'm living proof – but she never did anything like this. Will she even have me back? I am staring at my knees, contemplating my fate (which at this moment seems to involve – at best – adoption by kindly hippies who will let me earn my keep selling love beads out of the back of their weird-smelling van) when the bus starts to wobble again and I know that Jugs is back. Nathan hops up and goes downstairs to meet him. There is a certain amount of mumbling before they both return wearing extremely serious faces.

You know when people say the bottom has fallen out of their world? They really mean it. That's exactly how I feel. It's as if the floor has opened out underneath me. I'm falling and I'll keep falling because everything I thought would be there to catch me is gone now. Nathan makes his excuses (a round of interviews for the BBC's Glastonbury coverage beckons) and leaves us to it, promising to return as soon as possible. I am left alone with Jugs, whose previously raconteurish demeanour seems to have evaporated. He sits down beside me on the sofa and stares straight ahead like a huge zoo animal hit with a tranquiliser dart. Eventually he says, "Your mum is Maggie Valentine?"

I nod. "Yes. Sort of. It's Maggie Caine, really. Maggie Valentine was her modelling name. She lived in London and was a model until she, er, until she was going to have me. I've got a photo." I retrieve the printout photo and hand it over. Mum with her arms octopussed around Nathan, looking impossibly gorgeous. I think about Nathan, his hundred-grand tourbus, all his houses, superstar mates and the most amazing life that has yet to be made into a bestselling rock autobiography (if he can remember enough of it) and think: this kind of life should have been hers. Mum lost all this by choosing me instead. And I've left her – probably worried to death with no idea where I am or how to find me – to chase after a lie. A lie I invented myself.

Staring at the picture, Jugs shakes his big fluffy head with his mouth hanging open. He looks at me. "You're Maggie's daughter."

It's almost a whisper, really.

"Did you know her?" I ask, not really caring what the answer is. I suppose it made sense, if Jugs had been around when Mum and Nathan were friends that they would have known each other.

"Everybody knew Maggie, Candy. She was..." He tails off for a moment, looks back at the picture, tiny in his giant bear-paws. For a second I think he might cry but he laughs softly. "She was lovely."

The poor lump. Mum has this effect on a lot of blokes. Stupefying. And he knew her at her most potent. Jugs drifts off into his own thoughts and I try to make all of this make sense. To add it up. Our eyes. The photo, the salon... It doesn't fit. Unless... Unless Nathan's lying? Maybe Jugs can help me out. He was there...

"I came here because I think... I thought," I correct myself, "I thought Nathan was my dad. He says he isn't. Says it's impossible but look at us!" I affect the Oxblood dog's bum mouth. "And look at him and Mum in that picture!"

Jugs doesn't answer. He's staring at the photo. Mum didn't need to marry a hypnotherapist I think to myself, she's not too bad at it herself.

"Look," I press on, "maybe Nathan doesn't want to admit that he could be my dad because my mum wasn't special to him. Well that's fine," I say (although as the words come out they feel like a lie). "And I don't expect to be special to him either. I don't want anything from him. I just want to understand the way things are. To understand myself." Jugs doesn't say anything. I hope he can't tell I'm lying about that bit too – I really, really want to be special. "I was born eight months after this photograph was taken. Do you think he could be my dad?"

Jugs rubs a hand across his mouth and down over his chins. "Candy—" then his phone rings again. He answers it. "This better be important!" he says tersely. It must be, as there's a long silence before he says, "Adrian, stop panicking. No they're not joking. I know what to do. Are they with you now?" It must be the melons again. I'm not really listening, though, I'm thinking about Nathan. I find myself staring at the tattoos poking through the fur on Jugs' arms. There are a series of gruesome heavy metal ones (the word "SLAYER" features twice) but there's also a heart which sits incongruously among the dark stuff. I've just made out what the writing says (*M. Feb 14th*) when he turns and speaks to me.

"Wait there. Do you understand me? Don't go anywhere. I'll be back." He goes downstairs and outside. I spend five minutes that feel like an hour each, staring at my knees. Eventually I hear the door of the bus open but I don't look up. Not until she says, "Candy! Thank God you're OK!"

Mum. It's my mum. She's still in her wedding dress.

21
Found, Still Lost

I only see Mum for a second before she grabs me – her face is red and wet, her hair looks like a bird's nest. She envelops me in a vice-like hug and I think might break a rib. Her hair smells different – hairdresser-spray. She thought I was still in bed when the stylist came over to put the rollers in. It must have looked nice then, before she found out I was gone. She holds me tight against the sharp and starchy material of her wedding dress. How did she find me? She's shaking and crying too. Normally hearing Mum cry always gets me started but I'm actually too taken aback by the sound to know what to make of it. It's not the kind of cry I've ever heard from her before. Not a sad-film cry. Or a through-the-wall after a break-up cry. This cry is a bottomless-pit of a thing. It comes from somewhere deep and raw and it feels like it might never end. Which is made even worse by the fact that she's squeezing me so tight I can't I... I can't...

"Mum! I can't breathe!"

I manage to extricate myself from her grasp and swallow a few gallons of air. Mum grabs hold of my head (hard) with both hands and puts herself eye to eye with me. Her brown eyes are bloodshot, ringed red, sore and swollen with tears. She looks like she's gone ten rounds with Mike Tyson. She forces the words out through her tears.

"Never... never... do that... ever... again!"

It's frightening to see the power of her feelings. I knew she'd care but... not like this. I feel like a six-year-old doing ninety in a stolen car.

"I'm sorry, Mum!"

And I am. I really am. She pulls me back in and holds me against her chest. Hearing me speak seems to galvanise her somehow and she manages to get herself back under control. Her breath, still shaking, is coming out in little hiccoughy sobs that make her shiver every time they escape. She takes my face in her hands and holds it up to hers. Usually I'd say I'm the one who looks like a messed-up version of her but not today. And it's all my fault.

The reality of what I've done to my mum starts to dawn on me. I picture the abandoned church full of guests, the frantic call to the police, the fear, driving all the way here in tears imagining what could have happened, Mum replaying a hundred horrible news stories in her head. I am the worst daughter ever. Shame overwhelms me and hot tears prick the backs of my eyes. I try to look away but Mum's still holding my face right there and she's... I mean, her face is all messed up and she's still crying a bit, so it's actually quite hard to tell but it looks like she's... *smiling*?

I sniff back a sob. "Don't smile, Mum. Don't! Hit me or something."

Then she laughs which just makes it worse.

"I'm serious! Hit me! Shout at me! I've ruined everything! I'm totally selfish and stupid! I ruined your wedding and scared you and... and..." I want to say how it was all for nothing. How I was wrong anyway. How I thought I could find Nathan and that she could just go ahead and get married without me. But I can't make the words come out. It's all too much. It's suddenly crystal clear how childish and stupid I have been, when I thought I was being precisely the opposite. I dissolve into a shaky mess of snivelling tears.

Mum holds me tight and pats my back gently and rocks me, whispering, "Ssshhh. Everything's OK. It's OK now," over and over again, like she must have done a thousand times when I was a baby. And I think that if I don't belong to anybody else in the world it doesn't matter. I belong to her and she belongs to me. She is my mum and always will be. And that is enough to make me really, really lucky.

Eventually, I stop crying. When I manage to speak again, it's to try and explain. To tell her how sorry I am approximately a thousand times. I tell her that I came here looking for Nathan. (She knows. She and Ray turned my room upside down when they realised I was gone and found an extra copy of the map Calum printed off the internet in my bedroom, plus a box full of stuff about Nathan. Mum put two and two together.) I show her the photograph – the two of them together all those years ago. She looks like she might cry so I tell her I'm sorry again. Only every time I say it, so does she.

"No, *I'm* sorry, Candy. I should have told you about your dad. I just didn't know how. I still don't... I thought I could explain it to you better when you were older."

"I am older Mum," I say sadly. She slips her arm around my shoulders and rests her head on mine.

"I know you are, sweetheart."

A knock at the door a few minutes later announces Ray's arrival.

He comes into the room, closely followed by Glad. And Holly. Calum! Calum's here! For some reason just seeing his face makes me feel a bit better. Glad catches my eye – her face is a headmistressy mask of anger. "You are going to get it" her expression seems to say "and it is not going to be good". I can tell she's had a go at Hol already because my friend seems to have shrunk a good two inches and acquired the reticent bearing of a mouse with post-traumatic stress disorder.

"Hey," Hol squeaks before disappearing meekly into the shagpile.

Ray looks knackered. "Thank goodness you're all right!" he says as he comes in. And he actually sounds like he means it. His morning suit is creased and his forehead is etched with the worry that must have been gripping it all day. He bounds towards us but stops short of hugging me. Instead he places a hand on Mum's shoulder which she takes hold of gratefully. I am not just the worst daughter, I am literally the worst person in the world. Ever.

"*All right*?" Glad echoes shrilly, waddling towards me like a bowling ball trundling towards a strike. "I should say she's all right! What in the name of God were you thinking, lassie? What possessed you? Have you any idea what your mother and I have been through today? And Ray? Never in all my born days have I heard of anything approaching the selfishness—"

"I'm... sorry... I didn't mean to..."

The telltale listing of the vehicle announces that Jugs is back on board and sure enough, he arrives just in time to rescue me from the worst of Glad's inquisition.

"Hello again everyone," he says apologetically. "Just wondering if anybody needed a cup of tea?"

Mum runs over and throws her arms around him. His face twists up into a huge hairy smile that makes him look like a broken coconut.

"Oh, Norman," Mum sighs. "Thank you so, *so* much."

It isn't just the offer of tea, of course (although we could all do with a brew). It seems that Jugs's mysterious phone call was from his assistant Adrian who was with Mum, Ray, the Biscuits and the Police (and yes, I do mean the *actual* police and not Sting's old band). He delivered my family here and has spent the last half an hour trying to dissuade the boys in blue from arresting us. Momentarily distracted from her present pursuit of telling me off, Glad trots over and reaches up to pat Jugs on the forearm.

"What's happening with the officers, Jogs?"

"Jugs, Mrs Appleyard," he corrects her gently. "Short for Juggernaut. The officers are quite satisfied that there has been... an error. It appears that as well as their initial concern when you were reported missing, the local constabulary had some intelligence that you... that is to say that the band were here under..." Jugs searches for the right way to put it. I glance at Pirate, who looks at the floor. "Under – shall we say – false pretences? A complaint had been made. Luckily it seems that the complain*ants* are aspiring musicians. Some backstage passes for this weekend and VIP tickets to Nate's stadium tour seem to have... poured oil on troubled waters. They now realise that you are, in fact, not the people they believed you to be. *Voila*. Problem solved."

"Thank you Jugs," Mum says again, finally letting him go.

"Anything for you, Mags," he smiles shyly. "Just like always."

Glad is right about tea. It does have miraculous powers. Somehow, having a cup of tea makes everything feel a little bit more like the world is on the right way round. Even if it only lasts until the first sip breaks the spell.

Then we all notice where we are, sitting side by side in the freakiest bus of all time. Glad eyes the pole by the bar with obvious disapproval. Calum appears to be trying to figure out what the "iRide" is for. Ray clears his throat and looks up (a long way up) at Jugs.

"So! You and Maggie know each other?" he asks.

Jugs nods. Mum is in the middle of sipping her tea and it goes down the wrong way. She starts choking.

As Ray gives her a few firm slaps on the back Jugs says, "We're old friends." He turns back to Mum. "Nathan missed you, Mags. We all did. It's been a very long time."

"I know," Mum says, regaining her composure. She takes hold of my hand but looks up at Jugs. "I know it has. I'm sorry."

Ray clears his throat, which usually indicates he has an idea. Ordinarily I'd be cringing at this point – anticipating him saying something really embarrassing, but today I find myself listening. "Well – it's been an *interesting* day. Maybe not the one that we had planned..." He looks sad for a minute, "But you know what, Candy? It's my fault."

"No Ray!" Mum says turning to him, but he shushes her.

"Your mum and I got carried away. We were so happy to have found each other, we didn't think about how you might be feeling as much as we should. We knew you weren't happy but we chose to take your silence as acquiescence. That's not the way to go about things, though. It's not what families do." My eyes start to sting again. How many times is it possible to cry in one day without running out of tears?

I look at Ray, lost inside his rumpled hire suit, a good size too big. The flower pinned to his lapel has long since wilted in the

June heat and there's a small shaving cut just beside his right ear under the grey bits of hair at his temples. He's definitely not cool. But like Glad said, parents aren't cool. Maybe I will find my dad here today. It just might not be the dad I expected.

"I'm sorry," I say.

He smiles one of those sad upside-down smiles. "I'm sorry. I let you down. I won't do it again." And for the first time, we hug.

Ray turns to Mum, she's crying too. He touches her face tenderly. "Now, Maggie. No more silences. OK? It's time to tell her the truth."

Mum nods. I pass her Jasmine's skull-napkin to wipe her eyes with as Ray stands to address the others.

"OK everyone. Since we're here and Jugs has so kindly supplied us with these..." He lifts up the backstage pass that is hanging on a lanyard around his neck. "I think we should go out there and see a bit of what Glastonbury Festival has to offer." He bends his arm in an exaggerated gentlemanly fashion and offers it to Glad. "I think Spinning Rascal is playing shortly. Would you care to accompany me?"

Hol covers her eyes in horror but Glad smiles. "I must say I do have a soft spot for *Bonkers*."

Jugs grabs his keys. "How about I get my assistant to give you a lift? I've got the golf buggy outside, you can use that." Jugs looks at us. "Nathan should be back from the press run any minute, Mags. Shall I tell him to come straight up?"

Mum nods and watches them all file downstairs and out into the afternoon sunshine. Calum hangs behind for a minute.

"You need me to bring anything back for you, Candy? Mrs Caine?" he asks kindly.

I shake my head and Mum pats him on the arm. "We're fine thank you, Calum. Candy will be out to see you in a while."

He turns to leave. Once we hear the door close downstairs, Mum says, "Nice boy, Calum. Good friend is he?"

I give her a look that says, "Don't change the subject," then she breathes in deeply and starts to tell me about how she met my dad.

22
The Wierdest Family Reunion Ever

"I met your dad through my brother."

"Brother?" I ask. She nods.

"Your *uncle* Nathan. My big brother. Nathan Oxblood."

The sounds of the festival outside – which seemed to disappear when everybody was in here with us – come back again. I suddenly remember where I am.

Nathan Oxblood is my... uncle? I can hardly take it in. I look around the bus and catch sight of the shrine again. The pictures of my... *cousins*? Mum's face creases up with concern and she looks like she might cry again.

"I'm adopted, Candy. I found out by accident when I was seventeen. My birth mother was a lady called Eleanor Oxblood. She'd already had Nathan when I was born and she just couldn't cope with us both."

Mum takes another deep breath and lets out a heavy sigh.

"He didn't know who I was when we met. I'd gone to London looking for my birth mother and... it wasn't until after I found out she was dead..." Her voice wobbles and for a minute I'm scared she's going to stop, but she doesn't. "I sort of found Nathan by accident. He knew me as Valentine – the name I was modelling under. Anyway when I told him, we got really close, really fast. We were so similar it was uncanny. And we'd both felt so alone until we found each other. Him after his mum died and me... well always, really."

"So if Nathan's my uncle who is my—" The noise of the downstairs door opening stops me asking the question. It hangs suspended in the middle of the room. Nathan appears in the doorway at the top of the stairs.

"Hello Candy. Hello Mags." He smiles. Then Mum jumps up, runs over and throws her arms around him, enveloping him in a huge hug. They sway from side to side, saying things I can't quite hear in squashed and tearful voices.

Eventually they come unstuck and lean back to look at one another. Mum wipes the tears out of Nathan's eyes and he laughs, embarrassed. "Nice dress, by the way. Not exactly festival attire but..."

Mum looks down at herself and laughs too. "Well I did have

other plans for today but your niece..." They both turn to look at me and she wells up again, "...she brought us here instead; to find you. I'm..." her voice catches in her throat as she tries to stop herself crying again. "I'm so glad she did, Nathan."

Nathan slips an arm around her shoulders and they both look at me. She leans her head into him and I think of the picture. But now I know what I was really seeing: protectiveness not ownership. A brother who thought he had lost everything along with his mum, finding someone he was connected to again and guarding it fiercely. "You've told her then?"

"Almost all of it," Mum sniffs. She makes her way back over to the sofa and sits beside me, Nathan joins us, rubbing his face and running his hands through his hair as if he's a bird trying to smooth out some severely ruffled feathers. Mum's about to say something else when Jugs lumbers into the room. We look up, annoyed.

"Sorry. Bad time?" he asks.

"Yes!" Nathan snaps, but Mum lifts her hand.

"No Jugs. Come and sit down. I need you to hear this too."

All of our eyes are on Mum.

"God, this is hard. I never meant to hurt any of you. Life is strange and takes you places you never planned to go. At least my life has." Mum shifts in her seat and turns to Nathan. "You remember what it was like back then – we all do. If we'd taken odds on the likelihood of you lot making it, they would have been pretty long. But by the time you found out who I really was, things had started to happen and that kind of success has a life of its own. You had your own path to follow and all these opportunities open to you. But I started to want something else. Maybe it was roots, maybe something as simple and as bloody complicated as love. I didn't know what until I found it." That's when Mum looks up at Jugs. "Why didn't we tell him, Jugs?"

Jugs sighs. It sounds like a pipe organ being switched on.

"You know what me and you are like, Nate. We're like *this* but we're always butting heads. I knew you wouldn't like it – mixing business and… you wouldn't have been happy."

Jugs looks down sadly, tracing a couple of sausagey fingers across the tattoo on his forearm: *M. Feb 14th* As in *Maggie Valentine…*

Nathan's mouth drops open. Jugs shakes his huge bearish head. My brain feels like a blender somebody just switched on.

"Candy, darling…" Mum takes both my hands in hers. "You came here today to find your dad. Well, you did. It just isn't the dad you expected. Your dad is Jugs, darling."

I look from Mum to Jugs. He looks as shocked as I feel, even through all the hair. The hair! The bloody hair! That's why I can never keep mine under control! We stare at each other, each with an expression that looks something like a concussed goldfish. The long and hilarious life-story Jugs told me while he was keeping me company earlier flashes back through my mind. Jugs getting his first job as guitar tech for Motorhead. Jugs giving Slash from Guns 'n' Roses his first top hat... My dad did all those things. My big... hairy... dad.

"Why didn't you say something?" Jugs asks Mum without taking his eyes off me.

"I'm sorry... I thought Nathan needed you more than I did. And you were so good at your job even then. Look at this!" Mum throws open her hands, indicating not the tourbus but everything beyond it: the fame, the fortune, the fact that the only thing the entire country is talking about today is the gig that will take place on the Pyramid Stage in a few short hours.

"Look at everything you've achieved together. You needed each other to succeed and I didn't want to stop you – either of you – from living up to your potential. I'm sorry."

"I looked for you!" Nathan protests. "*We* looked for you!" He stares at Jugs in disbelief.

"I knew you would." Mum shakes her head. "That was why I changed my name back to Caine."

"But… but what about the salon?" I ask meekly. "Glad said someone who believed in you bought it for you."

Mum nods. "That's right. She did. It was her."

The four of us sit in silence. Because really, where do you even start? Me, my mum, my dad and my Uncle Nathan each squinting in silent concentration as we try to fit the new facts we've learned into the world as we know it. Everything is different now. It's like going to bed as usual one night and opening your curtains the next morning to find out your house has been relocated to Mars.

"Looks like I have got a family after all then," I say.

"One that's going to take a bit of getting used to," says Jugs.

"You can bloody well say that again," says Nathan.

Mum looks at the three of us together. She looks just like she used to on my birthdays – wet eyes and a big smile. But this time she's crying because she's happy.

23

Living Your Dreams, Enjoying Your Nightmares and L-O-V-E

It's half-past nine now. I'm in Nathan and Jasmine's bedroom, downstairs on the tourbus. I have been left alone to "freshen up" before The Rain take to the Pyramid Stage at ten. I'm alone for the first time since I found out the truth. Calum has returned The Beast to me. He saw me scarper leaving it behind and knew I'd want it back. And it looks none the worse for its ordeal. In fact it looks better – it's shining like a freshly polished apple. Now there's only one thing I want to do. I sit on the edge of the bed (which boasts not one but three different textures of coverlet/throw/duvet) and hit a hard harmonious B major.

Nothing happens. I hit it again.

"Clarence?" I call, panic rising in my throat. "Clarence, where are you?" I must be able tō get him back. Unless… what if this is one of those deals where the fairy gets you to meet your destiny and then sails off into the Great Beyond once it's completed? What if now that he's served his purpose here he has ascended to the next spiritual plain and is lost to me forever? What if this is it? Then I hear a little voice – high and thin and squeaky.

"…made my daring escape just in time! It reminded me of that story about your first attempt blowing up the toilets in the Waldorf-Astoria!"

"Clarence!" I say in one of those whispery-shouts couples do when they're annoyed with each other in public. "Is that you? Come here!"

Somewhere far off, the voice pauses. "Ah! Calling me now… Yes, I know, you loon! Well, we've all done it, haven't we? At least she only had to get away with a guitar! But your drums would have been easy to run away with, dear boy, they were always blown to bits too!"

There is sustained laughter then the familiar flash. And hovering midair before me is the final piece in the bizarre jigsaw puzzle that is my family: my fairy Godbrother.

"Clarence! Thank goodness you're all right!"

"Yes. No thanks to you, flibbertigibbet that you are! Imagine, leaving me in the sweaty paws of that dilettante adulterer! Luckily, as I was just saying to my good friend Keith, my feline reflexes impelled me to evanesce within moments of your own disappearance."

I have no idea what he's just said, but it's good to have him back. "How did you escape?" I ask.

"As I said, my dear. I vanished shortly after you did. I saw Calum go after my guitar. I knew he would get it to you. I must say, he may dress like a giant baby—"

"Hoodies aren't babygros, Clarence – we've been through this! Adults wear them and everything."

"Let me finish, Candypop. As I was saying… Calum may dress like a giant baby but despite this, I really am becoming rather fond of that young man. You could do worse for a boyfriend, you know." He pulls a face. "And from memory, you recently have. Quite how I'll ever recover from being cheek by jowl with that cut-price teen rebel I'll never know."

Ordinarily I'd be embarrassed to think of Clarence being so close when I was snogging Dan but after everything I've been through today… But, I'm thinking about something he just said.

"Hang on," I say, following him over to look at the growing throng of people passing outside our cordoned-off security perimeter. "You said *my* guitar. Like The Beast was *yours*."

"Ah."

"'Ah!' is right, Clarence. The Beast is yours, isn't it? Or it was when you were alive." Clarence looks at the guitar still around my neck. He floats over to it and touches one of his little white hands to a tuning peg. The instrument seems to answer, emitting a beautiful little hum. Clarence looks at it like a cowboy looking at his faithful old horse. "Yes," he says simply.

I point to the sticker. "So Photogenius is you? That's your band?" He nods.

"Why didn't you tell me?" I ask, incredulous.

He shrugs. "This instrument was fated to bring us together. To bring your life into my death and me into your life to the benefit of both, I hope. I came here to help you create *your* story. In which I am merely playing a small supporting role. My life is over. Yours is just beginning."

"But just look what you have been able to give back to my instrument." I look down at The Beast which is now so beautiful it would totally win guitar Crufts if such a thing existed. It seems to shiver proudly. "So that's why it's been getting less messed up?"

Clarence nods. "It's healing. The closer you get to where you're meant to be, the more it is restored to its former glory. It's not just the guitar, Candy. I feel it too. Thank you for everything." He places a hand on his chest, where his heart should be. For a second, I think he might be about to get emotional but then he says, "Now – let's not love each other. It gives you wrinkles. Fabulosity beckons. Are you ready to heed the call?"

I smile, and check myself in the mirror. Mum has reapplied my makeup (but less of it) and I have changed into another outfit that we rescued from my bag in the back of the dog-van (where we also found Kylie, Spooky and Dan). It's an old vintage dress of Mum's and one of my favourites. It must be from the 50s and is covered in flowers.

I turn to Clarence. "Do I look OK?"

He smiles. "Like an angel in her granny's coming out dress, dear. But if that's the look you're going for… Are you ready?"

"Yes. I think so," I laugh. "Are you?"

"I?" Clarence puts a Scarlett O'Hara hand to his chest and raises his eyebrows.

"Yes, you. You're coming with me."

◎

So that's how I came to be up here. On the Pyramid Stage. It's just like my dream, only bigger. Louder. Everything is just *more*.

In eight bars (thirteen and a bit seconds) my uncle Nathan's band, the biggest in the world, will launch into their most stupidly catchy single *The Wow*. JJ is on bass and in first. As he strikes up the first few notes the crowd scream in instant recognition of a song that became an anthem for a generation. At the front of the stage I can see Glad perched on a chair, wearing a The Rain T-shirt over the top of all her other clothes. She looks on wreathed in smiles with Mum and Ray behind her. *I guess this means I'm forgiven*, I think, relieved. Ray's arm is around Mum's shoulders and they're both in civilian clothes. Well, reasonably civilian clothes. Jasmine wasn't too chuffed about having to lend Mum something to wear, especially her Gucci coat. Ray almost looks cool in Nathan's Prada shirt and APC jeans. Almost...

Mum's eyes are sparkling with emotion, watching and waiting. She's shouting something – I can't hear what but it must be something good. The Biscuits are just beside them. Hol is waving and screaming, pointing madly at her best mate, about to run out centre-stage. JJ loops the bass part over and over as Nathan starts to speak.

"Ladies and gentlemen, I want you to welcome someone very special to the stage. She's a brand new talent and I want you to look out for her in the future. Give it up for CANDY CAINE!"

Forty thousand people cheering at the sound of your name is indescribable. Like the kinetic squeal of a hundred racing-cars taking a hairpin bend. Like an electricity pylon struck by lightning. I run towards Nathan, waving at the crowd. He smiles but archly, fully absorbed in his rock star persona. Jugs plugs The Beast into a stack of amps as Nathan says, "Three-Four!"

And we're off – racing into the most insane version of the most ridiculous (and ridiculously catchy) song ever written.

Don't try to hypnotise
Disguise the supersize
Lies behind your eyes now!
Surprised you recognise
Something you can't deny
Hits you between the eyes
POW!
You and me we're The Wow!

As I play along, The Beast seems to be helping me – adding harmonics and squeals I couldn't have dreamed up in a million years. Clarence's old band badge (which he told me he superglued on in a pub in Kilburn in 1985) glows brightly. The Beast is loving it. As we hit another chorus the lights really kick in and that's when I look up to see Clarence – he couldn't come all this way without getting up onstage after all. He was unconvinced until I told him about the strobe lights. I figured three minutes of insane flashing would be the perfect opportunity for Clarence to join us for the finale. And there he is, rocking out and glowing every-colour of the rainbow before flashing back to his usual white among the flickering light. If I didn't know any better I'd think he was a trick of it.

At the end of the song, the crowd roar like a storming sea. Nathan places a hand on my shoulder. He speaks to me but it's the crowd he's talking to really.

"So here's the thing. This kid is family. But we haven't seen each other in a long time... Ever in fact, CANDY CAINE, EVERYBODY – COME ON!" He cups a hand round his ear and cocks it towards the vast crowd who "WHOOOOO!!!" enthusiastically in response. He smiles at me again.

I glance down into the press pit where the rest of the Biscuits are. Holly and Calum are both cheering madly, shouting stuff I can't hear but that I know they will tell me about later. Between pouts, Kylie is smiling and clapping too. She looks more at home than ever with a selection of VIP passes strung about her neck. Dan is standing next to her trying to hold her handbag in a dignified fashion. He doesn't quite manage it. I'm trying to locate Spooky when I suddenly see her head emerge over the top of a bank of photographers: Jugs has lifted her on to his enormous shoulders. She waves and punches the air and he laughs, shaking off the dazed expression he's been wearing since he found out he was my dad. He actually looks kind of proud.

When the ringing in my ears has subsided and my heart rate has returned to normal and after Nathan has bought the entire VIP bar unlimited drinks and he is borne aloft for a victory lap of said bar by a crowd of drunken journo-types, ensuring The Rain get glowing write-ups in tomorrow's press) it's time to put right one last wrong. It's time for Mum and Ray to get married.

It was Pirate's idea. She read in the press about a place up at the top of the festival site in the Lost Vagueness field where impromptu marriage ceremonies are held. Apparently Kate Moss and Pete Doherty are just one of the rock n roll couples who have tied the knot up there. If the fact that the whole deal takes place in a boxing ring wasn't enough of a clue that it isn't *actually* legally binding, the fake beard on the lady dressed up as a vicar to perform the service might have given it away. After the events of today, though, I don't think it matters.

Having never wanted to see the thing again, I'm unbelievably glad I brought my bridesmaid's dress here. Glad gets the worst of the creases out with Nathan's mini-iron (he claims never to have seen it before) and Pirate and Spooky complete my look with a cool gold vintage hat with a little net at the front that they picked up from a fancy-dress stall. Clarence has appointed himself official photographer and is back in Polaroid camera form slung around my neck.

Glad stands back to survey me and dabs her eyes. "Lovely! You look every inch the bridesmaid, lassie."

I look down at her. The Rain T-shirt is gone and the blue floral dress, yellow jacket and matching hat she purchased from TOP CLASS BRIDES have been ironed again to within an inch of her life. For the first time I think about how much this – the wedding, finding me safe, being here to share everything else – means to her. Glad has invested in Mum and me since the day we first came into the lives. Buying the salon is the least of it. She's given us her time and made us both who we are. Today she's getting to see it all work out.

"You look every inch the mother of the bride, Glad." I say truthfully. "And every inch the bridesmaid's nan. I'm sorry for everything I put you through."

"Ach, away with you!" says Glad, particularly Scottishly. "It's been an adventure. Anyway..." she looks around her, "I rather like Glastonbury Festival. I think I might come back next year."

So everyone is standing around a boxing ring in a tent full of people dressed up like maniacs, waiting for Mum. I'm just outside behind her, waiting to make our entrance. I peek through the tent-flap to see how everyone is getting on and take a few snaps of the world's most bizarre congregation with Clarence. After some initial awkwardness, Spooky and Kylie have bonded with Jasmine (AKA my new auntie – not sure which of us feel weirder about that) about the perils of being unbelievably pretty (Kylie) and having chemically treated hair (Spooky). The three of them chatter in the second aisle, clutching huge bags of flower petals ready to throw at the appropriate moment. Dan Ashton stands to one side, casting surreptitious glances at Jasmine's humungous cleavage and looking unsure of what to do with himself. Glad turns back from the row in front where she is sitting with a giggling bubble-blowing Holly. Catching Dan's wandering gaze, she gives him a prod with her walking stick. She might not know exactly what happened between us, but there are no flies on Gladys Appleyard. Dan's eyes immediately find the floor and stay there.

Ray is in the middle of the boxing ring, pacing like a nervous featherweight about to defend his title. He's in his tails again, a fresh flower in his lapel. I see him swallow nervously. Jugs notices too and pats him on the shoulder with a force that almost knocks him over but gives visible comfort. When it comes to Best Men, Ray couldn't have better at his side than BioDad. He was delighted to accept the job.

"The only time I've ever been Best Man was at Nathan and Jasmine's wedding," he told Ray conspiratorially. "It'd be nice to do it and be able to remember it afterwards. With Nate's, everything's a blank after the first half an hour of the stag do..."

Calum jogs down the aisle and over to where we're waiting. He sees my getup and can't stop himself smiling. "Nice dress!" he says unconvincingly. "It's very... very... orange!"

Then he spots Mum who is a few feet away doing the same relaxing deep-breathing techniques as Ray is up the front. "Wow!" says Calum, more persuasively. "You look amazing, Mrs Caine. You ready?" Mum nods, then smiles at me. Calum is right – Mum looks more beautiful than ever in her wedding dress, all fresh and glowing, especially with the addition of a daisy chain or two. The huge smile reminds me of the photograph in my bag. Maggie Caine got a bit of Maggie Valentine back today and it suits her.

Calum pops back inside the tent, gives the signal to the DJ (a huge man dressed as a ballerina with facepaint of the Nightmare Clown variety) who strikes up the music: a thumping remix of *Love is in the Air*. That's the cue for the three of us to start walking. Mum makes her entrance, with me behind her, holding on to her brother's arm. When she first asked Nathan to give her away, he thought she was joking. Then he realised she was serious and I thought he was going to cry again. And so it is that, a little later than planned and 279 miles away from the church they booked, on a hot June night my mum and step-dad get married.

◎

Calum pulls up a deckchair next to me. It's late and soft sounds of far-off ongoing parties drift down the valley towards us, but all our lot are finally asleep. Apart from Glad and Hol who were last seen heading to the Silent Disco to "have a rave". We're outside of the tourbus. Our own that is, not Nathan's. Jugs somehow rustled one up when he persuaded us all to stay for the rest of the weekend. The campfire he built before he turned in for the night is still smouldering in front of us as we examine the wedding pictures I took with Clarence.

"It's mad how that camera puts rainbows on everything," Calum says, bringing a photo of Ray and Mum right up to the end of his nose so that he can examine it more closely (he's already got his glasses on). Mr and Mrs Hoppings are dancing (to an old Frank Sinatra song), bright clouds of colour in the middle of their chests. It's as if you can see their hearts, and how identical they are.

"Mad," I agree.

"The maddest thing of all, right…" Calum says, leafing back through the stack of Polaroids to an earlier shot of the entire wedding party, "is that Dan hasn't got any. Not in any of these. What's that about, then?"

"Dunno," I shrug, leaning back to look up at the stars. That's not actually true, of course. I do know. It just took me a while to work it out. Dan might say all the right things and wear all the right things and look the part – he even works in the record shop – but he's never *felt* music. I'm not sure if he's ever felt anything. He just doesn't have it in him – there's nothing there for Clarence to capture.

"I thought you'd come here for him, you know," Calum says softly.

I look up and meet his inkblot eyes. "I know you did, you idiot."

"You're the idiot," he says. "Although I must be one too. I came here for you." And then Calum Stainforth kisses me and I know he means it and feels it. And so do I. It isn't like kissing Dan – the first three seconds of Christmas morning. Kissing Calum is like a song that travels from his lips to mine then finds its way to my heart and it stays there, long after he's gone: sweet and soft and as warm as a candle flame.

As I'm falling asleep on the weirdest best and longest day of my life, I think how true it is what Glad said about family: "You don't get to pick, and maybe that's just as well." And what

Mum said about life, "it takes you places you never planned to go."

I marvel at the magic and madness of the life I've discovered and how much of it I already had, if only I'd seen it. I'm alive, it's today and unbelievably I get to be me.